FIGHTING FOR HIS FORBIDDEN MAIDEN

ELLA MATTHEWS

HISTORICAL

Recycling programs for this product may not exist in your area.

ISBN-13: 978-1-335-83189-7

Fighting for His Forbidden Maiden

For questions and comments about the quality of this book, please contact us at CustomerService@Harlequin.com.

Harlequin Enterprises ULC
22 Adelaide St. West, 41st Floor
Toronto, Ontario M5H 4E3, Canada
www.Harlequin.com

HarperCollins Publishers
Macken House, 39/40 Mayor Street Uppe
Dublin 1, D01 C9W8, Ireland
www.HarperCollins.com

Printed in U.S.A.

1 2 3 4 5 6 7 8 9 10 HDC 28 27 26 25

Lucan did not want to touch her; no, that was not quite right.

Every time he saw her, he wanted to brush his fingers along her skin or bury his face in her hair, but that was something very different from what he was going to have to do now. Not thinking it through, he took her hand in his. The shock of her touch sent a fire racing through him, racing through his veins, burning him from the inside. Surely it could not be because of one light touch. It had to be because of his heightened awareness of their surroundings. "Come along," he said gruffly.

"What is your plan?" Jehanne asked, her French accent making the English words sound lovelier than they were.

"Not let the wool-brained Lord get us killed."

If they hadn't been standing so close, he would not have heard her soft laugh. "That seems wise," was all she said in response.

Moving with him, she did not try to tug his hand in a different direction, confirming his guess that she was more than willing to come along with them. His heart hurt at the knowledge that he was about to let her down, that he was withholding his intention of not allowing her any farther than a little way off from the castle gates. She belonged to his enemy and he should feel no compassion for her. But although his mind knew that, it seemed his body was slower to catch on.

Author Note

Thank you for picking up Lucan and Jehanne's story. I hope you enjoy getting to know them as much as I did.

Did you know that the Hundred Years' War between France and England went on for even longer than that? It was a disagreement that spanned 116 years and started with Edward III's claim to the French throne in 1337. If you've read my other titles, you'll know that most of my medieval stories are set around this time period. King Edward III is known as the father of England, and not just because he had a lot of children with both his wife and his mistresses. Under him, a united England began to take shape, but alongside this achievement, Edward also believed he had a right to rule France.

Lucan and Jehanne's story is set during the first physical conflict of this long war. Edward III's men swept through Picardy, treating the land and its residents brutally, entirely unnecessarily. Lucan is an English baron, involved in the conflict against his will (the King's law was absolute in this period), and Jehanne is the daughter of a French Comte (a very powerful title in France at the time). I wanted these two natural enemies to fall in love despite their different backgrounds, and pitting them against each other and the troubles they found themselves in was great fun.

If you'd like to find out more about me and my other books, please visit my website, ella-matthews.com.

Ella Matthews lives and works in beautiful South Wales. When not thinking about handsome heroes, she can be found walking along the coast with her husband and their two children (probably still thinking about heroes, but at least pretending to be interested in everyone else).

Books by Ella Matthews

Harlequin Historical

The Knights' Missions

The Knight's Rebellious Maiden
The Knight's Bride Prize
The Disgraced Knight's Redemption

A Season to Wed

Their Second Chance Season

Brother and Rivals

Her Warrior's Surprise Return

The King's Knights

The Knight's Maiden in Disguise
The Knight's Tempting Ally
Secrets of Her Forbidden Knight

The House of Leofric

The Warrior Knight and the Widow
Under the Warrior's Protection
The Warrior's Innocent Captive

Visit the Author Profile page at Harlequin.com.

To Jeanne

Chapter One

September 1339, Picardy, France

High on the castle battlements, the autumnal wind tugged at Jehanne de Balladur's braid, pushing it over her shoulder as she stared out over the familiar landscape that surrounded her father's stronghold. The men moving across it looked like ants from her high vantage. She shifted, trying to shield her face from the insistent breeze. Her eyes were beginning to sting, and her cheeks were smarting from the cool air, but it would be some time before she was allowed back into the warmth of the Great Hall. There was a spectacle to watch. And as the daughter of the Comte de Balladur, and affianced to the man leading the display, Jehanne was duty-bound to observe it until it was all over.

Moving again, her arm brushed against her sister's hugely pregnant stomach. '*Désolée*,' she murmured, trying to turn so that she wasn't nudging Margot, but it was hard to find a spot, pressed as she was from every side. Not one member of the castle wanted to miss this triumph: the prisoners shuffling towards them, some in chains, their heads bowed. Or their captors riding alongside, their chests thrown out in triumph. Jehanne's betrothed, Urian, rode out in front, leading. Jehanne couldn't make out the features of his face, but she could imagine the cruelty of his satisfied smile. She shuddered, tugging her shawl tighter around her shoulders, lightly knocking her sister again.

Margot waved away her second apology. 'It is my fault for being this great size. There is almost nowhere I can stand that you will not be able to touch me.' Margot slowly ran her hand over her bump, her eyes shining with adoration for her unborn child. Her sister was already desperately in love with her baby. Jehanne could only hope she felt the same way about Urian's child when the time came. Thinking about it reminded her that she would have to lie with the man for it to happen; her whole body shuddered at the thought of the horrid man laying even a finger against her skin.

Trying to distract herself from the impending nightmare, Jehanne looked down at the approaching men. 'Or perhaps it is Père's fault for making all the castle inhabitants stand to observe this spectacle. I feel as if it is us on display as much as the captives.'

'Père wants to humiliate the English and he wants them to know that we have all witnessed their downfall. After their despicable actions over the last month, I am pleased to see them brought low.' The English King's war on French soil had been brutal, but the vitriol in her sister's normally sweet voice was still a shock. As was usual these days, she wondered if that was her sister talking or whether it was her husband putting words into her sister's mind. Jehanne swallowed, trying to shift a lump that had formed in her throat. It would not be long until she was married. Her future husband was meaner by far than Margot's. She did not want to allow Urian's darkness to infect her, but perhaps it was inevitable when all one heard was bitter words. Keeping a light of happiness burning within her was becoming increasingly difficult and she was not yet married. Heavens knew how hard it would be then.

'I know,' continued her sister, 'that living in England for as long as you did means you have some empathy with these people.' She gestured to the defeated soldiers below, as if Jehanne knew them personally, but these were strangers to her as they were to her sister. 'But do you really blame Père and Urian for treating them in this manner? You know the English would have treated us far worse if our situations were reversed.' Her sister's lips were twisted unnaturally, the distaste marring her delicate features. From the tales Jehanne had heard, she did not blame Margot for her look of horror. The English had moved through the French countryside with a brutality that had shocked everyone, especially Jehanne, who had lived among them and would not have thought them capable of such savagery. It didn't match with the people she had known, who were kind and gently reserved.

Jehanne turned her attention towards the far horizon, fixing her stare on a point where the sky met the land. By unspoken agreement, she and her family rarely spoke about Jehanne's time on English shores. During her tenth summer, her father had arranged a betrothal between her and the heir to an English fortress on the south coast of the country. She'd been terrified at being sent away to learn English and how to run a large fortress, but her pleas to remain had fallen on deaf ears. Her father wanted the alliance and she was the sacrifice he was prepared to make. The long, sleepless nights and the sickness that had plagued her body for weeks had all been for nothing in the end. The boy she was to marry, William, had been adorable with his quick, dimpled smile, and they had grown up together as the very best of friends. When it was clear the English were going to start a war with France, Jehanne's father had abruptly terminated the marriage contract. Within days, bewildered and grieving the loss of her friend, she had returned to her native France, almost a stranger to her relatives.

Her sister was kind to her face, but when Jehanne had been reprimanded by her father for a comment she'd though private, Jehanne had begun to keep herself at a distance. There was no one in this stronghold who was her confidante.

Pressing fingers to her heart, she tried to ease the familiar ache that plagued her whenever she thought of William and the place she had called home for so long. Finding Jehanne's previous connection to such a prominent English fortress embarrassing, her father acted as if her whole time there had never happened. Jehanne tried to hold on to all the times she had laughed with William, all the times his mother had braided her hair and sung to her and all the times the people of her adopted castle had treated her with kindness. She wanted to remember the English as good people, or at least as good as the French people she knew, but that belief had been harder to cling to with every day that had passed since the English had stepped onto French soil. Excuses for their King's behaviour sounded false even to her own ears after a month of him laying waste to the countryside, burning everything within his sight no matter what it was.

'No,' she said. 'I do not deny that Père's, and Urian's, wish to make our captives suffer in this way is not justified. The English destroyed the lives of innocents for no reason that I can fathom. I only hope the capture of these men does not turn violent. I do not want to see bloodshed within the castle walls.' As much as she would like to say it was because she abhorred violence in all ways, that was not the only reason she did not want fighting in her home. She did not want to see Urian succumb to it. It would be further evidence that the man she was supposed to marry was a brute, and she had enough of that already.

'You are too sweet, my sister. The English had no such qualms as they ravaged our countryside, destroying our villages and slaughtering our people.' Margot's words, kind though they were, were said in a tone that suggested her sister thought her brain was sized like a sparrow's. Once again, her words echoed that of her husband's, a man Jehanne found it hard to respect.

The column of men was nearing, the prisoners' chains ringing like bells in the late afternoon. Jehanne could make out more details now; there were not as many of them as they had been led to believe. This was barely even a small section of the English invading force: no more than twelve men in total. Out in front, there was one man, presumably their leader as he was unchained. He wore a richly embroidered cloak and held his head high as if he were not the defeated captive of the whole castle of enraged French people. She watched him for a moment, trying to see some hint of remorse on his face for what he and his fellow countrymen had done. If he felt any, it did not show.

Behind him, leading the column of chained men was

what appeared to be a giant, looming over the rest of them, his cloak only just covering his broad frame. Trying to make sense of what she was seeing, Jehanne peered closer. No, this was not a creature of legend but a tall, broad man with fiery red hair and a scowl so deep it seemed bottomless. His frown seemed focused, not on Urian, who rode alongside them, but on his own leader from whom his ferocious glower never wavered. Tethered to him, with a rope looped around his waist, was a young boy, one who could not long be past his tenth birthday. Jehanne's heart hurt for him; whatever the English had done, the boy was an innocent and did not deserve to be led like cattle.

'Why do you think there is a child with them?' she asked Margot.

Her sister shrugged. 'The English are strange, are they not?'

It was not really an answer, but as Margot was as knowledgeable as her about the situation, Jehanne did not press the issue.

Urian pulled ahead of the prisoners, his lips twisted into a triumphant smile. Clattering onto the drawbridge, he lifted his arm in acknowledgement of the cheers that rang out along the battlements. Jehanne knew she should join in but her mouth would not obey. She did not revel in this show of power, not in the way the others did. She knew all too well the unnecessary cruelty he would show to these men, who were already defeated. She glanced at the prisoners again. The red-headed one had turned his furious look towards Urian now. His wide shoulders were tensed, his fingers curled into tight fists, so strained she fancied she could see the whites of his knuckles from where she stood. In that moment, she knew that if the man's hands were not bound, he would rip Urian to pieces. God, how she wanted that power for herself. If she had that man's strength, nothing or nobody would stop her from getting exactly what she wanted.

Without warning, the giant's gaze flicked up. Before she could look away, his eyes met hers. The chattering crowd fell away, their voices a distant murmur. The wind died back, stilling as if to mark the moment. His eyes widened briefly, the frown disappearing into a look of surprise. One of her father's men poked him with the tip of his sheathed sword, breaking their shared look. Without another glance, the giant followed his leader onto the drawbridge. As the world rushed back in, Jehanne straightened, not realising that she had been leaning that far forward.

'What a nerve that man had, looking at you like that when he is no better than a dog.'

Jehanne's fingers tugged at her shawl but she did not comment. For an instant, it had seemed as if the world had somehow changed into something she did not recognise, somewhere safe and still; an illusion to be sure, but a powerful one that left her knees trembling.

'Your man has done well,' Margot continued when Jehanne said nothing in response to her retort. 'To capture so many men when no one else has is quite an achievement. King Philippe will reward him handsomely for this.'

Would he? Jehanne was not so sure that this supposed triumph would be as well thought about by the country's leader as the rest of her family believed. From what she had gathered, she thought that Philippe VI de Valois wanted the problem of the English to disappear. He had made no attempt to stop them in their rampage across his country and appeared to have retreated deeper into France. This capture would only make things worse in the long run. Mindful that this was an unpopular opinion, Jehanne did not voice her thoughts, only saying, 'Urian is not mine yet.'

Margot nudged her. 'It will not be long though. Père said last night there was no reason to wait. It could happen before the end of the month. Just think, soon you will be like me.' She rubbed her belly. 'Our babies will be close in age, closer than us. They will grow up together.' Margot sighed. 'You are lucky that you got a handsome one.'

Wool snagged under Jehanne's nails as her fingers curled into fists beneath her shawl. Many of the castle's inhabitants thought Urian a fine figure of a man. With golden hair and a square jaw, he did have the look of an angel, but Jehanne suspected his soul was blacker than night. As the days passed, she kept noticing things others seemed to miss: the quick cuff around the head of an innocent child, a casual kick to a hunting dog's flank and an unkind word to an elderly alewife. Small things but not inconsequential ones. Each small, malicious act building an image of a man she did not want to know better. Pinpricks rushed across her skin as she imagined him touching her, her body curling in on itself at the thought of performing the marital act. Although her relationship with William had never got so far, they'd discussed it at length, and she'd been prepared to lie with her closest friend, but now… Now, the thought of lying with Urian haunted her nightmares.

If only William had been a different man, maybe he would have fought for her. They could have married before her parents had forced her return to France. She missed his soft laughter, missed the way the way the sea shimmered blue and grey from her bedroom window, yearned for the small, bitter apples she could pick from the trees just outside the castle she still thought of as home.

Urian cantered to the centre of the courtyard, scattering people in his way. Those on the battlements stumbled awkwardly, turning, bumping into one another as they twisted, so that now they all peered down into the large courtyard at the centre of the castle rather than out over the landscape. The prisoners emerged through the gateway, trudging slowly after Urian and bunching together when they realised he had come to a stop. Only the red giant stood apart, the boy near him. Whether that proximity was due to a desire to be near someone strong or because they were tied together, it was hard to tell.

'The English,' cried Urian, sweeping his arms out over the eleven men and one boy as if they were the entirety of King Edward III's men. 'I have captured them and brought them here so that they may pay for their crimes. I dedicate this deed to my betrothed, Jehanne de Balladur.'

At the mention of her name, Jehanne jerked backwards, her head hitting the woman behind her. The crowd roared. Margot clapped her hands together, her wide smile directed at Urian, whose gaze was searching for Jehanne along the battlements.

'Pardon,' she murmured, but she needn't have worried, the woman was as fixated as everyone else on the goings-on below them. There wasn't a single person in the castle who didn't want the blood of the English to fall, not after the month of destruction wrought upon their country by the invading men.

The prisoners shuffled on their feet, all but the leader and the giant. It was doubtful the lower ranking captives understood what was being said. French was only spoken by the ruling classes in England, but they obviously understood the tone as they pressed closer together. Some of them appeared to try and shuffle behind the tallest man, as if using his bulk as a human shield. The leader, in his fine coat and unmanacled hands, still held his head high as if he expected to be treated as an honoured guest, and perhaps he would be. It was likely that he was the only one among the desultory group worthy of a ransom. The others might be used for work at best, or maybe executed as examples at worst. There was no way of telling how her father might want this to play out.

None of them held her attention for long. It was hard to take her eyes off the red-headed man. It seemed to Jehanne as if he were vibrating with fury. Every line in his body was rigid, as if one touch would cause him to snap. Next to him, the boy kept glancing up at his towering frame and then to the well-dressed leader and back. The huge man seemed not to notice the furtive glances. Standing in the centre of the courtyard as if this were a normal day, the English leader was oblivious to the intensity of the anger being directed his way.

Leaning forward, pressing her palms against the battlements, Jehanne peered closely at the giant, as if proximity would somehow explain his wrath to her. Whether it was her movement, or something else that caught his attention, the Englishman's eyes snapped to hers once more. Her lungs seized as if he had somehow squeezed the air out of her. As before, his frown faded and something in his stance relaxed, almost like he looked at her and saw someone familiar. Although she had never seen him in her life and would remember him if she had. Carved from stone, his face had sharp edges, with wide blue eyes that were startlingly clear underneath thick, red eyebrows.

This time, Urian noticed him look at her. Jehanne dropped her head, but it was too late, Urian was already on the move. He flung himself down from his saddle and stalked forwards. 'You dare to look at my betrothed,' he screamed, his skin turning purple.

Not wanting to look but unable to do anything else, Jehanne lifted her head. It was as much her fault as the man's and she owed it to him to witness any punishment, as if she could share in it somehow. The giant ignored Urian; he was less than an irritating fly to the man, such was the difference in their heights. At the sight of the foreigner's defiance, something flickered in Jehanne's chest, an ember in a fire she had long thought banked. It was gone almost as soon as it had started, lost as Urian pressed closer to the redhead's front. The contrast in size should have been laughable. Urian only came up to the man's shoulders but his arms weren't bound. There was nothing funny about his contorted face or the spittle that flew from his lips as he screamed at the prisoner to look at him.

When the big man continued to gaze up at her, Urian shoved him. Even with his hands manacled, the bigger man could have saved himself. But he was tethered to the young boy, and the force of the shove set the child off balance.

'Oh no.' Margot gasped as the boy crashed to the ground, pulling the bigger man with him. 'Not the child.'

The giant twisted his large body, falling so that he did not crush the small body, which now lay crumpled on the ground.

'Oh, that poor boy,' continued Margot. 'Why would the English bring someone that young on campaign? What brutes they are.'

'He wouldn't be hurt if it wasn't for Urian,' said Jehanne. She winced as her betrothed repeatedly kicked the ribs of the fallen man. His attack appeared to have no impact on the giant as he ignored the blows to his body, turning to speak to the boy instead. The smaller head nodded a few times, his shoulders shaking a little.

'The boy is bleeding,' said Margot, her lips trembling. Her maternal heart obviously caring for the child even if she did not seem to think twice about the man being beaten in front of them.

Jehanne pressed the tips of her fingers to her heart. 'Why won't he look at Urian? If he would only show him slight deference this would stop.'

Margot tsked in annoyance. 'Who cares about the English pig? I doubt he gave our people a second thought when his King ordered him to burn our land, kill our cattle and slaughter our people.'

Yes, Jehanne must remember that. She should push her care to one side and remember all that the invading force had done. The English had moved through France with terrible force. Destroying things that they could have left alone for they caused no harm. Nor were the places they destroyed even the property of the people they had come to fight. She should not feel any pity for their plight now, but it was difficult not to care for a man who was caring for a boy and not himself. No one else was putting a stop to this senseless violence, and Jehanne's father, someone Urian would normally hide his true nature from, was nowhere to be seen. Maybe he had returned inside once the prisoners were inside the castle walls; it was all right for his people to stand in the cold wind but not him. There was no one here to put a stop to Urian's behaviour other than herself.

'Monsieur le Chevalier Dupont,' she called down.

Her betrothed gave the giant one last violent kick before looking up at her and sweeping a deep courtly bow. 'Mademoiselle, I give you the English.'

She curtsied, although he would not be able to see most of the gesture as it was hidden behind the ramparts. Everyone around would be able to see her lowering herself before him, and that was the point he would want noticed. 'You have done well to bring us the English.' She bit her tongue to stop herself from pointing out the small number of them. 'My father has promised a great feast in your honour.'

'I have only done my duty, Mademoiselle.'

Less than that, in Jehanne's opinion. Urian should have been at Cambrais, helping to defend that castle from the English who had attacked it with force, despite the French King being elsewhere. Urian had not gone to their aid, not even when a request for help had been sent. It was not how Urian worked. He was a spider, spinning his webs, hoping to catch something but not attacking directly. Not unless his captive was already vulnerable, then he would sink his teeth in. She could say none of that. This man was to be her husband. He could make her life miserable if he so wished, and no one would do anything to stop him. For the rest of her life, she would have to pretend to support him in all things, even if those things were abhorrent to her. Although her soul rebelled against the idea, she had no choice but to accept her fate. 'You have made us proud,' she said, and those surrounding her cheered.

Below her, Urian preened, the fallen knight forgotten at his feet. She dared not look at the giant, dared not remind Urian of his conquest. She pushed her way lightly through the crowd of onlookers, most of them making way for her without her having to ask. As the daughter of the all-powerful Comte and the fiancée of the volatile chevalier, she was treated with the utmost respect and her route to the courtyard was unhindered.

Slipping her arm through Urian's she said to him, 'Let us go and see the Comte de Balladur now, so that you may regale Père with your morning's work. I know he is keen to hear how you defeated the English. Let others see to the captives.'

Urian stilled. Walking away from the audience of many was not in his style. He would want to soak up the adulation of the crowd for as long as possible, but to gain a favourable meeting with the castle's head was too good an opportunity to pass. As it stood, Jehanne's older brother stood to gain control of the castle on her father's death, but he had been plagued with ill health and had no heir of his own yet. Urian was ambitious. A younger son from a less noble house, he did not stand to inherit anything but this castle…leadership was tantalisingly within his reach and not a day passed when he wasn't working towards it.

'As you wish it, my beloved.'

Her spine tightened. There was no love between them, and it sickened her when Urian pretended otherwise. They barely knew one another, had been thrust together by circumstances outside their control. Other than making a show of adoration in front of everyone, he otherwise ignored her. Their betrothal had first come about through a negotiation of a parcel of land south of her father's. When he had arrived at the stronghold to await their wedding, she had tried to get to know him. It had not taken long to discover she did not like the man behind the bluster; cruelty came second nature to him, his words were cutting and abrasive. She avoided him as much as she could. There would come a time soon when she couldn't, and her soul wept for fear as to what that would do to her. But for now, she kept her distance.

As they walked away, Jehanne did not glance down at the man who must surely still be lying on the floor. If she showed interest, it would only draw Urian's attention and that was what she was trying to avoid. Though it did not stop her awareness of him. It was as if the air around him reverberated, calling to her to look, to recognise him as someone worthy. But she couldn't, that was not her path. She could only save him from another kick to his body. It was not enough.

Chapter Two

Lucan's ribs protested as he lowered himself to the ground. Why he had let that prick of a man take so many hits against them, he had no idea. He leaned back against the stone wall that currently separated him from freedom, shifting to try and find a position that didn't hurt.

Rolf watched him, his young eyes holding an expression far older than his years. The lad had attached himself to Lucan since the beginning of this godforsaken campaign. Lucan shouldn't have encouraged it, but Rolf had reminded him of his own son. So he kept him with him when he should have ignored him like he did the rest of the invading force. Now they were stuck in this senseless situation with no clear way out. 'You can go and sit by the fire, lad. I'll be all right.'

Rolf was loyal. Lucan would give him that, foolish but loyal. Even though Rolf was able to move away from him, Lucan knew that he wouldn't. Rolf still had the use of his hands; he was the only prisoner who didn't have chains around his wrists, only one around one ankle. Maybe the French didn't have any the right size, or maybe they had a shred of decency towards the innocent child. Rolf could move about, but could not run around and find something to get the rest of them loose.

'Why have they done that?' Rolf asked, nodding to where Lucan was chained tightly by his wrists to a section of the inner castle wall, nowhere near the rest of the English prisoners.

'They realise how fierce I am and want to keep me separate.' He winked at the lad, who seemed to take the answer at face value, which was sweetly complimentary.

Lucan thought his position away from others and, more importantly, the fire and the meagre warmth it provided, was punishment. Retribution for refusing to acknowledge the arrogant Frenchman who had attacked Lucan's ribs with the toe of his boot for daring to look up at his betrothed. In truth, Lucan knew he shouldn't have stared at her like that. It wasn't polite to look at a woman for that length of time, regardless of who she was. Yet for some reason, once he'd seen her, he hadn't wanted to look away. Long dark hair had framed a pale, unsmiling face. They were natural enemies, and yet there was something about her stillness that his soul latched on to. She was like a smooth pebble resting on the shoreline while a storm raged around it. For him, she'd been a fixed point to hold onto and he'd been like a drowning man, clinging to her look as if she might save him by sheer will alone.

Among her people, she was the only one who didn't glare at him and the rest of them with visceral hatred. He wondered at that. From the wreckage the English had caused, Lucan knew there was no shortage of reason for the French to hate them. Hell knew, he despised a lot of them himself. Right now, if he could get his hands on one Englishman in particular, he would be, if not a happier man, then potentially a less furious one.

He growled, remembering what their foolish leader

had done earlier. Rolf looked up at the noise. 'Are you thinking of Lord David again?'

He chuckled darkly. 'I cannot stop, lad.'

'He should have listened to you.'

'Aye.' If their leader had paid attention to what Lucan had said, not one of them would be inside this castle.

'Why didn't he?'

'Because he is our leader and he thought he knew best.' This was a polite way of saying it. That the man had a smaller brain than a sheep was another.

'But you are bigger than him. You could have overpowered him and...'

'Lad, I am a baron, he is a Lord. If word got back to the King that I had disobeyed him, then my head would be on a spike before I could protest my innocence. I would not be able to get back to England and...' He petered out. He had to get home, he had to. His life could not end here, not so far away from the only person he loved.

'You need to get back to your son,' Rolf finished for him.

'Aye.' In truth, Richard would be fine without Lucan. Before Lucan had left he had ensured Richard was surrounded by men Lucan trusted implicitly, they were too afraid of him to risk incurring Lucan's wrath. He did not need to worry about his son, but if he never heard Richard's innocent laugh again or saw his whole body light up in excitement when he caught sight of his father, Lucan would not be all right.

No one had ever looked at Lucan with such joy. He was the only person in the world who loved Lucan for who he was and not for what he could do for him., Lucan would be damned if a prick like David kept him from seeing his boy again. Getting home was all he had thought about from the moment he had left, and now it looked as if it was going to take even longer to achieve his dream.

During the weeks of the unnecessarily violent campaign, Lucan had not bonded with his fellow knights. His size seemed to frighten people off before they got the chance to know him. Over the years he'd become used to it, enjoyed the peace being left alone gave him. If he'd ever had the desire to change that, it had long since left him.

He certainly wasn't interested in the men he travelled with now. They had welcomed the destruction they had been ordered to create, while Lucan had mourned the pointlessness of it all. Clustered around the firepit the others had been given to keep them warm, he doubted any of them gave a thought for him at all; he had not given them any cause to like him. Still chained, at least they had warmth to keep them slightly more comfortable. Lord David was not among them. Somehow the rancid cur had managed to get himself within the castle, he was probably even being fed.

Lucan's stomach growled and Rolf grinned at him, his wide eyes luminous in the dark. 'That was loud.'

'Aye, I'm very hungry.' He pretended to appraise Rolf. 'There's not much of you, but I reckon you'd make a decent snack.'

Rolf giggled and then winced, touching a hand to his cheek. In the darkness, Lucan could not see the cut he knew to be there. Tied up as he was, he could not help the boy. The wound did not look deep but even the smallest graze could turn deadly if not treated properly.

Footsteps sounded behind him, soft as if the owner of the feet did not want to be heard. Lucan turned slowly to see who was coming; he did not want a knife in his back. Even chained, he knew he would try to protect himself and Rolf.

The woman from the battlements was approaching carrying a bowl in one hand.

'You don't speak French,' he said quickly to Rolf, no time to explain how it would be easier to learn the plans of their enemy if the French let down their guard in front of them. One of the easiest ways to do that was to pretend not to understand their language.

The boy nodded once. He was quick and clever and hopefully understood without further explanation.

The woman did not glance in Lucan's direction but that strange pull she seemed to exert on him came back, as if by her very presence she could soothe away some of the pain in his ribs and quiet the fury that raged in his veins. Kneeling down in front of Rolf, she gestured for him to come closer.

Rolf glanced at Lucan, questioning whether this was wise with the brief tilt of his head. 'Go on.' He nodded. He was fairly sure the lady meant no harm and, if she did… well, Lucan was chained but not incapable.

Her face was shades of grey in the feeble light of the crescent moon. She was not smiling, nor were her lips downturned, but something about her seemed resigned. Maybe he was projecting his own thoughts on her. Hell knew, he would be subdued if he was betrothed to the pig who thought it acceptable to kick a chained man when he was on the floor, who did not spare a glance for the child he had inadvertently hurt by his actions. Pointing to her chest, she said, 'Jehanne.'

Rolf paused, wetting his lips with his tongue.

'You can tell her your name,' Lucan told the boy. In some circles, the lad's name would be significant, but not here. Lucan doubted even Lord David would be as unwise as to blurt out the boy's lofty connections.

The boy nodded. 'Rolf,' he said, pointing to his own chest before gesturing backwards. 'Lucan.'

Mademoiselle Jehanne did not turn to look at him. Irritated that it mattered to him, Lucan looked away, staring into the blackness of the courtyard, only to turn back almost immediately. It had been a long time since he had been in the company of a woman. That must be why he wanted to look at this one so intently. There could be no other reason for it, or at least not one on which Lucan was willing to dwell. Besides, if she meant Rolf harm, Lucan would need to be watching; it was his duty to keep a close eye on the proceedings. Turning away would be negligent. Ignoring his relief at having a genuine reason to observe her, he settled back into position.

Jehanne placed her bowl on the ground and pointed to Rolf's cheek where the skin was grazed. '*Je veux voire votre visage.*'

Rolf frowned as if he did not understand her request to see his face. She beckoned him closer. 'She is going to check the wound on your face,' said Lucan.

Rolf looked back at him as if to say, *I know that, you imbecile*, but he continued to go along with Lucan's pretence of not understanding Jehanne words. Lucan shifted his back against the wall, uncomfortable at feeling foolish.

He rarely gave into introspection. There was no time for doubt when one had a castle to run, a boy to raise and a headstrong King to obey. But even he had to admit that it was unwise to show Jehanne he understood her intentions only moments after telling Rolf not to do so. Hopefully, the lady would not understand their silent communication or their spoken one. A nobly born Frenchwoman would have no reason to learn the language of the English peasants; even so, he would prefer not to come across as a halfwit to the lad.

Pulling some fabric out of the bowl, Lady Jehanne squeezed it tightly, the water running over her long fingers and into the fabric of her sleeve. She shuffled closer to Rolf and began to gently clean his wound. The boy's eyes fluttered closed at her ministrations, making him look even younger than his twelve years. Some lads looked like men at his age, but Rolf had been slow to grow and could have passed for ten or less. During their long days together, Lucan knew the boy lamented the fact that he did not look older, but his youth might save him. He'd be manacled to the wall like the others if he looked like any of the older pages.

Holding the boy's chin in her fingertips, Jehanne inspected the rest of his face. Seemingly satisfied with what she saw, she dropped her hold and returned her cloth to the bowl.

'*Attendez*,' she said, gesturing for them to remain where they were, as if the two of them had somewhere else they could go. All they could do was wait for her return.

'She is pretty,' said Rolf, when her footsteps had faded.

Lucan grunted. He did not want to think about the woman's deliciously soft-looking neck, or the way her long fingers might feel against his skin. He closed his eyes tightly. It had been a long time since he had held a woman, that was all this was. No one should go as long as he had without touching another person.

'Do you not think so?' asked the lad, for some reason not letting the subject go.

'Aye, she looks well enough.' Lucan made the mistake of opening his eyes and looking at the boy. He was squirming, and it was clear he had something else he wanted to say.

'You were looking at her on the battlements.' Rolf was fighting a smirk as if he had caught Lucan doing something naughty. 'Why was that?'

Not having a proper answer, Lucan settled on, 'It seemed to annoy her betrothed.'

'You were looking before that.' Rolf's grin appeared now. 'I may be young but I am not blind. You *do* think she's pretty.'

'It's irrelevant what I think, boy. I'm chained to a wall, an enemy of your fancy friend. She'd as likely spit on me than look at me.' He wished he hadn't been quite so harsh as the boy's smile faded. They were prisoners, but Lucan hadn't needed to ram it home quite so forcibly. 'But of course, I think she is lovely-looking. I'm not blind either.'

Rolf's whole body lifted at Lucan's admission. 'I knew it! I've never known you like a woman before. Is it because…'

Whatever Rolf had been about to ask was thankfully interrupted by Jehanne's return. This time, she was wearing a thick cloak, the type one would wear in the depths of winter. She glanced over her shoulder before dropping into a crouch next to Rolf again. '*Voilà*,' she said, pulling a loaf of bread out of a wide sleeve and handing it to the boy.

Rolf held it for a moment, as if unable to truly grasp its magnificence, before he tore into it, tearing off hunks and shoving them into his mouth. Jehanne watched him for a moment, a small smile finally breaking onto her face. Lucan briefly wished for sunlight so he could see her expression properly before dismissing the foolish notion. It did not matter what this woman looked like when she was happy, they were enemies.

Together they watched the boy enjoy his food. After a while, she turned to Lucan. As her look met his, a jolt ran through his body before it slowly stilled. A strange sense of calmness washed through him, as if she had somehow soothed away the horror of the last few weeks and replaced it with something else entirely.

She pointed to his hands. He blinked at her. Was she going to unlock the manacles? Surely not. She must know that if she did so, he would tear through her castle's defences and disappear into the night.

When he didn't move, he heard a snick of impatience, the sound coming from the back of Jehanne's throat. She reached over and encircled one of his hands with both of hers. The touch of her skin was a lick of fire that shot through his body, burning everything in its wake. Lucan made a noise, something between a grunt and a groan, but she ignored him, twisting his hand so that his palm was facing her. She snicked at him again and reached for the bowl. With neat, precise touches, she began to wash away the small stones that were embedded in his skin after he'd been pushed to the ground.

Lucan swallowed, trying to concentrate on the stinging of the water on the tiny cuts, trying desperately to ignore the way his heart was racing, almost falling over itself to beat quicker, urging him to do something, anything to keep this woman touching him. He shifted, the sensation almost too much to bear. Jehanne stalled, looking up at him from beneath long lashes, and raised an eyebrow. He shook his head, not wanting her to stop, even though he should.

As she moved to his other hand and began the whole process again, Lucan watched her bent head. Her braid was coming loose, revealing the swirl of her crown, and he fought the strangest urge to reach up and press his fingertip to it. Not only was that the oddest impulse he'd ever experienced, but it would also mean hitting her in the face with the chains that bound him. Hardly a fitting response for the kindness she was showing him.

She dropped his hands, evidently finished. His breathing was unsteady, his pulse still thundering in his neck. Jehanne was as calm as a pond on a summer's day, completely unaffected by the moment that had just passed. He was unable to take his eyes off her as she dropped the cloth back into the bowl and stood. Lightly she ruffled Rolf's hair, murmuring something to him that Lucan could not hear. The boy ducked his head, smiling slightly. Catching Lucan's look, his smile died as he held out half of the loaf. 'I saved this for you,' he said.

Lucan's skin burned as he took the food from the boy. He wished he could leave it all for the child, but his stomach was hollow. He could not remember the last time he had eaten. 'That is kind of you, Rolf,' he said.

Jehanne said something else quietly before moving away, fading into the darkness within a few steps. Lucan watched her go as he chewed on the bread.

'Well-enough looking,' snorted Rolf. 'You were like one of father's wolf-hounds right then.'

Rather than ask in what way he'd resembled the giant animals that were favourites of Rolf's father, Lucan took another mouthful. He did not want to know. Rolf carried on anyway. 'Those beasts always look like they want to rip your throat out, but give them some food and a belly rub and they are yours for always.'

Lucan swallowed, the bread sticking in his throat. He swallowed again. 'I was going to offer to lie next to you for warmth, but you can go wallow in the river for all I care. I'm not like a dog.'

Rolf laughed, coming closer, knowing that Lucan didn't mean it. Especially considering Rolf was right, that was a fairly accurate description of his behaviour. Even if it hadn't been, Lucan would want Rolf to be warm; they both knew that. From the moment Rolf had joined their band of men, Lucan had taken on the role of father to the lad. It wasn't that Rolf reminded him of his own son, the age difference was too large for that, but maybe becoming a father had changed Lucan in some way. Regardless, Rolf looked to him as a father figure and so that is what he had become.

'Is she like your wife?' asked Rolf as he settled next to him.

'Who?'

'Mademoiselle Jehanne. Does she remind you of your wife? Is that why you like to look at her?'

Lucan pondered the question; he rarely thought of Isabelle these days. It had been four years since his wife had passed away. He and Isabelle had not known each other before they had wed, but he had been lucky with his arranged marriage. The two of them got along well together. She occasionally made him smile, which, as she had pointed out, was difficult to do.

Together they had adored their son. He'd respected her deeply, and when she had taken violently ill, Lucan had searched for a cure. It had been no use. She had slowly faded before his eyes, one day simply not waking. It was the only time in his life that he had shed a tear, not that anyone else would know. By the time he had announced her death to his people, he was back to himself.

However he acted whenever he was around other people, he still carried her loss close to his heart. She was one of the few people he'd ever liked, and now she was gone. Knowing that the son she had adored with every fibre of her being would never remember her was one of the most brutal things Lucan had faced. The loss for his son was staggering.

Members of his stronghold had suggested to Lucan that he marry again. It had been implied, albeit only once, that Richard may not make it to adulthood, and should that happen it was Lucan's duty to provide his baronetcy with another heir. Lucan's rage at the suggestion had passed into legend; a story Lucan sometimes heard whispered as he passed by. The man who had suggested it still quivered whenever he caught sight of Lucan even years later.

It was not that Lucan did not want another woman in his life. There was the physical side of marriage he missed to the point of pain on some days, but it was a sacrifice he was prepared to make. He did not want to lose another person in his life, could not go through a wife's death again. He did not make friends easily and did not want the pain of losing someone he cared about. It was not only that which held him off finding someone new. The idea of conceiving a spare child, one that could replace Richard, was the worst thing imaginable to him. Richard was the only one whose love was pure. There would never be another wife; of this he was positive.

Emotion caused pain. Pain caused weakness and Lucan was not a weak man.

'No,' he said eventually in reply to Rolf. 'Mademoiselle Jehanne is nothing like Lady Isabelle. And,' he continued, forestalling the next comment, 'I was only looking at her because her head was very close to my hands.'

'I see,' said Rolf. 'Are they going to make us sleep outside?'

Lucan cleared his throat, surprised the subject had been dropped so quickly. Rolf was young, he probably had not spotted Lucan's lie. Because his response had been a falsehood. Lucan was finding it hard to keep his gaze from Jehanne, which had more to do with the physical side of marriage than the companionship side… 'Yes, we will have to sleep outside tonight. You have done that before, have you not?'

'Never without any sort of cover.'

'As you shared your bread with me, I suppose I could share my cloak with you.' It would not be enough to keep them from the coolness of the October night, but it would have to do. 'Or you could go and lie nearer the firepit.'

Rolf wrinkled his nose and laid his head down on the stone floor of the courtyard. Lucan flung some of his cloak around the boy. It was hard with his hands in chains but Rolf would feel the benefit of the extra cover during the night.

Gradually the noise from the other men slowed to a

low rumble, and then nothing at all. Next to him, Rolf's thin body went limp, snores Lucan would tease him about tomorrow falling from his lips. Lucan's ribs ached. If he could look at his skin, he was sure it would be covered in blossoming bruises. He didn't want to give that little pig of a man any credence, but he had to admit that the Frenchman had known where to aim his boot to cause the most amount of pain.

Lucan lay on his back, tracking the path of the moon as it crossed slowly across the sky. A plan would need to be formed, an escape attempted, but he was exhausted and hurt and could come up with nothing.

Noise from the castle gradually stopped altogether, only sounds of horses in the nearby stables could be heard over the grunts and snores of his English companions. At first he thought he was dreaming it, but he slowly became aware of soft footsteps sounding nearby again. He turned his head slowly, closing his eyes so they were nearly completely shut, not wanting to alert whoever was approaching that he was awake.

It was Mademoiselle Jehanne. Lucan slowed his breathing, giving every impression he was as deeply asleep as Rolf.

Through his barely opened eyes, he could make out a bulky shape held in one arm. Moments later, she threw a blanket over Rolf. It looked as if she might leave without sparing Lucan a glance but at the last moment, he felt the weight of her gaze on his skin as she looked him over.

Before he could even think of expressing his gratitude for the extra warmth, she turned and scurried away quickly. Gone so fast it was as if he had imagined her presence. Lucan reached over and slowly tucked the blanket around the boy and, against all odds, fell into a dreamless sleep.

Chapter Three

Lucan didn't mind hard work but pointless toil for no reason made his blood boil. As he pushed his way forward, he reminded himself he was a prisoner, and he wasn't dead. Every day he got up and did what he was told was another day that his head wasn't removed and stuck on a spike for all to see. He had to live because he had to get back to his son. He would toil and do what was asked of him, because he did not want to fall foul of his captors, but this…this was backbreaking and futile.

Lord David, the loathsome cur, spent his days inside the castle. Lucan had seen him twice. From the way his clothes still looked unmarked, it was clear that he was not spending the sennight since their capture labouring at some degrading task. The rest of the prisoners had been taken to mine iron ore. The Frenchmen seemed pleased to have their captives collect the material that would be used to make weapons, which would, in turn, be used to kill Englishmen.

Lucan had not been sent to the mine with the others. Perhaps because of his size, or because Monsieur le Chevalier Dupont had not yet forgiven him for his lack of deference. His task was meant to humiliate him, to reduce him to that of a mindless animal.

He stumbled, falling briefly to one knee. The man behind him yelled curses in French, curses which called into question his mother's morality. Still pretending not to understand the language, he did not respond, merely pushing himself to his feet. Up ahead of him, the unploughed ground seemed to stretch on forever into the grey horizon.

As a punishment, reducing him to the role of an ox was effective for more than just eroding his dignity. Shoulders screaming in protest, Lucan began to pull the plough behind him, his only focus on surviving the gruelling work. Later, his body would demand sleep and food. Thoughts of escape would be impossible to grasp through the thick fog of exhaustion.

Stepping forward, he forced himself to remember Richard's innocent, beaming smile, the one that suffused his whole body when he caught sight of his father. *That* was why Lucan was accepting this. Fighting back could result in his death, but if he held on, he would be ransomed eventually and he would see his son's face once more. Humiliation was a price worth paying; death was not.

The flutter of purple where it should not have been caught his eye. He knew who it would be; there was no reason to lift his head to look at Mademoiselle Jehanne, and yet he did. Just as he'd watched her pass in the opposite direction earlier, she now held his gaze again. Contained as always, Jehanne followed several other ladies as they made their way back to the castle. From the dampness of some of the ladies' hair, and because they carried no washing or barrels of water, he guessed they had been bathing at a nearby river.

Lucan could not be sure what it was about Jehanne

that held his attention. Certainly, it appeared that no one else in the castle paid her much notice, and yet he found himself captivated. He wanted to know her secrets, to unravel her mind until he understood how anyone could seem so calm.

If he hadn't pretended on that first night that he could not understand the language she spoke, he could ask her. Every night since, she brought food to Rolf and, he'd begun to suspect, himself too. Hunks of mouth-watering bread and sharply sweet fruit supplemented the meagre rations their captors doled out.

Visiting under the cover of darkness, Jehanne handed the food to Rolf, glancing at Lucan only briefly. Each time her eyes met his, his heart jolted and he had to look away to get rid of the uncomfortable feeling. It was a sensation he did not want to understand or dwell upon. He was too hardened by life to develop a young lad's infatuation with a woman. Surely his fascination was only because he was unused to such attention. Still, it was the quantity of food she brought that suggested she might be thinking of him as well as the boy, that maybe he occasionally crossed her mind too. Or perhaps Lucan was delusional, hoping that it was true because then it would justify the number of times a day he thought of her.

Her stillness intrigued him. Tired as he was, rage still flowed through his veins, as if his fury alone could transport him to his son. Jehanne's presence was a gentle breeze brushing against his skin, somehow soothing him, even from a distance. Impossible though it was, he wanted more of that, and so he struggled to pull his gaze from her, even out here, where it was so brazen of him to look.

Pain blossomed against his back, sharp and sudden.

Turning, he found the man watching over him wielding a whip meant to urge on a reluctant ox.

Red coloured his vision, thoughts and plans fading to nothing, only the cold, hard certainty of retribution. The overseer paled as Lucan stepped towards him, the leather of his harness creaking as it strained. It didn't matter, nothing would stop him getting to the man who thought he could treat him like a beast of burden and get away with it.

He was reaching for the man when he heard his name on the breeze.

'Sir Lucan.' Jehanne's voice, speaking directly to him for the first time was the only thing that had him stilling. 'Monsieur le Chevalier Dupont wishes to talk to you. You must come now.'

Heavily accented as it was, her English was perfect. Turning to the man with the whip, she repeated her instruction in French this time, calling him Matieu, who shook his head vehemently when Jehanne suggested he untie the yoke. Matieu was right to fear him; given half the chance, Lucan would make it very clear how furious he was.

'He will not hurt me,' argued Jehanne in French. Turning to Lucan, she added, 'Will you?'

He shifted his shoulders; she raised an eyebrow.

'*Non*,' he agreed, his ears burning as it dawned on him that she had known he had understood her this whole time.

'Even so,' replied Matieu, 'he will remain chained. I do not trust him not to come after me.' A valid concern, showing the man had some slight sense.

Matieu shot him one last worried glance before scurrying towards the safety of the castle, leaving Jehanne alone with him. For someone who did not trust Lucan, he had not seemed to want to hang around to protect Jehanne. Coward.

The leather yoke pressed against his shoulders as Jehanne appraised the ties that held it together, keeping it in place on his body.

'A helpful man,' he commented, as she stepped closer, her fingers running over the straps as she tried to work out how to unbind them.

'I suspect he thought you would rip him apart with your bare hands if you were free.' His gaze caught on that swirl on the crown of her head, the one he found oddly endearing. 'Would you have done?'

A faint breeze stirred her hair, pushing some strands onto the sleeve of his forearm. A strange desperate yearning to touch it was building inside him. If he lied, he fancied she would know. 'I'd like to think not.' He had to remember his son, had to remember his reason to keep living. 'But he whipped me, and I wouldn't do that to one of my animals, not even if provoked. In truth, I do not know what I would have done if you hadn't intervened.'

'It is good that I stopped you then, before you did something you regretted. I should not have liked to see your head on a spike.'

His heart turned over oddly and he cursed himself for a fool. 'I would not have thought you cared.'

'I don't. I dislike the smell of rotting flesh and I also think you would make a garish corpse.'

His smile shocked him; he had not thought himself capable of the gesture anymore. Her fingers finally tugged on the bindings, loosening the ties. Together they pulled him out of the yoke and it hit the ground with a heavy thud.

'I would offer to carry it back to the castle but…' He held up his hands to show why he was not able.

She raised a dark eyebrow. 'That is a poor attempt to get me to take them off you. I couldn't in any case. I do not have the key. Matieu would not have had it either in case you could overpower him.' Glancing at the yoke, she shrugged. 'I could also carry it, but I think we shall leave it for Matieu. He was chicken-hearted to run away; this can be his payment.'

'Are you not afraid I will hurt *you*?'

She began to walk towards the castle as if she expected him to meekly follow. He stayed where he was, looking towards the endless grasslands, the horizon beckoning him forward, wide and open.

'You could run,' she said without turning, 'but I would not recommend it. There is not a Frenchman alive in these parts who is not begging for the chance to run a sword through an Englishman's belly. Fierce though you undoubtedly are, you cannot fight them off with your hands bound.'

She was right, damn it. Good though his French was, his accent would give him away immediately. Besides, the manacles would mark him out as a prisoner, not to mention how heavy they were and would therefore slow him down. And there was Rolf. The lad didn't need him. The other men might not treat him as a son but they would look after him. Rolf had become attached to him though and would no doubt feel betrayed if Lucan disappeared without explanation. Not that the boy's feelings should matter to Lucan. Rolf was not his son; Richard was. With one last look at the open expanse, Lucan began to trudge after Jehanne.

One thick, dark braid rested against her back between her shoulder blades, barely stirring as she appeared to glide towards the castle gates. Catching up to her, he felt like a lumbering, cave-dwelling troll as he walked beside her. The kind of mythical beast your parents warned you about as a child so that you did not stray too far away from home.

'What does Monsieur le Chevalier Dupont want with me?'

'Nothing.'

His boots hit the drawbridge with a heavy thud. 'Then what…'

She glanced across at him. 'I saw your face and acted without thinking. I did not want to see yours and Matieu's lifeless bodies in the castle by the end of the day.'

'Because of the stench.'

She nodded briskly. 'Exactly that.'

A strange warmth began to spread through him. He couldn't remember anyone caring for him enough to step in when he was in trouble. Maybe his parents had, but he could barely recall them. They had died when he was a boy and he'd been raised by men who had taught him how to run a castle, but not how to deal with emotions. Isabelle had liked him well enough, but she had never put herself between him and a problem. His late wife had probably believed him capable of dealing with any given situation, and he had never found himself in one that had disproved that theory. Unless one counted this, which he didn't because it wasn't yet over.

To have someone care, even if they were hiding under

the guise of not wanting their home to smell, was a new experience and he wasn't sure how he felt about it yet. He could not believe that someone this good would have to wed Monsieur le Chevalier Dupont. Even if he wasn't Lucan's captor, Lucan would still loathe the man for the way he treated anyone he deemed his inferior.

'When will you wed the prick?' he asked, regretting the crude words as soon as they were out of his mouth, especially when her body jolted.

'Soon,' was all she said in reply.

The heavy metal on his wrists prevented him from scratching his arm, his irritation at not being able to alleviate the itch the only explanation for the dull ache in his chest. He dismissed the errant thought that he might be experiencing pity for this woman; compassion for people he did not know was not the way he was built.

Curious stares turned their way as they crossed the central courtyard.

'Where are we going?' he murmured.

'Inside,' was her frustratingly vague answer.

'What will you do with me when we get there?'

Another one of those raised eyebrows, this time accompanied with a slight smirk. Heat spilled across his face at her flirtatious glance, or was it? Had he wished it into existence through sheer desperation?

Now her face was turned forwards, her expression as calm as always, no hint she was imagining them pressed tightly together, their breath intermingling, as he was. He had not lain with a woman save for his wife, and she had been ill for a while before her death. Five long years without intimacy had him creating a scenario that would never happen.

Inside the castle, coldness seeped from the whitewashed stone walls. Sweat from his exertion dried on his skin, making him shiver.

'Why not act meeker?' she asked as they made their way along an empty passageway. 'You could be with the others rather than toiling by yourself.'

'Who said I wanted company?'

'A fair point,' she agreed. 'I am often not keen on it myself. But if you did not constantly give the impression that you wished to rip someone's head clean from their shoulders, you wouldn't have your hands continually manacled.'

She was right, of course. He knew that if he acted differently, then he might get some reprieve, but he had not found it within himself to pretend. 'I do not know how to be any other way.'

They came to a recess, obviously built as a place for soldiers to defend the keep, but currently empty. She gestured for him to step within the secluded alcove.

'What is your intention here?' he asked, remaining where he was.

She wetted her lips, the gesture surprisingly nervous for such a tranquil woman. 'To stay out of sight for a plausible amount of time for you to speak with Urian and then for you to return outside.'

'Are you not concerned Matieu and Urian will talk and discover your deception?'

'It is highly unlikely. Urian considers Matieu, and those like him, to be beneath him. Even if Matieu tried to stop him to ask, Urian would pretend not to see or hear him.'

Still Lucan did not step forward. The space was

cramped, so they would be close. Not touching, but nearer than was wise, although he could not pinpoint the source of his unease. Jehanne was tiny. If she tried to overpower him, she would fail. That could not be the reason he was reluctant to go any further. Yet something was telling him that taking another step would change things somehow. This woman might not be a physical match, but there was something about her that made him suspect she might be able to hurt him in a way no one else ever had before. Her kindness somehow made *him* vulnerable. It was not a sensation he was used to experiencing.

'Are you afraid of me?' she asked, amusement in her dark eyes.

'Should I be?'

He'd meant it half in jest, but she took the answer seriously, tilting her head to one side and regarding him thoughtfully. 'I have never hurt a soul,' she said eventually. 'Nor would I attack a person for no reason. And I certainly would not show violence to a man who shows such gentleness to a boy, who I suspect is not his own son, and who is ignored by others who should also care for him.'

Squirming, he took a step forward, hoping the movement would disguise his embarrassment over her assessment of him. Her next words showed she wasn't fooled. 'Why show the world your fierceness and yet hide your goodness?'

'Showing a child compassion hardly makes me a saint. If you think that's all it takes to make a man decent, you have been around Urian too long.'

Her shoulders dropped and he half-wished he'd not said anything. Reminding himself that she was betrothed to that pox-ridden pig would help him remain focused. Her thumb rubbed the palm of her hand, the gesture oddly mesmerising.

'You are right,' she said eventually. 'Urian is a problem. He is not a man I would wish to marry, should I have a choice in the matter.'

'Then you have my sympathies.'

Her brown eyes appraised him frankly and a pit opened up in his stomach. She'd been testing him this whole time. There was a reason she had brought him here and now he was about to find out. She hadn't been helping him after all. Or rather, she had, but there was a reason behind it. Being used wasn't new to him; being this disappointed was.

Her thumb moved quicker over her skin, the only outward sign that she was nervous. 'Are you sympathetic enough to help me?'

'You want me to kill him?'

She recoiled so quickly, her head smacked against the solid wall behind her. Wincing, she pressed her fingers to the back of her skull. 'Why would you think such a thing?' she asked, her accent stronger than ever.

'Your people think me a mindless brute. Or at least that is how I am being treated.' He held up his shackled hands in case there was any confusion as to what he meant. 'If you believe that to be true, then my assumption to your appeal is only logical.'

'My people have lived through weeks of horror while *your* people destroyed everything in their wake.' Her eyes were full of fire, her fingers taut. '*That* is why you are chained. Do not blame us for our response to the devastation you English have wreaked on our country.'

Lucan understood her anger. He had seen what had been done even if he'd had no hand in it, had vomited from the sight and stench of the total ruination of everything that had been good about the land. The damage was excessive and did not contribute towards the King's cause.

'I had nothing to do with that.'

An eye-roll suggested she did not believe him. He found himself wanting to make sure she did.

'The fires and the murders were a tremendous waste. I argued heavily against it, and when I was ignored by the King, I volunteered to travel with Lord David because I could not bear to be a part of something so awful. We were sent on a scouting mission. We were to look for signs of King Phillipe's fighters. He is rumoured to have retreated far further into France than here, we are to report back with any information. We had found no evidence when your betrothed came upon us. He bested me once, so as you can see, I am not the man to help you with whatever you have planned.'

Lucan did not mention how the capture had taken place. Not wanting to be part of any unnecessary violence, Lucan had not protested when Lord David had led them away from any potential conflict. Perhaps he should have exerted his authority, because the man did not listen when it came to good advice. If Lord David had heeded Lucan's words, none of them would be captives now. There was no point explaining all this to Jehanne. To suggest he was a better fighter than the French knight would sound arrogant, not to mention false, as he was the one in chains and Urian wasn't.

Some of the fire in her eyes dimmed but he was in no

doubt now that, despite her kindnesses to him, he was still her enemy.

'I don't want you to kill Urian,' she said. 'I would not ask for the price of your soul in return for what I have to offer.'

'Then what do you want from me?'

'If I release you from those chains and let you and Rolf out of the castle, I would like you to swear an oath, guaranteeing you will see me safely to England.'

The cold metal of his chains chaffed against his skin, reminding him how good it would feel to be free of them. 'What is in England?' he hedged, not yet sure of his answer. If the English were the enemy, what reason could she have for travelling there?

'My… I…' Her eyes darted to the side, another sign that she was not as composed as she appeared. She straightened. 'I was previously betrothed to someone else, William of Borne.' Her eyes softened, her fondness for the man shining in her expression. 'But the contract was severed when your King decided to make war with mine. I should like to return to…him.'

Lucan leaned against the wall, crossing his legs at the ankle, giving himself time to think about her request. His first instinct was to deny her. It was not in his nature to help ill-fated lovers, even if they were separated through no fault of their own. But of course that was not the only reason he was irritated by her request. It was proof that he had indeed imagined her coquettish look at him earlier and evidence against his errant thought that she might be bringing him food because she had a soft spot for him.

If she was desperate enough to risk travelling through a country in the grip of war to get to another man, then it was evident she did not think of Lucan any differently from Rolf.

'Well,' she demanded.

'I am thinking.'

'Think quicker.' She glanced along the still empty passageway but he would not be hurried.

'How would you be capable of getting Rolf and I out of here? And if you are able to do so, why not let yourself out.'

'I know where the keys to the manacles are kept. There are several ways out of the castle. I know them all. Getting you out is not a problem. As for me leaving… I am not a fighter, I have no skill with a sword. I could not get to the next castle by myself let alone another country.'

That was true. Travelling alone would make her vulnerable. She was in love with the man to whom she had previously been betrothed, but not to a foolish extent. She would be a good travelling companion, he was sure that she would obey his commands and she could aid in his disguise if he needed to communicate with anyone in French.

He could go home, see Richard sooner than if he waited for diplomacy to take place. That could take years and there was no guarantee the King would even be in the mood to intervene on the English captives' behalf, not after Edward's failed attempt to take Cambrais. There were many good reasons to take her up on her offer but several good ones not to, not least making himself the enemy of her vengeful fiancé.

Her eyes were wide and pleading and his chest ached for her.

'I appreciate your offer,' he said eventually, 'but I am afraid I am going to decline.'

'You will not help me?'

'I will not.'

Chapter Four

High within the castle keep, Jehanne sat amongst the other gently bred women of the Balladur fortress, her mother and sister, the constable's wife and the like, their needles sinking in and out of the silk as they used gold cloth to weave an intricate design around the edges. The repetitive swish of the thread being pulled through the fabric was almost soothing in its rhythm, as was the soft chatter between some of the older women washing over the room, with no need for anyone else to join in.

Jehanne tried to pretend they were working on any old garment and not the dress in which she was to be married to Urian, that the pattern they were following was merely a pretty decoration and not the symbolism of unity, peace and longevity.

Her days were numbered now. Every beat of her heart taking her closer to the time when she would have to join with a man whose cold eyes held the promise of a bleak future. There had to be a way out of it, but if there was, she could not conjure it up.

Her spontaneous request of the red-headed giant two days ago had gone very badly wrong. Blurting out her offer to help him escape if he would only aid her in return had been a mistake. She'd known it as soon as the words had left her mouth and his blue eyes had turned stormy.

Acting impulsively was deeply unlike her. Normally, she would think through a plan from back to front and left to right and round again a thousand times before acting on it, but this time it had blurted from her as soon as the thought had appeared in her mind.

As they'd sat in that secluded alcove, she had been unable to stop her gaze from returning to the deep red marks on the skin of his wrists. Where the chains he wore had rubbed against his skin, causing it to look raw. There was no way it was not painful, and yet he made no comment on it and did not wince whenever he moved. She wanted to remove them, to bring him a poultice to soothe it, even though she didn't quite trust him.

A man may be kind to a child, may protect him from the cold night air with his own cloak but that did not make him a peaceful creature. A fire burned in Lucan's eyes that no amount of spirit-breaking toil could douse. Trying not to look at him, somehow, proved impossible. Something about the sheer power of him drew her eye whenever she walked past him, and, much to her annoyance, she found herself making excuses to do so more often than necessary. She could see his anger burning within him day after long day, even as some of his fellow countrymen looked defeated by the lack of attempted rescue or even a word of hope from the English.

Nevertheless, that chaffed skin had triggered the idea in her mind, a way in which they could both be free, and she'd spoken without thinking. Though as she'd said it, the idea developed, becoming something she wanted more than anything. To pull off such a feat would be difficult, there was no doubt of that. It could end with both of them imprisoned or dead, but even those dire thoughts hadn't stopped the hope surging through her. Her heart had raced at the thought that she might be able to get away from Urian after all, that marriage to a man who made her skin crawl might not be inevitable.

Lucan's refusal was a pail of cold water, thrown unexpectedly over her head, a shock she felt to the core of her soul. With no prior knowledge to fall back on, she was still sure that a captive refusing to be let go was unheard of. If someone gave her the option of running away this afternoon, this very moment, she would take it without hesitation, whatever the terms, and that was even taking into consideration her cautious nature. To stay here and marry Urian was to die; a slow, painful death in which her body still lived but her soul slowly disappeared. One day she would become like her mother, so beaten down by her dictatorial husband she appeared to have no thought of her own, and that could not happen.

There had to be a way out of here, there *had* to be. She just could not think of one, or at least she could not think of one that did not involve having the giant help her in some way.

Next to her, Margot hummed softly, occasionally running a hand over her stomach, an indulgent smile on her face as she carried out her work. Jehanne's fingers tightened on her needle as she wondered what her sister would say if Jehanne told her the truth, that she did not want to marry Urian, that she was frightened of him and what he would do to her, not just physically but to her soul too. She tugged on the clothes she was wearing, trying to loosen the material where it had become tight around her ribcage.

'Did you ever consider becoming a nun?' she asked Margot, dropping her sewing to her lap. It was a possible way out; it might be the only way.

Margot stopped mid-stroke. 'Goodness me, no. I always knew I wanted to be a mother.' Margot reached out and smoothed her fingers over the back of Jehanne's hand, her smile full of love. 'It is normal to be nervous about becoming a wife, especially the wedding night itself. But there is no need to be afraid, it's not as unpleasant as some say. It can be over quickly and the result is the most wonderful...' Margot took her hand back, resuming the smooth stroke of her stomach, her eyes taking on a far-away look.

Jehanne resumed the steady stitching she had been working on, keeping her stare on the gold thread as a heavy weight pressed against her chest. The life of a nun had never appealed to her before, but it had to be better than marrying Urian.

A commotion sounded, loud and abrupt, breaking into the peace of the room. Heads raised quickly, the women gazing about as if to find an answer for the noise. It sounded from somewhere outside the chamber, from the bottom of the keep, Jehanne guessed. Male voices, alarmed and frantic by the sounds of it.

Her mother put her sewing down and the rest of the women followed suit. The urgent sounds were reminiscent of the early days of the English invasion when they had not been sure whether their castle would be safe or come under attack. Shouting had flared up regularly, keeping everyone on edge until it was clear danger, if there had been any, had passed. But the English had been in retreat for days now, as far as everyone knew, they should not be at the castle gates. Unless…unless they had come for the prisoners after all.

Colour drained from Margot's face, her hands protectively curling around her stomach, all hint of dreamy happiness gone. 'The invaders…' her sister wheezed, her thoughts obviously following the same direction as Jehanne's.

'It may not be them and, even if it is, it will be all right,' said Jehanne, trying to reassure Margot even as her heart thundered in her chest, panic turning her knees to water.

'No, the English…they show no mercy, not to women, not to children…'

'It is probably nothing. Perhaps Matieu spilled the ale again and now there is no beer to be had.' Jehanne did not believe that either. If it was as simple as that there would have been one man yelling and then nothing. But the shouting was ongoing, building, becoming more frantic, not less. Margot whimpered, her spine curling as if she could protect her unborn child by hunching over her stomach.

'The English were last seen heading north. It would not make sense for them to be here. We are far in the opposite direction to where they are based,' said Jehanne.

'They have come for their men. I knew it was a bad idea to keep them prisoner. I said, didn't I say?'

Until this moment, Margot had been thrilled that theirs was the only castle in France that had managed to best any of the English. Proudly announcing during the meal last night that she would be ashamed to belong to any other family. There had not been one instance of her sister suggesting that keeping captives was a bad idea.

Jehanne held her tongue; her sister was afraid and not

for herself but for the babe in her belly. Her terror was stark in her pale skin and wide eyes. If the stories they'd heard were true, then Margot was right to be fearful. But they could not be here, not even for the men the Balladur family had captured. Scouts would have seen them days ago. They would have warned them of an incoming attack. Perhaps this was something else, something unforeseen, and in the chaos there might be opportunities for those desperate enough to exploit them.

Pushing the fabric she'd been working on off her lap, Jehanne stood, decision made. 'I will go and find out what is happening.'

'No.' Margot made to grab her hand, but Jehanne was faster, moving quickly away. 'Jehanne, you cannot go, I forbid it.'

Jehanne knew Margot cared about her, but her docile sister was very different from her and would not understand this overwhelming need to do something, anything, that might change her current situation. 'I am sure it is not the English, and the sooner we find that out, the quicker you can relax,' she said, adopting the calmest, softest voice she could manage in the circumstances.

'Jehanne…' Margot whimpered, but she was already turning away, not wanting to see the anguish in her sister's eyes.

Murmuring to the woman nearest the door to lock it after her, Jehanne slipped out of the chamber before anyone else could try to stop her. Pinpricks of fear skittered over her skin, the smooth wall surrounding the spiral staircase grounding her as she skimmed her hand along it, moving downwards towards the source of the commotion.

When amongst the other women, in the shelter of the

chamber, Jehanne had believed that the castle was safe from the invaders, that this move to find out what was going on was not dangerous, that there might be something here that could help her. But the shouting had not abated, the harsh guttural tones of furious men becoming clearer the closer she got, and her confidence ebbed away.

She was either audacious or foolish, but she was not entirely sure which one. Then she remembered the glint of amusement in Urian's eyes as he'd watched a young lad spill boiling water over his fingers and she pushed herself to keep going. She was not going to find any opportunity to change her fate if she stayed locked in a high chamber, hiding from the fear of the unknown.

Reaching the bottom of the stairs, she crept over the small entranceway, her soft footsteps not necessary in light of the din outside. Opening the door slightly, she peered through the small crack she had made. It was hard to see anything through the narrow gap, but she could not make out anyone running towards the battlements, nor could she hear the ominous grinding of the portcullis being lowered in a hurry. That noise would be easy to hear even over the clamouring uproar.

Pulling open the door fully, she leaned out, keeping her feet inside so that she could quickly move behind the solid door. When there was still nothing to see or hear but the shouting coming from the direction of the central courtyard, she stepped outside and moved out of the shadows.

Seeing that the gate was open and no English men appeared to be surrounding the castle, her knees began to tremble, finally giving way to the fear rushing through her veins. She leaned against the nearest wall, the cold stone rough against her arm even through her long sleeves. How strange that her strength was abandoning her now that she could see the English were not at the gates.

A stable lad scurried past, his head down, eyes fixed on the floor.

'What is happening?' she asked him.

'The English captives have escaped,' he muttered, as he kept walking, not looking in her direction. 'Comte de Balladur is furious. I would not go near him if I were you.'

The boy picked up speed, disappearing around a corner before she could question him further.

Jehanne should return upstairs to warn her mother and reassure Margot; this was a humiliation for them but not a lethal one. Despite knowing she should go, she could not move. Her stomach swooped, diving and falling in a way that felt very close to disappointment. Until now, she hadn't realised how much hope she had still been pinning on Lucan. The disappointment of him refusing to help her had given way to the belief that, given time she could talk him round to helping her get away from Urian. Now that slim expectation was dashed, gone before she could shape it into anything real.

There really was no other option, she would have to marry Urian. Bile rose in her throat and she clutched her neck as if to stop herself from being sick. As far as everyone was concerned, she was the calm member of the de Balladur family, not given to flashes of emotion like the rest of them. Most of the time that was true but not in this endless moment, where her future stretched out before her. A lifetime of Urian, no way to escape.

Stumbling, her knees still watery with shock, she made her way back towards the keep. Now she knew what was happening, she could make out her father's roar of fury above the rest of the din. Someone was being blamed for the escaped captives but she was not going to wait to find out who. Her father's temper was not something she wanted directed at herself, not even a tiny fragment of it.

Making it into the keep without anyone seeing her, she rushed up to the first level before stopping, her breath coming in pants, far quicker than the brief run up the stairs should have caused.

Panic was flooding through her, a delayed reaction to the knowledge that there was nothing here to help her, nothing she could use to change her situation. Swirling around with that was grief and the oddest sense that she would miss the red-headed giant, even though she barely knew him. The sharp pang of a life she'd thought she might lead was gone before she could really get a hold of it.

She leaned her head against the stone, needing more than a brief moment to collect herself. Sooner than she would like, she was going to have to face the women at the top of the keep and relay the news, with emotion they would expect: shock, horror and dismay. None of them could know about the deep, desperate dread surging through her.

Even though Lucan had turned her down, she'd really thought that he was her way out of the castle. The conversation in which he had rejected her had been the only one they'd had. Up until that point she had pretended she could not understand what he was talking about, but every night she had taken him and Rolf food and listened to them talk. The teasing warmth in his voice as he spoke to the lad, the way he let the boy eat first and made sure he had the juiciest cut of meat or the sweetest fruit, contrasted with the fire that raged in the depths of his eyes. Everyone else might see him as a brute, but she had begun to think of him as a man with a hard outer shell, but a softer inside.

When he'd sympathised over her betrothal to Urian, she had thought that they'd had a connection. Of course, she should have known better. Connections meant nothing in reality, the ending of her previous engagement should have shown her that. The family that she'd thought she would belong to forever had given her up without a word of protest. If you could not see something, it was best to assume it did not exist.

For the briefest moment in time, Lucan had been her best hope, her *only* hope, to escape. She should have known not to dwell on romantic images of racing across the country with the red-headed giant. Fanciful imaginings had never got her very far before, and giving into them had been a weak indulgence that had given her false hope. Despair washed through her, but she would not give in, she could not. There had to be another way for her to stop her wedding to Urian, even if she could not think of it in this moment.

Beneath her, the door to the keep crashed open, heavy footfalls sounding on the stone floor, heading towards the base of the spiral staircase. Leaping forward, Jehanne began to climb again, rushing, almost tripping over herself to get to the top. All thoughts of her escape from Urian fleeing.

If the newcomer was her father, she would need to warn the women of his impending fury, her mother in particular, who would need to find the words to soothe him. Facing the brunt of his anger was not something she wanted to do on a day when her world was falling apart.

Today he would be able to make her cry and she hated to give him that satisfaction. Making those he deemed weaker than himself show any sign of vulnerability was something he seemed to enjoy. Once, she had realised that, he had ceased to hold power over her, which was when she had been shipped off to England. Maintaining a cool façade in front of him was the only thing keeping her from spiralling into despair and appeared to have won his grudging respect.

The tight corners of the staircase made running difficult. The loud crash of boots on the stairs following behind her, had her slipping in her hurry. By the time she reached the second level, the person was catching up. Rushing on, she raced upwards, only to trip over the hem of her dress, stumbling, cursing under her breath as her shin hit the edge of a step, the pain stunning her for a moment. Pushing herself to her feet, she rubbed the skin, trying to take the sting away. It was not blindingly awful; already the discomfort was fading and calmness was beginning to reassert itself. She need not run. The footsteps were coming quicker, so the person coming up behind her could not be her father. Fit though he was for his age, he was not able to move with that much speed. There was no real need for her to be afraid, if there were no English in the castle, then there was no one who had an argument with her.

She hadn't made it to the top floor when a hand curled around her arm, fingers biting into her skin. 'Just the woman I wanted to see.'

Urian. The cold fury of his tone, slithered across her skin. They were alone. That had never happened before; it was something she had always dreaded and had avoided at all costs. Without waiting for her to respond, he began to pull her back down the stairs she had just hurriedly climbed.

'What is going on?' she asked, fighting to keep her tone placid. Having witnessed Urian's furious temper when confronted, she always treated him with calmly, trying to soothe rather than escalate the situation. But it was so hard, so very, very hard, when all she wanted to do was shout at him for hurting her, for not giving her even the barest hint of consideration before dragging her away from her destination. How she *loathed* him for stripping away yet another layer of her personality even before they were wed.

His fingers pressed tighter, pinching, starting to hurt now. 'Your *father*,' he snarled, 'blames *me* for the incompetencies of others. The English have escaped while mining for ore and somehow, that is *my* fault.' Even if Urian was responsible, he would not believe himself guilty of this, so there was no point questioning about what had happened. He would not tell her the truth.

'Surely not,' she said, hating herself for pandering to him. 'Perhaps there has been some misunderstanding.'

'No,' Urian snarled, his spittle hitting her on the ear. 'He made it very clear in front of everyone that he believes it is my fault the escape took place. Everyone witnessed the way he yelled at me as if I were a child. I will not stand for it, Jehanne.' He shook her arm. 'Do you understand?'

Biting her lip to stop herself from crying out in pain, Jehanne sought for the words to appease his mood. 'You know what my father is like. He has a terrible temper but when he has calmed down, I am sure he will apologise for his rash words.' This was a lie. Comte de Balladur never backed down, never admitted he was wrong. To do so would show a weakness he did not believe he had.

Urian snorted, clearly not believing her words either. 'He told me that he could not allow anyone so incompetent to join his family. He threatened *me*, you understand. Told *me* that I was fortunate to have parents who owned land he wanted, otherwise our union would be off immediately. In front of *everyone* he reviewed the terms of our betrothal contract, as the land might not be worth binding me into this family.' Jehanne bit her lips to stop any sound escaping as hope burst through her, like sun finally pouring through a gap on an otherwise cloud-covered day. 'And yet, you only have to look at your sister's husband to see that is a lie. He is a disgrace, his only thoughts are about finding something, anything, to rut.'

Margot's husband was no military genius, but her father had signed the marriage contracts believing the union would add to his lands. It had, but afterwards his only son had become sick, and now there was a need for a strong second heir, should his first choice fail him by dying. Until now, everyone had believed that person would be Urian, but maybe, just maybe, this would be the thing that got her out of the dreadful union.

'Would you like me to speak with him?' she offered, knowing that she would have to do so behind closed doors. If her father was having second thoughts about Urian, she would add third and fourth thoughts to those, until the wedding was called off.

'Your father is past reasoning,' Urian told her, his grip tightening. 'No. We will consummate this marriage and then he will have no choice.'

'What?' She did not want to believe what she had just

heard, could not believe it. Lying with him was the one thing she had been dreading above all others, and he wanted it to happen today. Now.

'You heard what I said,' he snarled. 'I have been patient. I could have pushed this matter before, but I chose to wait until we were officially married. I wanted to do this properly, for the whole world to see that we were wed. Well, no more.'

'No, I…' Her fingers scrambled, trying to find purchase on the smooth wall, desperate to find something to hold on to so that she could stop them where they were. *This* could not happen, *this* was the worst of all worlds. Her skin burned, even as her veins turned to ice. Her hands found nothing to grip as he continued to pull her along.

'You are not in a position to deny me.' He jerked her harder and she stumbled against him, his body a wall of tightly coiled muscle. 'We will consummate our relationship and you will become my wife whether your father wants it or not.'

'I…' He was too strong for her to fight; she would lose if she refused but this could not happen, not now, not ever. Urian was right. Once they had shared the marital bed, she would be as good as married without the ceremony needing to take place. She'd been prepared to lie with him before, knowing that it was part of the marriage that she would have to suffer through, but now every part of her body screamed out in protest. 'Urian. Wait…'

'I told you, I have done enough of that.'

They were getting closer to the bottom of the keep. Her mind scrambled as she desperately sought any other viable option.

'The English Lord,' she blurted out, just before his hand reached out to open the door to the courtyard.

'What?' growled Urian, half-twisting to look down at her.

'The English Lord cannot have escaped as well. He has been in the castle all this time. He must still be here.'

Urian grunted, his hand still gripping her arm, but at least he had stopped trying to drag her along. 'What good will that do me?'

Think, Jehanne, think. 'Do you know his family name yet?'

'No, the scrawny runt only talks around the matter, never giving a proper answer.' Urian spat dismissively on the floor. 'He suggests we send a message to his King, but your father wants to wait. That's all he ever wants to do.' Urian's disgust for that idea was evident from his tone.

But this finally gave Jehanne a shred of hope. If there was more to be found out, then there might be something here to save her from this dreadful fate. 'Let us go and talk to him. Maybe, if we can find out something new, that knowledge will bring my father round, especially if the Lord is someone high-ranking within England. A large ransom for one man has to be better than all the smaller men who managed to get away. Who cares about them anyway? Probably not even the English King does. My father will be proud, knowing that it was you who got the information from him.'

For all his faults, Urian was not a dull man. Ambitious, cruel and callous he might be, but not one to rush into mistakes. He was always on the lookout for an advantage, not caring who he destroyed in the process of getting there. The grip of his hand on her arm never loosened as the moment dragged on, only the muffled sounds of men still shouting sounded through the thick stone walls. Slowly, his lip curled. 'What difference do you think you could make when others have failed?'

Jehanne could hear the hope behind his sneer. Despite his words, he was still clinging to the belief that he could redeem himself in the Comte's eyes. Better to have the leader of the castle on his side than force his daughter into marriage. Urian had never given her any indication that he desperately wanted to marry her, any more than she wanted the union. She was a means to an end for him, more object than human.

'I do not think I will make the difference, I think you will.' She hated her obsequiousness, knowing this was either the first step in losing herself or a way to save her soul. 'You will tell him that his countrymen have abandoned him, you will make him see that he has no choice but to talk to you if he ever wants to leave. By making him realise just how alone he is, you will finally break him. If I show fear of you, then maybe that would help reinforce the idea that you are a man to be feared.'

It would not be an act for her, not like the calm acceptance she pretended to feel around him. She was frightened of him, terrified of the dark shadows that lingered in his eyes, of what they would do to her when she could no longer escape him.

Urian pondered her suggestion, candlelight throwing even more dark shadows across his face. He jerked her elbow. 'Very well, we'll try your way, but if it doesn't work, we shall go back to mine.' He leered at her, his eyes filled with cruel possession, no hint that he wanted her the way a man truly wanted a woman. 'You've made me wait long enough as it is. Most men would not be as patient.'

Biting back a retort wasn't easy. Given the option, she'd make him wait for her body forever. Like all women, there had been no choice for her. The contract for her betrothal to Urian had been signed before she'd returned from England and her previous engagement. Her father and the man in front of her had more control over her than she had over herself. But she was not about to go down without a fight.

'Let's go.' He pushed her in front of him as if he didn't trust her not to run away if unwatched. Perhaps he knew her better than she'd believed.

Behind her, he continued to rant about how the English had escaped while at the mine and how unfair it was that Comte de Balladur was blaming him. The words filled the narrow passageway and were easy to ignore. In the short time it took them to move from the keep to a locked room inside the castle walls, Jehanne turned over and dismissed a dozen ideas. Her thoughts tumbled over one another, fragmented and insubstantial, like the whisps of an unfinished dream. Months of waiting and hoping for an opportunity to change her fate, and here was one in front of her. Yet, infuriatingly, she could not see how to use it to her advantage.

Lord David leapt up from his straw mattress when Urian barged through the chamber door. The bewildered expression on his face was almost comical, as his gaze flitted between Urian and herself. She wondered if he had guessed from the shouting that he had been abandoned by his countrymen. There was clearly no love lost between the men. From the very beginning, Lord David had set himself apart from the others by choosing to stay inside, while his men were confined to the courtyard. In all her trips to take food to the boy and Lucan, she had not once seen him visiting the others with any supplies or even a quick word of support.

Still, it must be shocking to realise that you were left, that your fellow countrymen had run away from you without a backwards glance. She remembered what it was like to leave England and the place she had called home for many years—the sense of bewilderment that those who cared for her did not want to fight to keep her with them. Although she could find nothing to redeem the man in this chamber, she could empathise a little with what he might be feeling, or be about to feel, in this moment.

Urian wasted no time in launching his attack, switching between telling Lord David all about how desperate his situation was to yelling, demanding to know where he was from and who they should contact to demand a ransom. When the Lord only blinked at him in bemusement, Urian began to shout about all the ways in which he would use torture to uncover the information he wanted to know. Her betrothed was in a rage now, he would not stop until he had worn himself out; there was little Jehanne could do to stem the tide.

Instead, she moved around the cramped chamber, her presence seemingly forgotten by both men. On the far side, there was a small window, barely wider than her face. The glass was badly warped and almost impossible to see through. Peering through it, she tried to make out the shapes moving around the courtyard below, but they were blurry and indistinct. About to move away, she caught a flash of red hair and the glimpse of impossibly wide shoulders. Her heart stopped, before beginning to thunder rapidly, beating almost painfully beneath her ribs. Pressing her fingers to the cold glass, she tried to make sense of what she thought she saw.

That fiery hair should not be possible, not if the English had escaped. Lucan should have got away with the rest of them. Surely they wouldn't have been able to pull such a thing off without his powerful body doing some of the work. They must know that they would need him to protect them out in the French countryside.

Not once had it occurred to her that they might leave him, because she wouldn't. Not just because of his size and what he could do for her but also by virtue of him being a good man. She could not countenance abandoning someone like him; it was unthinkable. His fellow countrymen might see him like the rest of her castle did, as a large, immoveable object with no feelings, but she thought there might be more to him than that. It was why she had blurted out her request to him. Even after his rejection, she still believed there was more to him than his bulk. What he must be feeling right now as a result of being abandoned must be awful, soul-crushing in its harsh reality. If, indeed, that brief impression of red had been him.

Shifting closer to the window, she tried to get a better look, but the glass remained frustratingly difficult to see through no matter what direction she tilted her head. All the while, her thoughts raced. Trying to tamp down the feelings building inside her, hope she could understand, joy was harder to explain.

To work in the mine, the English would have needed their hands unchained to hold the pickaxes essential to complete the gruelling work. But Lucan's wrists were never unshackled. Even more than two weeks after his arrival at the castle, his fury at being captured was still evident in every scowl and burning gaze. His staggering height and breadth made him a real threat to the people of the castle should he be set free. Most likely he had not been at the mine when the others had escaped, in which case…

Even as she told herself to stay calm, not to hold out for the impossible, her heart refused to listen. It raced beneath her ribs, hammering faster than it ever had before, urging her to run from the room to find out right now if he was still here. And if he was…if he was, then her life wasn't over, her chance to get him to help her wasn't finished. Surely now that the others had escaped, he would be desperate to be gone himself, perhaps reckless enough to agree to her plan.

Moving quickly would be essential. Getting the result she wanted might be easier if she asked for his help now, while he was angry at the injustice of being left behind. From what she'd seen of him so far, his anger bubbled close to the surface as it was. She hoped this was the tipping point to urge him into action, an action that would potentially benefit them both.

The happiness building inside her had to be the thought that they could both get away. It could not be because she would see him again. She barely knew him, any connection she thought they had was in her mind. To get free, she could not allow herself to dwell on feelings that would be best left buried very deeply inside her. To let them out would only lead to disappointment.

'If you don't tell me what I want to know,' screamed Urian, his voice louder and more high-pitched than she had ever heard it, 'I will remove your—' Urian spluttered '—your…your…toes.'

Only paying half a mind to what Urian was screaming, Jehanne stared out of the glass, hoping for another sight of the red hair, praying that it meant what she thought it did. Plans flitted around her mind, some fanciful, others more realistic.

The door slammed.

Whirling round, not sure what to expect, she could only gape at the chamber. All thoughts of escape fleeing.

Urian had gone.

She was alone with the English prisoner, a man who was not bound in any way, a man who was at least twice as strong as her and a man who undoubtedly loathed her fiancé after facing the very real threat of torture.

Chest tight, it was almost impossible to inhale. Her mind urged her to run, but her legs refused to take up the command, as if believing that if she stayed completely still, this man, this enemy, would not see her.

Lord David was staring at the door, his stance frozen. Slowly, almost painfully so, his head turned towards her. His wide eyes met hers, and time seemed to stretch as their stares locked.

Before she had time to react, to even attempt to get out of the room, Lord David snapped into action. Striding over to her in less than four steps, his hand closed over her upper arm, his thick fingers pressing into the soft skin there. Ignoring her gasp of pain, he half-dragged, half-pushed her towards the door.

'If the imbecile is too soft in the head to realise he's left his affianced behind, then I'd be foolish not to make use of her.' Lord David muttered to himself, the cords in his neck protruding from the skin. Blood pounding in her ears, Jehanne pulled against his hold. He jerked her against him. '*Arrêtez*,' he commanded. 'Stop struggling.'

'*Non.*' Throwing herself forward, she caught him off balance, and he staggered forward, his wrist banging against the door.

Swearing viciously, he reached for her once more. Not quick enough to scramble away from him, she could only stare in horror as his hand closed around her once more.

'Trying to get away won't help you. I need to get out of this godforsaken castle and you are going to help me.'

Out of this godforsaken castle. The words bounced around her mind as Lord David pushed out into the corridor. It wasn't the way she would have chosen, but could this be it, the opportunity that she had been waiting for. Even if her father did end the marriage contract with Urian, there was no telling who he would align her with next. The only certain thing was that her preference would not be taken into account.

Right now, she could scream for him, someone would hear her and come running. Tempers were high, goodness knows what would happen to Lord David; it would not end well for the man. Even as his grip bruised her skin, she held her tongue.

For so long, she had dreamed of ways to get out of this castle. William had not fought for her when their betrothal ended, but he was older now, nearly a year so. If she returned, if he believed her family thought she was lost to them, it was possible the boy she had known for most of her life would take her in. The family had done so once before; there was no reason to believe they would not do so again.

Rounding a corner in a narrow passageway, she heard some of her father's men, their voices slurred from too much drink. Lord David paid them no attention, his stare was fixed on the door ahead, the door that led to the courtyard, the door that led to Lucan. Jehanne did not call for help, instead, she turned and started to speak to her captor.

Chapter Five

A cruel wind whipped through the courtyard, Rolf's small body shivered as he pressed into Lucan's side. Any confidence the boy had possessed had drained from him and, as the afternoon turned to dusk, he reminded Lucan more of a small child than the young man he was becoming at the start of this campaign.

Lucan's wrists burned where the manacles dug into his skin. In their fury over losing most of their English captives, some of Comte de Balladur's men had shackled the other end of his chains to a point higher up on the wall, leaving his arms stretched above him, making it impossible for him to slump to the ground and rest. It could have been worse, but the unnatural position he had to stand in made the metal of his chains cut into him and caused his shoulders to throb. No amount of shifting position could alleviate the discomfort. The firepit that had been lit for the captives had long since gone out and the cold was beginning to seep into his bones, adding to the agony. And yet, he could not give in, could not allow despair to take control. He could not let Rolf or his son down by giving up.

'What do you think they are going to do with us?' whispered Rolf, turning his wide eyes up to look at Lucan.

He wished he could give the boy some reassurance, some hope that they would get out of here too, but the others had left without a second thought of him or Rolf. In truth, it was hard to blame them, Lucan may have done the same in their position. No, that wasn't true, he would never have left Rolf behind, and although he had not bothered to get to know the men, he would not have abandoned his fellow countrymen either. 'In all that shouting earlier, we were not mentioned,' was the only response he could manage.

'I know that,' Rolf's brow furrowed, his irritation at odds with his young features. 'I listened as well as you did. But now they have gone inside they probably are discussing us. It would be strange if they weren't. What do you *think* they are going to do with us.'

Lucan didn't know, but he agreed with the lad's assessment that they probably hadn't been forgotten, not if the burning across his back was any indication of how they thought about him right now. He wasn't about to share with Rolf what he expected might happen to them. The ideas were twisting his own gut and there was no need to share them with the boy. And yet… Rolf was free, he was not chained in any way and he was small enough to move around mostly unnoticed.

While the Frenchmen argued amongst themselves, Rolf might be able to sneak out of the castle gates and run. If he was quick, he might even be able to catch up with the others. Although…if it was that easy, would the French not have already found the fleeing men? If Lucan sent the boy off into the wilderness, he might be sentencing him to an early death.

Bah! This was what Lucan got for caring about others; his thoughts flipping back and forwards like a fish pulled from the river. And his insides were tied up in knots, twisted in and around themselves in a way that hurt almost as much as his arms.

If the boy stayed, Lucan should be able to keep him safe. If his hands weren't bound, that *should* would become a *definitely*. Jehanne would help. He swallowed, trying not to remember the desperate hope in her eyes that had faded to pain when he had refused to help her. If she hated him now, she would still protect Rolf. There was a kindness in her soul, which made his brutal rejection of her worse.

The only reason he had not collapsed from exhaustion was because of the food Jehanne had brought him. She was the only person who had showed him any kind of mercy since his arrival at her father's fortress. That she'd continued to bring him and Rolf food after that did not help his conscience. The lady was as much a prisoner as he and Rolf, only her fate might be worse than death. Slowly shaking his head, he tried to dismiss the image of her soulful eyes from his mind. Refusing her aid may have been a hard stance to take, but it was the right one. Helping her was not something he could do whether he wanted to or not. Getting back to his son and keeping Rolf safe were his priorities, and he could not help her return to her lost love, no matter how much kindness she showed.

'There's no good guessing, lad,' he said, when he felt Rolf twitch impatiently next to him, waiting for his response. 'All we can do is wait.' Patience was not a virtue Lucan had mastered, but there was little else he could do unless presented with a key to his chains.

'We could tell them who I am.' Rolf's voice was less than a whisper, so soft the words were barely there.

'If it comes to it, I think we are going to have to,' Lucan agreed. He'd thought much the same himself. 'But let us hold on to that information for as long as we can. At the moment, the French have barely registered your existence and I think you benefit from that for now.' Lucan hoped he was making the right decision. King Edward had trusted very few people with the knowledge that Rolf was one of his son's from outside of his marriage to Queen Philippa. The King certainly hadn't told Lucan, who was far enough beneath him as to be insignificant. For reasons Lucan couldn't understand, his liege seemed to trust Lord David and had assigned care for one of his illegitimate sons to him. Lord David had in turn trusted Lucan with the knowledge, and Rolf had confirmed it once the two of them had formed a bond, a few days before their capture.

Lucan had no idea how Edward would react to having one of his children as a captive. Perhaps he would rage against the insult or pretend that Rolf was of no relation to him. Either way, Lucan had been keeping the boy's identity a secret and would continue to do so unless the situation could be improved by the French knowing the truth.

Lucan's eyes stung, his lids heavy. His blinks were becoming longer as he fought to stay alert. Forced to remain standing, it should not be hard to stay awake, not when danger pressed on every side, but tiredness was weighing him down. Hazy thoughts plagued his mind, the soft laughter of his son racing towards a river and a woman, not his late wife, walking beside him, her dark eyes smiling.

Footsteps approached and he jerked upright from an

awkward doze. Whoever was heading their way was in a hurry, the sound of their approach, two people perhaps, was quick but quiet. Having heard the noise too, Rolf pressed deeper into his side. Wishing he had as much confidence in himself as the lad seemed to, Lucan shuffled so that the boy was slightly between him and the wall. If he could not use his hands to protect the boy, he would use his body until he was no longer able.

As the shapes revealed themselves, Lucan's pulse quickened. The darkness made it hard to make out individuals, but Lucan would recognise the shape of one of them anywhere; he'd been dreaming of her only moments ago. Jehanne was heading towards him with…he blinked a few times but the image remained the same. It should be an impossible combination, but Mademoiselle Jehanne and Lord David were heading in his direction.

'We don't have much time,' David said by want of a greeting. 'Unlock his chains,' he said to Jehanne pushing her forward so that she stumbled slightly. Lucan growled, the inhuman noise instinctive and from somewhere deep inside him. Lord David tsked in annoyance, as if basic courtesy to a woman was something to be ashamed of. 'I'm rescuing you, man. You could at least sound grateful.'

Jehanne's slender fingers were reaching out to him and he could just make out the shape of a key in her hand. Her face was averted from his and he could not read her expression. From the set of her shoulders it was difficult to tell whether she was upset or resigned. Obviously not moving fast enough for Lord David, he pushed at her again.

'Don't hurt her,' Lucan snapped, his patience dangerously thin.

'For goodness sake, man. Now is not the time for chivalry. We have to get out of here before they realise we are missing. That bastard knight is searching for something to remove my fingernails one by one and you want to discuss niceties. You're lucky we walked past the key room, else you would have been the only Englishman left here.'

Jehanne's long fingers were tracing over the chains now, searching for the lock. Her skin was not touching his but he fancied he could feel her anyway. The hairs on his forearm stood to attention, as if she had run her fingertips along the inside of his arm in a loving touch. Her braid tickled his chin and he clenched his fists to stop himself turning towards her. It was not as if she could lend him strength—she was tiny, a mere whisp of a woman—so why his body had the urge to lean on her as if she could give him exactly what he needed in this moment was absurd. Perhaps it was because she was always bringing him food and he was perpetually hungry, maybe that had evoked this response to her. So used to relying on himself to get what he needed, he was in danger of becoming dependent on this woman, in danger of letting her take up too much of his attention.

The key sounded in the lock, and finally, blessedly, his hands were released, the weight from the heavy metal disappearing immediately. Off balance, he staggered forward, bumping into Jehanne, all of her pushing up against the length of him. Curves and softness pressed against him, the sensation shockingly delicious after so long without. For a moment, his thoughts went, his mind blank, only the loveliness of a woman's body against his mattered.

'Someone's coming,' Rolf's panicked whisper was

the only thing to get through to him in this endless point in time.

Stepping slowly back from Jehanne, he ignored the way the skin around his wrists burned now that he was focussing on something that wasn't her. He tilted his head to one side, trying to hear what had caught Rolf's attention. From across the courtyard came the sound a deep rumbling voice, followed by another. Two men talking at least, but not close enough that Lucan could make out the words.

'We need to go,' hissed Lord David, crowding him. 'I'm not waiting around for that little prick to come and lord it over me. The arrogant flea-spit thinks he could best me, but put us in a real fight and I would show him… But there is no time and he has the men of the castle on his side. I would be at a disadvantage and for that reason, we must go. *Now.*'

Lucan grunted, in total agreement that they should leave and that they should do so urgently but not quite able to agree that Lord David would win a fight between him and Urian. As much as it pained him to admit it, Urian was a good fighter. Having seen him in combat firsthand, he knew the man was an expert swordsman. There was a wildness in him that made him even more of a threat, a desperation that would not be satisfied until the blood of his enemy was at his feet. The Frenchman would not have been able to catch them in the first place if he had been a weak man. It would make their escape all the more dangerous, but staying would be worse.

'Let's go then,' said Lucan, putting his hand on Rolf's back, knowing that his presence reassured the boy, as it should. Lucan would do whatever it took to keep the boy safe.

Clinging to the shadows, the four of them began to make their way towards the castle gates. Every few paces, they stopped to listen for sounds that they had been discovered. Jehanne gasped in pain when they began to walk again, David's grip on her upper arm obviously hurting her. The urge to punch the man in the gut surged inside Lucan; the strength of his reaction taking him by surprise. Her next hiss of pain was too much. 'There is no need to hold her so tightly,' he snapped.

David's head whipped round to glare at him. 'Do you want her to go running off and alerting them that we are escaping?'

'I do not, but I also do not think you need to leave a mark on her skin.'

'You hold her then, I'll take the boy.' Not giving Lucan time to respond, Lord David shoved her in his direction. Once again she stumbled against him, once again, his mind went blank, his body reminding him of how long it had been since he had held a woman in his arms. Years. It had been years. And Jehanne was…

Shaking his head, he couldn't believe the nonsense he had been about to spout even in his own mind. He'd practically been writing Jehanne courtly love poetry while the world crashed down around him. In the time he'd been becoming a different man from the person he was normally, David and Rolf were already several steps ahead.

In truth, Jehanne could have run away from him in the long moments he'd been acting like a green boy next to her, but she had not. Possibly because she believed that this was her chance to escape, exactly as she had asked him only two days ago. It wasn't. As soon as they had made it out from the castle, he was going to make sure she did not come with them. Taking her across the French countryside would ensure that her fiancé would follow them to the ends of the Earth, her father too, and he could not take that risk. Maybe if it was just himself, he would take her, but there was Rolf to consider and putting the boy into any extra risk was not something he would countenance.

Right now, he had to bring Jehanne along with them. Although she seemed like a good woman, there was no telling what she would do if he let her go. They could ill afford for her to alert anyone to their escape attempt.

He did not want to touch her; no, that was not quite right. Every time he saw her, he wanted to brush his fingers along her skin or bury his face in her hair, but that was something very different from what he was going to have to do now. Not thinking it through, he took her hand in his. The shock of her touch sent a fire racing through him, rushing through his veins, burning him from the inside. Surely it could not be because he was lightly touching one hand. It had to be because of his heightened awareness of their surroundings. 'Come along,' he said gruffly.

'What is your plan?' she asked, her French accent making the English words sound lovelier than they were.

'Not to let the wool-brained Lord get us killed.'

If they hadn't been standing so close, he would not have heard her soft laugh. 'That seems wise,' was all she said in response.

Moving with him, she did not try and tug his hand in a different direction, confirming his guess that she was more than willing to come along with them. His heart hurt at the knowledge that he was about to let her down, that he was withholding his intention of not allowing her any further than a little way off from the castle gates. She belonged to his enemy and he should feel no compassion for her. But although his mind knew that, it seemed his body was slower to catch on.

The gates were almost in touching distance when they came to a stop. There were only two guards at the post, both facing outwards towards the French countryside, presumably waiting for the return of those who had left the castle in search of the English.

'What now?' murmured Lucan, knowing what David's answer would be even before he asked. It was always up to Lucan to do any fighting. Men seemed to assume that, because of his size, he relished violence. That was not the case. His height and natural strength certainly made it easier for him to win a battle, but he would prefer not to hurt anyone, given the choice.

'Subdue them,' said Lord David without even sparing him a glance, 'and we will get out of here.'

'Are you going to aid me?' he asked, already knowing the answer.

'One of us needs to guard the girl. This will be over before it begins if she gives us away.' Then turning to Jehanne, David added, 'Make a sound, Mademoiselle, and I will slit your throat.'

'Don't,' snapped Lucan, 'or it will be the last thing that you ever do.' The threat was instinctive, but damn it all to hell, he did care what happened to the woman. It would plague his conscience forever if she got hurt.

Not wanting to dwell on *that* thought for a moment

longer, Lucan pushed himself out of the darkness and descended on the first guard. The man was unconscious before the second guard even realised anything was happening. Lucan had seen enough of death, he did not want to be responsible for more, so while his opponent waved his sword at him, he dodged the blade, twisting to the left and lunging for the man's unprotected side. The guard went down as quickly as his companion, only a muffled grunt made in protest before he too was lying on the ground.

It had barely been more than a few blinks of the eye and already they were free to escape. Glancing quickly at Jehanne, he found her regarding him calmly, as if she hadn't watched him dispatch two of her countrymen. Something uncomfortable twitched in his stomach, a sensation he decided to ignore.

Without giving it any more thought, Lucan whirled around and grabbed Rolf around the waist. Picking the young lad up, he ran with him through the open gates, not waiting to see if David was following and certainly not looking towards Jehanne.

Chapter Six

Jehanne had to bite the inside of her cheek to stop her smile from splitting across her face. She was out of the castle, away from the watching eyes of her family and Urian's painful hold over her life. The English Lord tugging her along might think he needed a firm hold on her to stop her from escaping, but he could not be more wrong. Now, if he tried to get her *back* inside the castle, then there would be an issue.

Without discussing their direction, the four of them rushed towards the copse of trees not far from the castle gates. Wind whipped against her cheeks and, in the darkness, she allowed her smile to break, her face almost aching from the sheer joy of the moment. Happiness gave power to her movements and it was almost as if she were flying across the uneven ground, racing towards her freedom.

Lord David had been fairly easy to manipulate. The haughty Englishman had believed it his idea to unchain Lucan and bring him with them. Left to his own devices, David might have only thought of freeing himself. Watching the way Lucan had moved when dealing with the guards, she had been right to think the Lord would not have got very far on his own. Intimating that Lucan would be an asset, while also pretending she didn't want to leave the castle at all, could be the greatest thing she had ever achieved. Not that it was anything she could share with anyone.

Now all she had to do was make sure that Lucan didn't try to abandon her, and she would be a step further along with her plan to return to England. The English might be her country's enemies but her friends at Borne had loved her once, perhaps they would again. She wondered what Lucan's home was like but she dismissed the thought before she could linger on it; she would never know.

Lucan slowed as they neared the line of trees. The darkness under the cover of the wide branches was absolute. No matter how many times she blinked, there was no way to see anything other than unending blackness. As soon as they were under the canopy, Lucan brought them to an abrupt stop.

'What now?' grunted David, dropping her arm.

Rubbing the spot where he had been holding her, Jehanne tried to make out the two men, but even close to them, she could not see the expressions on their faces. There was no way of telling what their relationship to one another was; it did not appear to be amicable and, with his finer clothing, David had to be a more important man in the system of governance.

It was Lucan, however, whose physical presence dominated all those around him. No wonder the Lord had considered leaving Lucan behind; despite being his superior in title, it was clear he could not order Lucan to do anything the bigger man did not want to do.

The outline of Lucan's wide shoulders was still and

it appeared he was facing her, then he shook them and turned towards David. 'The woman goes no further.'

Her breath caught at Lucan's pronouncement, panic surging through her. She'd expected something like this, but not so close to the castle walls. It was hardly an escape if she could still see her family's fortress. It was not part of her plan to argue with Lucan yet. The longer it took to persuade him to take her with them, the more likely they were to be spotted by someone from inside the castle walls, making their recapture more likely. And if she could not convince him… She would not think of that, it did not bear contemplating.

'Don't be ridiculous,' David argued. 'Having her with us means we have something of value to exchange should it come to it. Her presence could save our lives and, if we could present her to the King as a hostage for ransom, it might make our capture less humiliating having something to show for it.'

'This woman is not a *something*.' Lucan virtually spat the words, any joy she experienced from his defence was soon dashed by his next words. 'Mademoiselle Jehanne is Monsieur le Chevalier Dupont's betrothed. You've seen the man. Where most of us have a heart, he has serpents. He will not rest until she is returned to him and we are dead. As it is, he will hunt us, but if we take his fiancée we may as well run headlong into his outstretched sword. She returns to the castle now.'

'I…' David blustered.

'This is not up for discussion. Not only is she that wool-for-brains bastard's affianced, she is also the Comte de Balladur's daughter. If the knight wants us dead, what do you think the father will do to you when he catches up with you. And yes, I meant to say *you* and not *us* because if you proceed with this empty-barrelled plan, I shall leave you from this moment forth.'

Lucan was towering over David now. The smaller man was shuffling backwards, conceding ground. But his chest was still puffed up, he wasn't giving up just yet. There was still a chance she would not be forced to return. 'You will not go it alone because you will not leave the boy.'

Jehanne's heart ached at the truth of it. Lucan would turn his back on her without a thought. The strange connection she felt towards him was clearly one-sided; he did not feel the same pull towards her as she did to him. If he walked away from her in this moment, that would be it, he would never think of her again. But he would not leave the child. Proof that he was a good man beneath his scowling exterior, but also further evidence that he did not care about her.

Right now, she was fighting for the survival of her soul and the right to give her body to someone who deserved it. It shouldn't matter that a man she barely knew did not care for her, but for some reason it hurt badly, almost physically.

Perhaps it was because there was no one in this world who would put themselves out for her, not a single soul who would put her needs before theirs. Not wanting to risk a battle with the French, the family whom she had thought she would live with for the rest of her life, had let her go. Her best friend's eyes, those of the man she had believed she would one day marry, had shone with tears. He had wished things were different but he had not battled for her. Returning to him now was a risk she had to take because she could think of nowhere better, but although she was sure they cared about her, William and his family would never put her first.

What Lucan said was true: her father and Urian would indeed hunt these men forever if they made off with her. Neither man would let her go so easily, but it was not for her person. They did not know her, did not care enough to find out. They would not rest in their pursuit because her capture would be perceived as an insult perpetuated against *them*. She was nothing to anybody.

'I will take the boy,' growled Lucan. Rolf shifted closer to him, as if silently confirming the truth of the statement.

'And go against the express wishes of your King. That's treason and you'll hang.'

In the strained silence that followed, a small splinter lodged itself in her heart. In a world where nobody thought about her, she would have to take care of herself.

'Lucan,' she said into the darkness. The two men stilled at the sound of her voice but neither turned in her direction. 'Every time I brought you food, I took a risk. Every act of kindness was to help you and Rolf. I did not do it for any other reason than to ease your suffering, and now you discuss my fate, and you won't even look in my direction.' The words flew out of her unheeded. She spoke French, knowing that all three of them could understand her but her message was for Lucan only. He already knew how desperate she was to get away from Urian. There had to be a heart under that gruff exterior, she'd seen it in all the sweetness he had shown Rolf. All she wanted was a tiny bit of that. She would beg if she had to.

For an age, she did not think he would look at her, that he would carry on acting as if she was not there.

But, finally, his large body tilted in her direction. In the dark, his face was only dark planes and angles, giving the sense he was made of stone. As the silence stretched, hope drained from her. The sweetness she believed was buried deep down inside of him was not for her; he was not going to show her any mercy. 'And how much of that help was given freely?' he rasped.

'All of it. Truthfully, all of it.'

Nothing in his stance softened. 'If that were the case, you would not be demanding my assistance now. You would know that the cost of your escape is a threat to Rolf's existence.'

'If it comes to it, I will sacrifice myself for Rolf.' She hoped he could hear the sincerity in her voice because she did mean it; she would not be able to live with herself if harm befell the boy. Everything about this escape was about trying to stay true to her values, to the core beliefs that made her the person she was. 'But why can we not try for my freedom too?'

David's gaze was whipping back and forth between the two of them. Despite being shorter than Lucan, his presence loomed ominously in the darkness. Rolf was standing slightly behind Lucan but closer to him than anyone else. There was no doubt in Jehanne's mind that the boy would side with Lucan and whatever the large man decided.

'We cannot have this discussion this close to the castle,' said David, breaking into the argument. The anger and irritation had faded from his voice, he sounded calm and conciliatory, completely different from a moment ago. 'Let us get further away and then discuss Mademoiselle Jehanne's future with us.'

Lucan rumbled something deep and incoherent. Perhaps he would have said more, but a shout sounded from the castle, followed by another. Even from this distance it was clear that the noise was urgent. Perhaps the unconscious guards had been discovered or Urian had realised both she and David were not where he had left them.

Cringing, she imagined his fury, the humiliation at being bested by a man he thought his inferior would only fuel his rage. People would suffer because of it, but if she was forced to return, it might be that this latest failing would be enough to dim his reputation enough that he would be banished from her father's fortress. Avoiding him until that happened would not be difficult. She had reason to hope, perhaps all she needed to do was avoid going back anytime soon.

'If we head through the woods in that direction,' she said, pointing towards the north, figuring the men could use her knowledge of the surrounding area as another reason to keep her with them, 'we will find a shallow part of the river. We can either cross there or travel downstream for a while. Whichever we decide, it should be enough to confuse my father's hunting dogs for a while.'

The shouting from within the castle walls became louder, more frantic, and it appeared the decision was made. Without further discussion, the four of them turned in the direction she had indicated and began to run.

Chapter Seven

Wading through water had been successful in throwing those hunting them off their track; there had been no sound of anyone following them for a while now. They'd travelled downstream until the river had come up to her waist, far further than she had intended, but Lucan had argued that they did not want to do anything their enemy could predict and, for once, David had agreed with him. Climbing out onto the bank had coated her legs in thick mud, but there had been no time to do any more than scrape the worst of it off with a large leaf and even then she had been subjected to Lucan's deep sighs of annoyance at the delay.

Plunging through the undergrowth, not stopping for rest, her wet skirts slapped against her skin. Cutting off her tongue would be preferable to letting Lucan know that the cold was burrowing deep into her bones and that all she could think about was warm blankets and a roaring fire. Conditions worsened as they emerged from the forest to find wide, open scrubland. Without the shelter of thick tree trunks, wind whipped around them, the temperature dropping with every laboured step.

There was nothing for it now. The further they got from the castle, the less likely she would be able to return. Even now, she would have trouble finding her father's fortress by herself. This part of the countryside was as unfamiliar to her as it was to them.

No one had said a word since they had clambered out of the water and continued heading northwards. Lucan was leading the way and she watched the way his large body strode through the countryside. There was something mesmerising about the way he moved, lithe despite his size, his strength seeming to cut through the air around him. He appeared to be heading towards another dense patch of trees. It made sense; out in the open like this they were vulnerable. But she was ready to sleep where she stood, the adrenaline she'd experienced at the beginning of the night had been swept away by the gusts of wind that buffeted them from every side.

'When will we stop?' asked Rolf, who was walking beside her. She almost kissed the lad for asking, desperate to know the answer herself.

'We need to find somewhere to rest,' Lucan replied, and she wished he would turn to them so she could feel his blue eyes on her. 'Somewhere that's hidden away from the Comte's men. Hopefully we'll find somewhere in the next woodland, but if not, we'll keep going for as long as needed.'

Trudging forward, the shelter of the trees seemed to be getting further away no matter how much distance they covered. Jehanne pressed her lips together to prevent herself from groaning at the effort.

'When will we eat?' asked Rolf.

'There's no food,' growled Lucan. 'And before you ask, there are no dry clothes either.'

The boy's shoulders sagged, his thin body curling in

on itself. Jehanne reached over and rested a hand on his shoulder. There was nothing she could say to contradict Lucan—he was right on all counts—but there was no need for him to be so harsh. 'Is he always this grumpy?' she asked.

Rolf grinned at the man's back, but he said solemnly: 'This is his cheerful side. When he gets really foul-tempered, he gets two deep lines here.' The lad traced his fingers over his cheeks to demonstrate. 'I'd recommend staying out of his way then, or when he starts to sound like a hungry wolf howling into the night.' He winked at Jehanne, who smiled back at him, enjoying Lucan's huff of annoyance more than she should.

'A wolf, you say. Is it like this?' She howled but only softly, wanting to annoy Lucan without drawing attention to their position.

Rolf's grin was wide now. 'You're very close. You just need to put a hint of desperation into it to truly match him.'

'I'll throw you both to the wolves if you're not careful.'

Rolf made a face at Lucan's back and the two of them giggled quietly.

'Don't think I didn't see that.'

Rolf stared at Lucan's back as if trying to work out whether the giant man was lying or whether he could see through the back of his skull. Although half-convinced that Lucan had made a lucky guess, Jehanne couldn't help but wonder if the man did have some kind of supernatural power. Shaking her head, she winked at Rolf. Despite looking like someone from a heroic legend, Lucan was not otherworldly; Jehanne's thoughts had only taken the strange turn because she was exhausted.

They fell silent again, the momentary respite of laughter fading quickly as they plodded onwards. Only Lucan showed no signs of tiring, his shoulders remained squarely upright, his head fixed in the direction they were headed. Eventually they passed under the boughs of a lone tree. 'Wait a moment,' Jehanne called to the men. 'This fruit is edible, I think.'

'You think?' Lucan turned to her, one eyebrow raised.

Reaching up to touch the rounded fruit, she said, 'It's an apple tree. They are not poisonous. Are they?' It occurred to her then just how sheltered she was, her life was in the confines of either her father's castle or her previous betrothed's. Apples she had plucked from trees had always been near one of those strongholds and eaten by all of the inhabitants of both. It did not follow that *all* apples were safe to eat.

Lucan watched her face, where she was sure all her doubt was playing out across her features. She thought he might contradict her, but instead he reached up and plucked one from the tree, his gaze never leaving hers. He twirled it round in his long fingers then took a large bite, the crunch sounding loud in the quiet of the night.

'I know this one,' he said after he swallowed. 'I ate some like this a few weeks ago and I am still alive. Grab as many as you can manage to carry, who knows when we will eat again.'

Lucan didn't comment as Rolf and Jehanne quickly ate an apple each. Jehanne murmured something to Rolf, which made him grin, before wiping her chin with her long fingers. He clenched his fists before he could do something foolish, like walk over to her and use his own fingers to brush away the juice of the apple. Even having the urge to do something like that was deeply unsettling.

He moved away from them, eating two himself in quick succession, before plucking enough to fit into his hand. With no other way of carrying the food, that would have to do for now. Witless fool that he was, he had not voiced any protest at Jehanne coming with them since his initial attempt to stop her. He should not have let her leave the castle, let alone walk through the small forest with them. By the time they had reached the river, he should have put his foot down. From there, she would have known how to return to her home. If she had refused his order, he could have tied her to a tree and left her for the Frenchmen to find. Those all would have been better ideas than allowing her to come this far.

Yet no sooner had those thoughts popped into his mind, he dismissed them. He could argue that David was right; she would make a good exchange if they found themselves in a tight corner. Or, he could reassure himself that he had heard Rolf's quiet pleading that they take her with them because she was clearly scared of her spiteful fiancé. But neither was entirely true. It had been in the way she had spoken to him, as if she could not believe he was so cruel as to deny her what she wished for, as if she believed it was he alone who could save her from her fate.

In that moment, he wanted to be a chivalrous knight for her, like some prize coxcomb from one of those indulgent courtly love poems. The type that normally made his skin crawl with embarrassment for the ballad spouting from them and the way a rapt audience would listen in spellbound attention, seeming to believe what he was saying about love was true. Not once had he found those poems to speak to truth.

And yet he had acted like some witless knight, turning his quest on its head because a pretty woman had believed in his power to help her. He deserved to be standing in a wasteland, so cold his balls had probably shrivelled to the size of a broad bean seed. It was just as well he did not intend to have any more children; he doubted that part of him still worked. Not that he was going to admit to everyone how cold it was; it had been his insistence that they keep wading through the stream after all.

His gaze drifted back to Jehanne, who was loosening the bindings around her sleeves and using the material there to create a small storage place to hold more apples than she could carry in just her hands. Rolf was talking quietly to her, the flash of his teeth now and then suggesting that he was smiling at her.

The lad was fond of her and would not like it if Lucan insisted she come no further. Turning her away was likely to be impossible now, anyway. They were too far away from her father's castle so that leaving her alone was likely sending her to her death. He could not live with that on his conscience. Living with his flash of weakness was all that he could do now. It was the only mistake he could allow himself to make.

Whatever it was that kept him glancing at her far more than was normal, had to stop. From now until they were safe, the three of them were going to have to rely on him to get them out of this situation and he needed to concentrate. David was as useful as a twig in a raging river, and as sweet and funny as Rolf and Jehanne were, they were not going to be much better. Once again, it was up to him to be the leader, and once again, it was in an almost impossible situation. The burden of it rested on his shoulders but there was nothing he could do to relieve it.

'Come on,' he said. 'We have dallied long enough.'

They found the cave just as the sky was turning a watery pink. 'It looks dry enough,' said Jehanne peering into its murky depths.

There were dark smudges underneath her eyes and Lucan didn't think she would be able to go for much longer without resting. Rolf had stopped teasing him a while ago and from the way the lad's shoulders drooped, Lucan didn't think he would manage much further either. He didn't bother to look at David; he didn't care if the man couldn't walk another step or not.

'Dry or not,' Lucan said, stooping to miss hitting his head on the rocky overhang, 'we need to rest and we cannot do that out in the open.'

'Can we have a fire?' asked Rolf. 'My clothes are still wet from the river.'

'Sorry, lad, we cannot risk the smoke.' Jehanne's whole body sagged but she said nothing in protest. Making her feel better was not his responsibility, and yet he found himself saying, 'We're out of the wind, so that will help.'

He paused, trying to stifle the words his body was screaming out for him to say. It was no use, they came out anyway. 'If we all stay close, that will help too.' At least he'd managed to use the word *all* and not suggest Jehanne lie next to him, and only him. There had to be some blessing in that, surely.

David thankfully took himself to the other side of the

cave, settling down with his back to the rest of them and apparently falling asleep almost immediately.

Jehanne was still standing in the entrance to the cave, her body silhouetted against the mouth of the entrance. Rolf crumpled to the ground where he stood, his eyes fluttering closed almost the moment his head hit the ground. Lucan picked the boy up and placed him against the wall of the cave, arranging himself so that there was no space on the other side of Rolf for Jehanne to lie. All the while not listening to the voice telling him that it would be a spectacularly bad idea if Jehanne lay next to him on the ground.

Snores filled the cave and still she hadn't moved.

'We're not going to hurt you,' he murmured, suddenly regretting the way he had arranged the sleeping boy now. Perhaps she would have felt better if she hadn't had to lie down near him. Tiredness, and some other nameless emotion, was making it hard for him to think clearly.

'I know you're not going to harm me. If you'd wanted to, you would have done so before now.' Still, she did not move.

'Come and lie down then.'

'Where?' Her hands fluttered out in front of her, as if to demonstrate the lack of space.

He nodded to his left, trying to appear practical and in control of the situation, even as his body twitched excitedly. 'Here.' Clearing his throat, he added, 'We need to stay together for warmth.'

Her first step towards him was hesitant as though still distrustful, then she came forward in a rush, as if her movement had snapped a cord in her, allowing her freedom.

Lowering herself to the ground, her fingers brushed against his arm and he hissed in a breath. 'You are freezing.'

'It's the skirts,' she said apologetically. 'They do not seem to have dried; they have allowed the cool air to move about my legs.'

Pushing himself upright into a half-sitting position, he tugged at the binding of his cloak, Pleased for once that his body was so large that his clothes were too; there would be plenty of material to cover her.

'Oh, there is no need…'

'There is every need,' he argued, pulling it free and draping it over her body. 'I can't have the daughter of the Comte de Balladur dying of the ague,' he added, should she begin to think that he cared about her.

He didn't want to discuss how he had watched his wife fade away from him, how painful that was, and that if he could prevent that for her, then he would do so. That would only send a message to her that he did not want to give.

'I am grateful,' she said, curling into it. He grunted, turning slightly away from her so that he did not have to witness her hair spilling over his cloak as she turned on her side to face him. 'Would you like to share it?'

'It is not necessary.'

'I thought you said we should stay close to keep warm.'

'This is close enough.' It was already too much. Years had passed since he had last lain next to someone soft and never anyone as captivating as Jehanne. His body was reminding him of all the things a man and a woman could do together. Any closer and all sense would flee from his mind.

'What about Rolf? Do you think he should share the warmth?'

'The cloak won't reach that far.'

'We could swap places.'

They could, but as they moved, no doubt their bodies would touch. There would be the soft press of her arm against him, the whisper of breath against his skin. He was clinging to his self-control by the thinnest of threads. It wasn't that he would turn into some sort of savage beast if she so much as touched a sliver of him. It was only that he would then know what her skin felt like against his. He knew the sensation would never be wiped from his memory, that it would haunt him when he slept and remind him of all that was missing from his life. Better that he not know.

'The lad's asleep, let's not wake him. Rest now, tomorrow night will be as hard as this one. Harder probably because we will be hungry.'

Her silent laughter shifted the cloak above her. 'Are you always this optimistic?'

'There is no use pretending otherwise. It is not as if tomorrow will be a festival day with feasting and merriment.'

Silence greeted his statement, a quietness he tried to convince himself was a good thing. Engaging with her was a bad idea. If he wasn't careful, she'd slip beneath his defences and muddle his mind. The next thing he'd know, he'd personally be fighting both King Phillipe and King Edward, just to hand her the English and French throne.

'Tomorrow,' she said, when she'd been quiet for so long he thought she'd fallen asleep, 'will be my first day free from the shackles of Monsieur le Chevalier Dupont. For the first time in nearly seven months, I will not have to pretend that it does not matter to me that at any moment my life will be irrevocably tied to a man who finds the suffering of others amusing, who cares only for himself and who would end my life without a second thought if it meant his advancement. It may not be a festival, it may be cold, wet, miserable and exhausting but it will still be better than any other day I have lived through during the last year.'

There was nothing he could say to that, no words he could offer in comfort, no way he could express his fury at that prick's treatment of her and of those around him. 'Aye, well at least you are prepared for tomorrow's problems,' was all he managed.

Her quiet huff of laughter made him smile. Turning his head away from her, he made sure that she couldn't see his amusement; he didn't want her to think he was going soft on her.

Chapter Eight

Jehanne woke to find her nose pressed against Lucan's shoulder. The rough fabric of his tunic scratched her skin, and this close she could sense the firmness of his muscles. His soft breathing caused his body to move slightly, pressing against her and away again in a steady rhythm.

This close, she could identify the different scents that made up his smell: leather, metal and the salt of his sweat. Before falling asleep, she'd made sure to leave a gap between them. She hadn't wanted him to think that she was trying to get close to him. It was one thing for her to admire his physique but quite another for him to know about it.

Over the years, she'd learned that the less people knew about her thoughts the better. When you bared your soul to someone and they still sent you away, it caused a little part of your soul to die. Jehanne didn't want to lose any more of herself. Not when she needed all her wits to survive.

Unless her family caught up with them, she could not return to her father's fortress now. This must have occurred to Lucan as they got further and further away from the Balladur castle. He might pretend to act the brute everyone saw him as, but she'd been paying attention to his actions, big and small. Lucan was a kind, honourable man underneath a hard shell.

She believed, or at the very least, hoped, that Lucan, would not send her off to roam the countryside by herself. She would not know how to return now, they had travelled so far, and to let her go would most likely be a death sentence. Lucan had to know that. Or perhaps he had known from the moment they had hurried towards the river right at the beginning of the journey. Whatever the case, he had made no further attempt to get rid of her, and last night, he had seen to her comfort over his own.

Now her face was pressed against his arm and although she had been awake a while, she had kept it there. Perhaps she should move away, but he was warm and solid—and lickable.

Her eyes flew open and she jerked her head backwards. Hell's teeth, where had that thought come from? She was not in the habit of putting her mouth on a man's skin, let alone her tongue! The very idea was...unpleasant. Of course it was. Overwhelmingly disgusting. Completely vile.

Waking in a cave was obviously meddling with her thoughts, because her mind seemed to be arguing that it wasn't as unpleasant an idea as she might have previously believed. Her whole body was urging her to press her lips to his skin and discover if he tasted as delicious as he smelled. Her sense had clearly been destroyed, that was the only explanation. It had fled during the day they had slept through.

'You're awake,' came his gravelly voice, the sound tugging at the pit of her stomach. Her desire to roll back towards him was almost overwhelming.

'I am.'

'Good.' He paused and she stilled, sensing he was about to say something. The weight of the silence grew heavy, almost palpable. She held her breath. 'You snore.'

Laughter cracked out of her, the sound echoing around the cave. She thought she heard a deep, answering chuckle but before she could look at his face, Rolf woke. Sitting up abruptly, he knocked his head on some protruding rock, putting an end to whatever had been passing between her and Lucan.

'Ow,' he grumbled, rubbing his head and lying back down almost immediately. 'That really hurt.'

'If you think that's bad, wait until we are cold, wet, miserable and hungry,' she told him, laughter still bubbling through her.

In the darkness, she could still make out the flash of Rolf's teeth as he grinned. 'Is that what Lucan told you? It sounds like the sort of thing he would say.'

'I understand that is Lucan's plans for today. If we also prepare for tired feet, aching bones and an itch that cannot be scratched no matter what, then his day, or rather his long, miserable night, will be complete.'

'When you put it like that, his thoughts on the night's activities sound positively festival-like. I am looking forward to getting started.'

'You both realise I can hear you.' Lucan's voice was a deep reassuring rumble. Her chest tightened as the urge to rest her head against his chest became almost overwhelming.

Since her return to France nearly a year ago, she had been relying on herself, trusting nobody. Having his solid presence was making her want to rely on him too much.

As soon as he was able to, Lucan would become like the rest and get rid of her. So instead of giving in to her strange craving, she rolled to her feet, catching his cloak before it fell to the floor.

'I slept well because of this,' she said, holding it out to him. 'I hope you were able to get some rest too.'

'In between the bone-rattling snores, I managed to get a little.' His lips twitched, the closest she'd ever seen to a grin.

She dropped the cloak on his head and was pleased to hear Rolf's giggle, the innocent sound almost as refreshing as a cool drink in the height of summer.

Watching Lucan struggle to untangle himself from the material was a surprisingly good way to start the night too. His dark glower when he emerged was very satisfying and she bit the inside of her cheek to stop herself laughing out loud. He might be able to take some humour at his expense, but she didn't want to push it too far in case it pushed him over an edge she could not yet see. Glancing towards the entrance to the cave, she could see that the sky was already darkening and her spirits slowly sank.

She made her way to the opening, not needing to crouch to get underneath the sloping roof. A soft mist had descended, coating the world in grey. It wasn't possible to see more than the first line of trees not far from where she was standing. The sound of the birds calling to one another, high in the branches above was undisturbed by men crashing about the undergrowth. For now, it seemed as if their pursuers were nowhere nearby.

'What happens next?' she asked, without turning to look at the others, she didn't want to see Lucan's face in case he was about to suggest she return to the fortress again.

'We need horses,' said David. She flinched at the sound of his voice. In her humorous start to the day, she had almost forgotten about that man's presence. The idea that he had heard what had passed between her and Lucan scalded the skin of her cheeks. That moment was private, and to realise that it hadn't been made her uncomfortable.

She did not trust David. The Lord had been keen to run from the fortress last night without stopping to get Lucan or Rolf. The only side David was on was his own.

'Where do you plan on us getting horses?' asked Lucan, pushing himself to his feet, stooping so he did not hit his head.

'We take them, obviously.'

Of course that was what the Lord wanted; he would not care what he did or whom he hurt, so long as he was fine. 'From whom do you plan to take them?' she asked before Lucan could respond. She could guess but she wanted him to confirm.

Even though the light in the cave was dim, she could still make out his careless lift on one shoulder, as if her question was irrelevant. 'We get them from wherever we find them. We need to move quicker than we did yesterday, and horses are the only way to manage it.'

Her fingernails dug into her palms, fury coating her heart at his cursory response. It did not matter to him who was impacted by his actions. 'Don't you think you English have done enough? Burning our land and destroying our crops hasn't caused enough destruction, so now you want to steal from innocents.'

'This isn't the time for morals, my dear girl. It's...'

Her anger was molten, a red-hot river that burned through her. It was men like him who took and took from those who could not defend themselves, who had no say over their future. He was as bad as Urian. 'Do not patronise me. You will take the horses from some of the poorest of my countrymen, people who have almost nothing except their animals. You will justify it with your need to stay alive. This senseless greed is what has made us French despise you and yours.'

In response to her words, he only raised his shoulder again. How dare he treat her people and her with such blatant contempt. She took a step towards him, not sure what she intended to do when she reached him but knowing she could not stand still and do nothing while he disregarded the French people.

She never reached him. A large arm slipped around her waist, not holding her tightly but not allowing her to move forward by even half a step. 'He is not worth it,' said a deep voice near her ear, the whisper of breath against skin. 'The man could not find a fish in a well-stocked lake. You do not need to worry about him stealing horses.'

Muttering a curse under her breath, she felt Lucan's laughter rumble through her. His amusement cooled her fury. In the short time she had known him, she had never seen him entertained. She wished she didn't have her back to him, she would have liked to see his eyes crinkle in a smile and his soft lips curved. 'I quite agree with that sentiment,' he said quietly. It took her a moment to remember her swear word as his breath tickled her cheek, the air moving down towards her neck. The soft caress caused an eruption of goose bumps in their wake. 'I'm going to let you go now, but I would beg you not to kill him. For reasons nobody can understand, King Edward is fond of the man.'

Glancing across at David, she found the man scowling at them both. Catching her look, he said, 'When you two have stopped dallying around with one another, it is time we get going.'

Lucan whipped his arm away faster than if she had been on fire, as if caught indulging in some courtly love ritual.

Jehanne shivered, missing the warmth of him against her back. David's words were pointless anyway. Lucan wouldn't dally with her; he was far too practical a man for that. He obviously didn't want her to think that he would either, if the speed of his movement was any indication. The tiny pang in her breastbone was ridiculous. She could not afford to get attached to yet another person who would eventually leave her. Lucan might have the physical strength of a pack of wolves, but he was still a man. Urian's dark behaviour might be worse than others, but that didn't mean that others weren't as bad in different ways.

'Any horses we might find amongst the peasants will be draught animals used for ploughing fields,' said Lucan. 'We'd be quicker crawling than riding one of those.' It wasn't a robust defence against stealing from her countrymen, but at least Lucan didn't agree with David. It helped remind her that, although they were working towards a common goal, they were not friends or even on the same side.

'Then what's your suggestion, oh, Great Leader.' David's voice was heavy with sarcasm, but that didn't quite hide the fact that the man had no more ideas of his own.

'I suggest we continue to make our way north,' said Lucan, ignoring David's contemptuous tone. 'If we are lucky we will encounter the English men as they retreat. If we don't, then at least we will find the coast. If we head east from there we will come to Port Einon, a place unaffected by the troubles in the rest of the country. From there we should be able to find a boat to take us back to England.'

'What about her?' David nodded towards Jehanne, obviously deciding she was not worth bothering talking to directly, after she'd had the audacity to argue against him over the horses.

'What do you mean?' Lucan's voice was as cold as ice.

'Taking her with us will only slow us down,' said David, talking about her as if she could not hear, dismissing her as if she were worthless; she was used to it. It didn't crush her like it used to, but she had a horrible feeling that if Lucan were to act in the same way, he could hurt her more than anyone ever had. 'Nothing can be gained from keeping her with us. I suggest we leave her.'

Rolf's soft gasp at David's words was echoed by her own.

'I thought you wanted her to come with us.' Lucan's reply gave no hint as to what he thought.

'I wanted her for the security holding her hostage would give us. It's unlikely that Comte de Balladur's people will have followed us this far, and the further we get without detection, it becomes even less probable.'

Jehanne risked a glance towards Lucan, but his face was inscrutable. All the warmth she'd felt as she'd woken up from lying next to him, fled. A chill crept up her legs and a fine tremor ran through her. Hadn't Lucan wanted to leave her from the beginning? Now that David agreed with him…

'Does it not bother you,' asked Lucan, 'that if we leave her here, the chances are fairly high she will die?'

His words seemed to echo around the cave, appearing to keep bouncing back to her as if the word *die* was repeated a hundred times. A lump formed in her throat. She swallowed, trying to dislodge it but it stayed, wedged there as if she had swallowed a large pip. For the first time, the idea that her life might end seemed possible. And yet, hadn't she been prepared to take that risk, to leave the safety of her father's protection? In the warmth and comfort of the place her family lived, leaving and facing death had seemed preferable over the possibility of marrying Urian.

Squaring her shoulders, she forced herself to meet David's scornful eyes. She had reached this far, she would not lie down and accept whatever fate the Lord chose. And if Lucan—she couldn't finish that thought. Jehanne needed him on her side, because if he wasn't…

'Her life or death is not of my concern,' sneered David. His gaze flicked between them, an evil smile playing around his lips. 'But then it's not been so long since *I…*'

'Do not finish that sentence,' growled Lucan. He shifted forward, his hard body brushing against hers.

David stopped speaking, but his supercilious smirk told Jehanne that he was pleased with the reaction he had elicited. Jehanne had no idea what the man had been about to say, but she doubted it was complimentary to either her or to Lucan.

'We brought her from the castle,' continued Lucan when it was clear that David was not going to say any more, 'and so she will come with us until she is somewhere safe.'

'Borne,' she said quickly. 'I should like to go to Borne. It's on the east coast of England. It's where my…' Her what? William was no longer her fiancé but he was still her friend. He would look after her, at least she hoped so. At the very least, she was sure he would see her somewhere safe. Though, she could no longer call William hers. 'I should be very grateful if you could take me to Borne,' she finished quietly, her confidence slowly ebbing away.

'There are white cliffs at Borne,' said Rolf with false cheer. 'At home, the coast is grey and boring, so I would like to see those unusual formations again. We can go there, can't we, Lord David?'

Jehanne's heart squeezed with affection for the young boy. As an excuse to visit a place, it was fairly weak and would probably not persuade these two giant men, but she appreciated his effort.

She waited for one of the men, David, most likely, to dismiss the lad's comments but nothing happened. Well, not quite nothing at all. A long pause ensued, becoming heavier with every passing moment.

David's glower flicked between Lucan's taut body and Rolf's hopeful one. Lucan continued to radiate menace but made no attempt at any further argument either way. Jehanne couldn't understand why they were giving Rolf's immature comment even the slightest of considerations, but it appeared that David was thinking hard about it.

The dynamics of this group were almost impossible to understand. Why should it matter what Rolf wanted to do to a man who had been prepared to leave him to the mercy of the French?

'I suppose it could be on our way,' agreed David after an age.

'Excellent,' Rolf jumped up from his place on the floor. 'Are there any more of those apples left? My stomach is growling.'

Chapter Nine

Two long nights passed, broken up by days of fretful sleeping. Moving through the darkness was a hard, dispiriting slog. A thick mist covered the land, seeming to clump between the densely packed trees, sometimes disguising blocked routes, so that they had to turn around and come at the path from a different angle.

Clothes were damp and there was little to be done to dry them off. Food was hard to come by and a diet of mainly fruit scavenged from the woodland they passed through did very little to assuage the hunger that gnawed at Lucan's belly.

Rolf was worryingly quiet, his ready smile showing less frequently as time went by. When David had the energy, which was thankfully becoming increasingly rare, he complained about everything. As if the coldness of his bones was somehow Lucan's fault.

David's resentment of Jehanne was growing with every day that passed. He did not even try to hide the way he despised the Frenchwoman, curling his lip whenever he caught a conversation between Lucan and her. Lucan ignored him because, as far as he was concerned, the only ray of light in this whole endeavour *was* Jehanne. He did not want to dwell on how the brief conversations they managed to have without David or Rolf were the highlight of his day. The sparkle in her eyes when she teased him for his grumpiness, the slight hitch in her breath when he did something that impressed her or the way her dark hair swayed as she moved. All of it combined helped to keep him going forward.

But it wasn't only those things which drew him to her. It was also in the way she showed she cared without saying a word. When Rolf was struggling, she was the first to place a reassuring hand on his shoulder, the first to make him laugh—usually at Lucan's expense—and the first to find somewhere for the boy to sleep at night.

As they trudged through the woodland, Lucan found his gaze returning to her every few steps. Even when he was leading their small group, he found himself twisting round to try and catch a glimpse of her smile, the soft curve of her lips coming more frequently the further they moved from her father's fortress. He was clearly losing his mind in this endless tramp through trees that all looked depressingly the same.

Even if the gazes he kept throwing at Jehanne, that he refused to call longing even in the privacy of his mind, meant something, even if he ever considered taking another wife, it was entirely irrelevant anyway. Jehanne was running away from her current fiancé because she was running *to* her previous one. Whoever that man was, it was he who would get to look at her for the rest of their lives together, not Lucan. He wasn't sad about that, no matter how much his gut might protest otherwise. He'd not take on the responsibility of caring for another human, his son and the people of his castle were enough. One more person who depended on him for their survival and livelihood was one too many. The sooner he reunited her with her lost love, the better for his peace of mind.

As the sun began to rise on the third day, Lucan suggested they rest under an overhang. It wasn't much, but it was better than being out in the open.

David rounded on him, his teeth bared. 'This is pathetic. If someone passes us, we'll be spotted immediately.'

'It will have to do,' answered Jehanne.

'Of course you think so. You'd agree with anything that lumbering beast said.'

Lucan was used to slurs on his size and he let the insult slide off him, but Jehanne took a step towards David, her finger raised. 'If it wasn't for Lucan you'd still be locked up in my father's castle. I do not see you complaining about his strength when he lifts large logs out of our way, so that we don't have to turn around and walk another way. Yesterday, you sat and watched him as he arranged somewhere safe for us all to rest. It's about time you showed him the respect he has earned.'

Stunned at being defended in such a way, Lucan was momentarily speechless. Nobody had ever spoken up like that before. He was used to his strength being taken for granted and realising she had noticed his efforts lit something within him.

David's mouth twisted into a cruel sneer. 'You think he is some sort of heroic knight, rescuing you from an imagined distress. You are nothing but a spoiled lady with ridiculous romantic notions from listening to too much courtly love poetry. It's filled your empty little head and made Lucan someone he is not. But perhaps you deserve each other. Not only does he look like a rock, he has the intelligence and the personality of one.'

With that overblown speech, David turned and strode under the overhang. His dramatic exit somewhat hampered by having to duck only a few paces in.

When Jehanne turned to Lucan, the whites of her eyes were pink, her shoulders stiff. He longed to pull her to him, to offer her comfort, but he could not. She belonged to another man, and he was not strong enough to hold her and then let her go.

'Do not get upset by David,' he said gruffly, wishing he was the sort of man who could express all he was feeling. 'He is almost universally regarded with contempt.'

'He is horrid and he is wrong.' Her voice cracked as she spoke. 'You are much more than he says.'

The flame within him grew larger, despite the voice in his head telling him not to be a fool. 'You do not know me well enough. Perhaps he is right.' Lucan wasn't sure why he was pointing out that he might have very little personality. It surely could not be that he was hoping for more compliments from her, although he feared it might be.

'I do not need to know you better to see how you care for Rolf, how you have looked after me, even though you did not want to.'

'Aye, well…' He glanced across at Rolf who had lain down on the ground and fallen into a deep sleep. 'Anyone would do the same.'

'Why are you finding it hard to take a compliment?' The red had faded from her eyes and now amusement shone from them.

'I have little practice in receiving any. I cannot remember the last time I had praise.' A red bug landed on her sleeve and he stepped forward to brush it off.

'Then I shall do it more often.' She didn't step away, and he was close enough to see a tinge of blue on her collarbone, the remnants of a bruise that had no place on her soft skin. He wanted to press his lips to it, to soothe her, but he held himself still before he could give in to the strange impulse.

His gaze swept up her long neck, taking in the pale skin dotted with two freckles close to one another, a small, faded scar on her jawline, the dip at the centre of her top lip. Her dark eyes watched him intently. Even though he towered over her, there was no fear in her gaze, only curiosity and something else he did not understand. Or, perhaps he did, but he turned away from it, unwilling to take a step towards anything that could upset his finely tuned balance.

Now there was only Richard who held a place within his heart, only Richard had the power to destroy him. Lucan would not hand this power to anyone else, even someone as breathtakingly lovely as Jehanne, *especially* someone as breathtakingly lovely as Jehanne.

'We should rest,' he said, hoping she would move away from him because he appeared to have lost the ability to pull himself out of her orbit.

'We should.'

Neither of them moved.

'I will have to carry the boy. I do not think he can manage another step.'

'I am the same.'

'You would like me to carry you too?' He raised an eyebrow in jest, and her soft smile made his heart kick.

'I know you are strong, but I think I am too heavy for that. I can manage the few steps to the shelter.'

'Too heavy! You cannot weigh much more than Rolf.'

Laughter bubbled out of her, soft and sweet like a summer's breeze. 'Four of him, maybe.'

Knowing it would be a mistake to touch her, he held out his arms anyway. 'Let me see.'

Still laughing, she stepped into his hold. Taking a deep breath, his hands slid around her waist, resting above her hips, fingers brushing against her ribs. Her amusement faded, and all he could hear was his rough breathing. 'Ready?'

As she nodded, some of her hair brushed against his skin, and he temporarily forgot where he was and what he was meant to be doing. Her head tilted up to look at him, her eyes wide, her lips slightly parted, the stance reminiscent of a woman waiting to be kissed. *Pick her up* screamed his mind but his body refused to look at him. It had been such a long time since he had held a woman, so long since his mouth had touched another. But he could no longer give this excuse to himself. It was Jehanne whose lips he wanted to taste, no one else's.

Slowly, he lifted her, his body barely registering the weight, until her face was level with his and they were looking eye to eye. His knees shook, but it had nothing to do with effort and all to do with the restraint of not giving in to his deepest desire.

'There, see,' he whispered, for no other reason than the situation seemed to require quiet acknowledgement.

'I see,' she said, her breath brushing over his skin. He wasn't convinced either of them were talking about his strength anymore.

'What are you doing?' Rolf's question broke the moment. In truth, he'd forgotten the boy was there. He lowered her to the ground and dropped his hands.

'Lucan was demonstrating how insignificant I am,' Jehanne told the boy.

'That's not what...' Her fingers lightly brushed the back of his hand, the gesture reassuring and private, telling him what he already knew. That moment had been for them alone. 'Aye,' he agreed with her, 'the lady weighs little more than a feather.'

Rolf laughed, pushing himself up to sitting, taking their explanation without further comment. 'Are we staying here?'

'We are,' said Jehanne. 'Do you think you can manage to get underneath the overhang. Or does Lucan need to see how light you are too?'

'I can manage.' Rolf was able to take the few steps further. Jehanne followed close behind with Lucan taking up the rear.

The shallow cave was gloomy, but it was light enough outside that they could see what they were doing. David was still awake; he shot Lucan a glare before turning on his side, facing away from them all. Lucan's skin burned as he realised the man must have heard all that had passed between him and Jehanne. Their conversation had been innocent enough but it hadn't felt so in the moment.

Rolf and Jehanne settled down to sleep, seeming to gather comfort and support from their proximity. Lucan's legs trembled with the effort of holding himself back from joining them. It was his cloak they were using as a blanket, but he was not sure of his welcome. It was as well that he kept his distance. Too close and he did not trust himself not to bury his face in her hair and breathe her in. As fantasies went, it was very tame, but it was still a craving from which he was having a hard time moving on.

Instead he settled down near them, near but not so close that he might roll over in his sleep and pull her to his chest without meaning to.

'When do you think it will be safe enough to risk a fire?' Jehanne asked, turning her head to look at him.

'If we could find dry twigs, we could probably risk it tomorrow during the day.' He meant to leave it there. Every time they conversed, he found out things about her that he suspected might stay with him for the rest of his life. He knew that she loved the sound of rain against a roof, but only if she could also hear the crackle of a fire burning; that she gagged at the smell of fish once it had been out of the river for more than a day and that she once fell down a hole so deep, she couldn't get out of it without someone called Harold coming along with ropes. That they had been laughing so hard she'd had difficulty forming the knots around her waist. But he found that he didn't want to stop speaking to her. 'It's been three days of travelling. I'm surprised that we have not heard anyone following us.'

For a while she said nothing in reply. He didn't blame her; it was not as if he had asked a question, he'd only blurted out words with no real thought to them other than trying to engage her for a little while longer. Eventually she said, 'I have been worrying about that.'

'Worrying?' That was not a response he had expected.

'The Comte de Balladur is not a man who takes insults lightly. Your escape would have been bad enough, but the fact that I am missing too is not something he would let lie. His rage would have been a sight to behold, and I would have thought he would have sent every able-bodied man after us.' She paused and then added softly, 'And perhaps those not able too.'

Lucan had thought as much himself. He had not encountered much of the Comte, but what he had, suggested a temper worse than Lucan's own. At least Lucan only saved his fury for those who deserved it; the Comte de Balladur seemed to dish it out to everyone. 'What do you think it means that we have not heard anyone yet?'

His cloak shifted as she tucked her knees higher and rolled so that she was facing him again. 'I have given it a lot of thought, and I think it could mean several things.'

'Go on.'

'His best hunters would already have been out searching for the rest of the Englishmen. They have more skill in tracking than anyone else in the castle. Urian would have discovered we were missing fairly quickly, and although I was hoping this might diminish his stock with my father, I have realised that only I know it was Urian's fault I was left unprotected with David. In the hopes of building bridges with my father, he would have set off quickly. He is very good with a sword, but tracking is not one of his skills.'

Lucan grunted in acknowledgement. As much as he did not like the man, Urian was a good fighter. 'Your father would have sent his better trackers after us now.'

'He would. Of course. He will not like that the larger group of Englishmen have escaped, but we will be more important. Well…' She paused as if considering her next words. 'He would consider David and I to be the greater importance.'

She shot him an apologetic look and he smiled reassuringly back, realising that he smiled at her more than he ever had at anyone else. In this case, he wanted to be sure she didn't worry about his feelings. He understood his place in the world, brute-force protector was how he was seen by everyone. 'I agree he will not take kindly to your absence. I also think we should assume that the other English have been recaptured. We've seen no evidence of them wandering around the countryside either.'

'Do you really think so?'

'Unlike us, there were lots of them. Unless they split up, they would be moving slowly, they'd need more food than us and they are more likely to argue amongst themselves as they get tired. They'd also leave wide trails for the skilled trackers to follow. If your father's men are any good, they may have rounded them up on the first day. But, if that's true, then we should expect to see or hear more people coming after us now, and that is not the case. Do you have a theory for why?' He did, but he wanted it, if not confirmed, at least supported. It would make planning the next few days easier.

'I do.' She lapsed into silence, staring out towards the entrance of their shelter.

'Are you going to tell me what it is?' he prompted.

'I don't know for sure, I have not travelled much other than between Borne and Picardy on two separate occasions. Both times I spent much of the journey thinking of other things than where we were going. Only—' she paused, pressing her lips together '—only, I've been wondering about how to leave my father's castle for some time and so I've been paying attention, and I think I have a reasonable idea of the layout of the land. Not perfect, or even good, but…' She trailed off again.

'I am not expecting you to know everything, it would be impossible in any case. Tell me your guess, then maybe we can put what you know and what I know together and come up with a plan.'

She nodded contemplatively, her gaze darting to him and away again. It was irritating, distracting even, to want her look to stay on him for longer, to see if there was any longing reflected back at him in her eyes.

'I wonder if they have gone on ahead of us,' she said. 'They will be expecting you to head to the English, and there will only be a few routes open to us. Less if we want to get some decent food from somewhere.'

'There is no need to chase us when they can wait for us to arrive,' he agreed. When there had been no real sign of anyone pursuing them, he had thought this himself.

'I'm sure my father will send people behind us. He is thorough and will leave nothing to chance.'

'Perhaps we should try and cross into England somewhere else.' Not that Lucan was an expert on the country. This was only his first time out of England but there had to be more than one way in and out. There was a huge section of coastline he knew nothing about, but it was likely to be inhabited by seafaring people.

'Perhaps,' was the only answer he got.

'You do not seem enthusiastic about that idea.'

A strand of hair fell across her cheek and she brushed it off, tucking it behind her ear. The simple braid which had fallen neatly down her back was unravelling as the days passed. Instead of distracting from her beauty, the slow undoing of the calm, collected lady he had met was somehow becoming even more alluring. It made no sense.

'There will be other ways to get to England,' she agreed, 'but where we are heading is the shortest crossing that I am aware of. Unless you know differently.'

He shook his head.

'I thought so,' she said quietly. 'More time on the sea will never be something I will rush towards. Being tossed around on a ship crossing between our two countries is the worst I have ever felt in my life. Even so, I would do it, but...how would we get passage? You speak French with such a strong English accent that your origin would be obvious. Bad news travels quickly, so unless you have gold sown into your clothes, you won't find many French people open to ferrying you across the water, and they would not expect a woman to speak on your behalf.'

'Aye, you're right. Any true Frenchman is more likely to slit my throat after what Edward did.'

She stared at him for a long time; he thought she might question him but eventually she turned away, looking out towards the mist once more.

Depressing though this conversation had been, it only reinforced what he'd already thought himself. The only way out of the country was via a ship, and they needed to leave from a port that was friendly towards the English, if such a place still existed.

Rubbing his hands over his face, he suppressed a groan. The desperate gnawing in his belly was making it hard to concentrate, and paired with his odd desire to keep glancing at Jehanne, he was slowly going out of his mind.

Food was a priority. Tomorrow they would have to get something other than fruit. With his spears, horse and hunting dogs, Lucan knew he was a skilled hunter. Put him in a forest where he knew nothing of the terrain, without anything to catch or kill an animal, not to mention two people he had to keep safe, and he knew he would not fare so well.

The alternative would be to find a settlement and beg, but as Jehanne had already pointed out, his accent was strong enough to mark him as a foreigner. Of course, there was always taking it from someone, but he would not pilfer from those who did not have much to start with. Even if he was desperate, he would not do it, not if it would bring down Jehanne's estimation of him.

'Do you hear that?' While he'd been pondering all the problems he was facing, Jehanne had pushed herself up to sitting.

'What?'

'Listen.'

Nearby, David didn't stir. The man had the ability to fall into a deep, unbreakable sleep the moment he closed his eyes. Thankfully he wasn't snoring. Rolf mumbled something incoherent, before settling once more. Jehanne and Lucan stayed absolutely still, barely even breathing.

'Voices,' he murmured.

'Yes,' she breathed, 'and coming closer, I think.'

They both leaned forward, as if trying to get closer to the source of the sound without moving from their hiding place.

She said something, but so quietly he could not make it out. He beckoned her closer. With his large body, he was more likely to make a noise should he move. Making sure to tuck his cloak around the sleeping boy, she shifted over to Lucan. Her long fingers settled on his shoulder, using him to steady herself. He closed his eyes, reminding himself of the danger that surrounded them, that he needed to concentrate on keeping all of them safe and alive. It wasn't easy though. Jehanne's breath brushed against the shell of his ear and he almost embarrassed himself with a whimper, managing to stop it from escaping only by clamping his jaw together so tightly his teeth hurt. Heat coursed through his body at his momentary weakness. He could not be undone by the simplest of touches.

'Should I move closer?'

'Huh?'

'To the people,' she clarified, and he was glad for the darkness because it hid the blush that surely must be staining his cheeks. Jehanne was able to concentrate on what was happening to them, so why wasn't he? It had to be the lack of food, because there surely was no other explanation.

'To what end?' he asked.

'I may be able to tell from their voices whether they are from my father's castle or whether they are passing through.'

Was it worth the risk of discovering who travelled through the forest? If they stayed where they were, there was no reason for the voices to find them. The danger could pass them by without a problem. Yet, if the men were from the castle, they might say something that would reveal Comte de Balladur's plans and that knowledge could be invaluable.

There was no way she could go alone, however. If it was her father's men, then they might take her away, a situation that had once seemed the perfect solution now appeared to be intolerable to him. Or else it might be strangers, and what would they do when they discovered a woman? Nothing good.

Turning his head to tell her he would come with her, he'd forgotten how close she was. Their noses were virtually touching, her mouth barely a whisper away. Their breath mingled and for a heartbeat he forgot everything: his own name, her lost love, even that they were running for their lives. In the dim light of the overhang, he thought he saw her gaze drop to his mouth; he swallowed, palms tingling with the need to touch, the need to feel.

A twig snapped and they sprang apart as if shoved by an invisible force.

More sounds reached them, the heavy thud of horses' hooves on the forest floor, the rapid sound of a male voice cursing. Going to listen to what the newcomers were saying was irrelevant; they were coming their way regardless. Lucan had never missed the reassuring weight of his sword more.

'The rain's getting up, should we shelter under this?' asked one voice, the sound so close the man might as well have been under the overhang with them.

'And get caught resting?' A second man snorted, as if incredulous that his companion could be so unwise. 'The way things are back at the castle, we'd be dead in an instant if we were spotted doing anything other than searching behind every blessed tree in this damned wood.'

There was a rumble of discontent from the first man, followed by a whinny of protest from an irritated horse.

A light tap on Lucan's arm pulled him from his thoughts.

'I know them,' mouthed Jehanne, or at least that's what he thought she said. It didn't really matter whether she had recognised them or not. From the conversation it was safe to believe that those voices belonged to Comte de Balladur's men. Either that, or there was more than one furious leader sending men out to search the countryside. Given the war in France, that wasn't entirely as wild a thought as it could have been.

That wasn't what occupied his mind though. It didn't really matter where these men were from, it was what they brought with them that was significant. Horses could mean supplies being carried: food, weapons, something which could be used to light a fire.

Lucan's fists slowly clenched, his knuckles tightening. A fight might take the edge off the strange discontent running through him, might take his mind off the feelings he did not want to name or think about. Having two horses would speed up their journey. They might be able to meet up with the English invaders within two days, be across the channel within the week. It would not take long to get to Borne after that. Hell, they might even land in that part of England. Jehanne could be back with her beloved within a sennight, and then all he need do was ride home. He could see Richard, could hold his son in his arms and forget he had ever been on French soil. By the spring, he would think no more of Jehanne, he would not remember that he had longed for something more, something he had never had and would never have.

He gradually released his hands, letting them unfurl softly. Rubbing his brow did nothing to alleviate the tension building there, but it did give him a moment of pause. A clash between him and the unknown riders might result in some food and possibly other assets, but he would have to kill the men. There would be no other option. Let them live and they would be able to give their liege a definite location as to where he was last seen, and therefore reveal the location of the others he was with. It would narrow the area in which the Comte de Balladur was hunting and increase the chances of recapture. Lucan would not survive that. The Comte would want someone to blame for the abduction of his daughter, and David would be quick to pass the blame on to him. Lucan would likely hang without ever seeing his son again.

Everyone might think Lucan a brute but he was not a mindless killer. Ending the life of these travellers was not something he could do without provocation. Even if these men had been complicit in keeping him half-starved and chained to a wall, they had not hurt him directly and he could not take out his anger on them. Besides, they were part of Jehanne's kin, and she would not take kindly to violence towards them. When her feelings on matters had become something he needed to consider before proceeding, he didn't know and didn't care to dwell on.

While he was busy mulling over his choice of inaction over action, he'd forgotten that he shared his hiding place with a man who had less common sense than a fly.

With no warning or sign he was awake, David leapt up from his prone position on the ground and ran from under the overhang.

For a brief flash, Lucan could only stare at the space the deranged Lord had occupied.

'What on…' Jehanne began.

'He's going to get us all killed.' Lucan sprang to his feet, hitting his head on the low roof. He ignored the stinging pain in his scalp. 'Look after Rolf for me. I'll try and stop this before it turns into a catastrophe.'

Not waiting for a reply, he raced out of the overhang, his legs flying over the uneven ground. The sun was rising but the mist had turned into a heavier downpour. The world was a dark grey and the woodland a dense patch of trees, their branches intermingling. It quickly became impossible to run or even move quickly, but it was obvious from the shouting where David had already met up with the riders.

For a man who dragged his heels for most of the day, David had been able to move with speed and precision, no doubt motivated by the thought of transport or food. A horse screamed in fury or pain and Lucan ran, heedless of the branches clawing at him.

Entering a small clearing, he found one man already lying prone on the floor, his horse unharmed but breathing heavily several paces away. A second rider had pulled free his sword and was bearing down on David, his face set in a steely grimace.

'What on God's Earth were you thinking?' Lucan screamed, pushing the Lord to one side before the irritating man was skewered. The horse thundered past without causing harm, and the rider grappled with the reins trying to keep it under control.

'Food, transport, extra clothes,' gasped David, clasping his side. 'Practical things you should have been thinking about instead of gazing into that woman's eyes, like a lovesick swain.'

Lucan's skin burned. 'I was doing no such thing.' David only smirked at him, not improving Lucan's mood one bit. 'Get that horse and the man's sword,' he barked, gesturing to the riderless one. 'Calm it down before it does itself a damage and makes this whole exercise pointless.'

Lucan knew how David fought; he had only one style and if that was thwarted he folded easily. It was not worth him getting involved in whatever happened next. That there was already one unconscious man was a miracle because it was not possible for the Lord to have defeated him in open battle. It was more likely the man had been taken by surprise as David had charged through the woodland and been thrown from his horse, but there was no time to ask for details.

The remaining Frenchman had turned his horse around and was coming back towards Lucan, his skin mottled in anger, his sword swinging dangerously, although fortunately with not much purpose. Scrabbling around on the floor of the forest, Lucan found a solid-looking branch and held it aloft. The enemy blade sliced right through it, the impact vibrating through his arm. He dropped the split stump. It might no longer be useful but it had saved his life and he was unhurt. Without an animal to control, he was also able to move quicker than his attacker, whose horse had become entangled in some of the low-lying vines. The beast, snorting in fury, was trying to unseat his rider, who was barely clinging on while shouting at the horse in a way that only panicked the animal further.

Seizing the opportunity, Lucan rushed to the man's side and pulled violently on his arm. Already unbalanced, the Frenchman crashed into Lucan, yelling obscenities as he fell. Grabbing his opponent's sword, he managed to fling it away from them into the undergrowth.

The world became nothing but fists and the heavy thud of punches finding their mark. A sharp jab to his stomach had Lucan gasping for air. But though his opponent was skilled and furious, Lucan was still the superior fighter, even more so with size and strength on his side. Eventually, the Frenchman fell limp against him.

Rain dripped from a nearby leaf, repeatedly hitting Lucan in the side of his forehead. He sucked in huge lungfuls of air, his heart racing. Lying crumpled on the ground, his assailant's chest rose and fell; the man would live but he would have an almighty headache when he awoke. Really, Lucan should finish him off and his companion too, but he could not bring himself to do it. If he and the others managed to escape while the two men were unconscious, then they would still have a good chance of evading capture.

Pushing against the tree he was slumped against, Lucan stood to his full height and looked around the small clearing, searching for the discarded sword, but there was no sign of it and no time to waste hunting for the blade. He had another look around and… He blinked. There was no sign of David or the horse Lucan had sent him to calm down. He looked around again, not truly believing what he was seeing, but he had been right the first time. David had gone.

The two Frenchmen forgotten, blood pounding in his ears, Lucan shoved his way back through the thick forest. Panic made his movements jerky and slower than they could have been and it seemed to take forever to retrace his steps. He hadn't even reached the overhang when Jehanne came towards him, her hands outstretched, her face pale and wet with tears.

'He's taken Rolf.'

Lucan barely heard words, even as a leaden ball sunk to the pit of his stomach. 'What happened to your face?'

Closer now, he could see the smear of a streak of blood on her chin and the swelling on the right of her bottom lip.

'I tried to stop him taking Rolf and he hit me. It was more like the swatting of an irritating fly for him. But I… I could do nothing.' Her voice was trembling, and Lucan's world turned red, fury coating everything. 'I stumbled and fell and before I could get to my feet, he just took him. Rolf was calling for me, screaming, but Lord David had a horse and they were away before I could get to them.' A sob burst out of her, and she clamped a hand over her mouth.

Lucan cursed softly, his body becoming completely rigid. He desperately wished he was the sort of man who knew what to say in this moment, perhaps he should offer to hold her, but his arms refused to move in any sort of gesture at all. A comforting word would be better than nothing, but his mind was a blank, no words of any sort forthcoming. Only rage consumed him. If David stood before him now, there would be nothing to stop him from ripping the man in half. All he could do was stare at her, as if she was some mystic creature of legend and her sadness had turned him to stone.

There was no time to soothe her anyway. They had to get moving before more of her father's men came and discovered them. There was no time to waste in going after David either. It was imperative Lucan found him, and not just because he was so angry with him, he wanted nothing more than to destroy the man. It wasn't clear why the Lord had decided to strike out on his own, and Lucan needed to get after them before he did anything foolish that would hurt Rolf.

'Can you walk?' he asked. A quick nod was all the

confirmation he needed. 'There's a horse. We can ride him if we get to him quickly. Come on.'

She wiped her tears away with the back of her hand and he thought she might argue but all she said was, 'Wait one moment.'

Disappearing into the overhang, she returned with his cloak clasped in her hands, her gaze fixed on the ground.

'Do not fret,' he said. 'You did what you could.' He meant that as a compliment; not everyone would try to save the boy.

From her jerky nod, she did not seem to agree.

'This way,' he said, moving away without a word on the tears that flowed down her cheeks unheeded. His stomach squirmed with the need to say something more, anything, that might ease her pain but, his mind remained blank. It was a good thing that he had decided not to remarry; he did not know how to be around a woman and didn't deserve the companionship such a relationship would give.

Even though the rain was making it hard to see more than a few steps ahead, the agitated stomping of the horse made finding the small clearing reasonably straightforward. Lucan busied himself soothing the animal, all the while listening to Jehanne's quiet sobs behind him. For the first time in his life, he longed to be a different man, one who knew what to say that would make the tears stop. With every shuddery sigh, his soul shrivelled. He wanted to fall to his knees, to offer her anything, everything, just to make her happy again. Her sadness was his torture.

He was sure her English love would know what to do, how to make her laugh. He'd not liked the sound of the man before, but for some reason, he loathed him now. To inspire such devotion in someone like Jehanne must make him truly special. No one would try and cross a country savaged by war to get to Lucan, and yet she was prepared to risk everything to see this man again. With his brusque manner and inability to offer anything in the way of a kind, reassuring word, she was more like to cross a country to *avoid* seeing him again.

Chapter Ten

Misery was the only thing keeping Jehanne from tumbling into a deep, fathomless sleep. That and the only place she would be able to rest her head was on Lucan's broad back as they rode through the endless woodland. If she'd been quicker or stronger, maybe she could have stopped David from taking Rolf. Only she hadn't expected the man to move that quickly or to be so aggressive. Although he'd dragged her out of the castle, she had felt that was more because she had been able to manipulate him into doing so and not because he was strong enough to truly master her. As they'd navigated the corridors of her father's fortress, she'd believed that, if she'd really wanted to, she could have pulled herself free from his grasp. It was humbling to know that perhaps she had been wrong about that after all.

Knowing she was defenceless against the English lord did not stop the weight that seemed to press on her shoulders or the knife that seemed to have plunged itself deep into her ribs, causing unending agony. It had not been very long at all, but she missed Rolf's cheeky smile and the way he tried to make her laugh. She could not stop picturing his face as David had dragged him away, or the way his fingers had stretched out towards her in a silent plea for her to do something, anything other than just let him go.

If that wasn't agony enough, she was forced to ride with the man whom she had let down so badly. She'd failed in the one thing he had asked her to do, and now Lucan was unable to bring himself to speak to her. Their ride through this endless morning had been conducted in a brutal silence, one so painful it almost seemed to slice at her skin.

Not that she could blame Lucan for his muteness. She expected no comfort from him when this disaster had happened because of her inability to keep Rolf safe. Back at the castle, she had watched them both. In the weeks she'd known him, Lucan had taken great care over Rolf's comfort. He always made sure the boy was fed before he was. If the night had a chill to it, it was always Rolf who wore the cloak or had the spare blanket wrapped around him. Over the last three days, Lucan always made sure that Rolf had more than a quarter of the food they found and that he was comfortable in whatever shelter they found. In the few moments where Lucan had left Rolf with her, she had failed to keep him safe from what should have been the mildest of threats.

'Is he your son?' she asked, when it started to feel as if the silence had become a living, breathing entity.

'Who? Oh, you mean Rolf. No, he is not mine.'

'I did not think so.' Although she had begun to doubt that assumption over the long, quiet ride. 'You look nothing alike. But you are close, yes?'

'I only met him at the start of the campaign, but I like the lad, and for some reason, he seems to want to be around me.' The broad shoulders lifted slightly, as if to indicate that he couldn't understand Rolf's preference, which was absurd. There were many reasons why anyone would prefer to spend time with Lucan than anyone else. His steady kindness was one of them, but she didn't think Lucan was in the mood to hear that, especially from her.

'Do you think Lord David will keep him safe?' she asked.

'I think he will *try*.'

Her stomach squirmed; that was what she was worried about. For whatever reason, David wanted Rolf, and if he'd gone to the effort of keeping the boy with him, then it stood to reason he would look after him. But David was an incompetent fool who cared more about himself than anyone else. If their lives were on the line, David would choose himself over Rolf every time.

Rain continued to fall, but the thick canopy of leaves above them stopped the worst of the water reaching them. Even that small mercy couldn't penetrate her misery.

'I…' she began. 'I…know I should have done more. You'll never know how much I regret what happened. If there was anything I could do to make it up to you and to Rolf, I would do it in an instant. Even if it meant giving myself up to Urian. Of course, that would not help. I only want to illustrate how very wretched I am about the whole thing. I should have moved faster, stopped him before he got too close. It's just, I've never been hit before. I did not know how to react. Before this, Lord David seemed so…'

Even though Lucan couldn't see her, she waved her hand around to illustrate how pathetic she had found the man prior to this morning.

About to carry on with her desperate ramble, she

stopped when Lucan said, 'I could tear him apart with my hands for so much as laying a finger on you.'

'Oh, I…but…' She wasn't sure how to respond. Why would he protect her if he was so very furious with her?

'If I hadn't let him hit me…'

'What?' Lucan's shoulders tightened even further. 'You think his violence towards you was somehow *your* fault? That you *let* him put his hands on you?'

'Don't you?'

'No!'

'Then why are you displeased with me?'

'What! I am not angry at you.' He half-twisted in his saddle, peering down at her from his large height, fury flashing in his eyes despite his words. 'Do you really think that?'

Of course she did. 'You have not said a word in ages. Besides, it is my fault Rolf is no longer with us. I failed to protect him even after you'd asked me to. I…'

He made a low rumbling sound from deep inside his chest. 'You are not to blame, and the only person I am truly annoyed with at the moment is myself.'

'But…'

Lucan pulled the horse to a stop, twisting further in the saddle so that he was almost completely turned towards her. 'I knew Lord David was a conniving little toad. I should not have taken my eyes off him for a moment. Instead of telling him to take care of the horse that was running free, I should have tied him to a tree. Or better yet, as soon as we were a sufficient distance from the castle, I should have made off with you and Rolf and left him to rot. We could be days away from him by now. In all our time together, and unfortunately I have had to be his travelling companion for months, I found him to be witless and incompetent, but I did not think him capable of hurting a woman.'

At this, Lucan's jaw tightened and he glanced away from her, as if unable to look at the damage Lord David had caused. 'It is my fault he took Rolf. It is my fault he hit you. I am livid with him and also myself.' He turned back to her and she could see the anguish burning in his blue eyes. 'But I am not angry at you, never you.'

His large fingers reached up to the edge of her lips, his touch featherlight, even as it sent sparks shooting through her. 'The swelling is going down, soon you will look as normal.' His voice softened even if his eyes still burned.

'It doesn't hurt as much now.'

He half-smiled. 'Good.' He twisted back round, kicking the horse into motion. 'I will still never forgive him.'

They rode for a while longer, the silence no longer painful, his shoulders softer.

'I do have a son,' he said as the rain began to ease and the day edged into the afternoon.

It was the first time he had volunteered information about himself in the entire time that she had known him, and she was not about to allow him to lapse back into silence. 'What's his name?'

'Richard. This will be his fifth winter. I want… I *need* to be home to see him. This pointless war is a distraction from all that is important and I…' His voice petered off as he navigated the horse around tangled branches too thick to penetrate.

A horrible thought dawned on her; an idea that shouldn't make her stomach twist and turn but somehow did. 'What about his mother?'

His right arm jerked and the horse nickered in irritation. 'She passed away, four summers ago now.'

A small puff of some emotion brushed past her heart, which surely must be pity. It could not be relief, as that would make her the most vile woman on earth. Perhaps his wife's death was what explained his gruffness; maybe he was still grieving his lost love. 'I am sad to hear it.'

He grunted softly.

'What was she like?' It definitely wasn't jealousy she was experiencing, not if she was this curious about a woman she would never meet. Now she was reassured about herself; she wasn't a bad person after all. That weird feeling she had experienced had to be down to the bone-weary tiredness tugging on every part of her body and not relief that Lucan was not a married man. She did not think of him in that way for herself after all, and so there was no reason to think on it at all.

'Like?' The question seemed to take him by surprise, as if his wife's personality was not something he'd considered before. After a long pause, he said, 'She had brown hair and brown eyes.'

Jehanne bit her lips to stop herself from laughing, but she must have made some noise because he said, 'What's funny about that?'

'Nothing. It's only…that is the sort of unobservant answer I would expect from a man. I meant was she quiet and shy or loud and boisterous? Did she despair of your grumpiness? Or was she exempt from that side of you. Perhaps you treated her like a queen.'

His hands twitched on the reins, the only sign he had heard her and her smile fell. Maybe she had gone too far with her questions, perhaps his grief was such that talking about her was painful. In trying to find out more about him, she had trodden thoughtlessly on subjects that were better avoided. It was hard to know with this man, he gave virtually nothing away.

After an age in which she scrambled for something else to talk about, he said, 'I felt sorry for her, my wife that is, lumbered with a husband like me. Isabelle was her name. I can still recall the way her eyes went wide enough to split her face in half when she first caught sight of me. Probably thought she was about to be wed to a mountain troll.'

'Don't be daft. You look nothing like a mythical monster.' He really didn't. Sure, his eyes had burned with suppressed rage for most of the time she had known him, but that was hardly surprising, given that he had been chained with those heavy manacles for most of that time.

During his imprisonment at her father's castle, she'd had a difficult time keeping her gaze from his wide shoulders. Her fascination had only grown as the days in his company had passed. The power his body possessed was intoxicating to be around, and she didn't believe she could be the only person to experience this phenomenon. He was quickly becoming her lodestone and it would be very difficult to tear herself away when the time came. Not that she would have to. He would leave her as surely as everyone else in the end.

'I know what I look like, you don't need to be kind.'

'Fine,' she sighed softly. 'You are right, you look like a troll. Go on with your story.' It wasn't true at all, but she sensed he would not believe compliments about his body. Perhaps his perception of himself as a monster was too far ingrained for him to appreciate the truth. Enough people must have commented on the way he looked for him to believe such things, but they were wrong too. Indeed many of the women of the castle admired Urian's golden hair; the same women had sniggered about the brute chained up in the castle courtyard. From what she knew of both men, there was no competition. As far as Jehanne was concerned, Lucan was the more beautiful of the two in every way.

Thankfully he laughed at her attempt at humour, his wide shoulders shaking. Once again, she was not able to see his smile, a sight she believed must surely change his features completely. She would like to see it for herself sometime soon.

'Aye, well Isabelle bore the wedding well and once she got used to my size, we got on fine.'

'Oh, Lucan. You're still not describing her to me. All I know is that she was not keen on your height at first. Were you kind to her? I cannot imagine that you were anything otherwise. Despite your gruff demeanour, I think you are softer than you give yourself credit.' He grunted a denial, but she ignored him. 'You were wed long enough for her to bear you a son. You must have picked up something about her in that time.'

That deep rumbling in his chest sounded again and she waited. Last time, he'd sounded like that, she'd got lots of information out of him. On this occasion, he didn't disappoint her either.

'She liked vegetables rather than fruit, she didn't really enjoy meat. Her favourite time of the year was autumn because she believed that the light turned everything golden, but also because the leaves turned red. When we were together, I tried to make my bulk less obvious. I would sit rather than stand, not make sudden movements in case they startled her. Eventually she relaxed around me, and our life settled into a pleasant routine.'

There was nothing wrong with what Lucan was saying. He was describing a marriage that sounded a lot more congenial than anything Jehanne could have hoped for with Urian but…but it didn't seem right that a man of Lucan's passion should live with something that sounded fine but also limited. It wasn't right that he made himself small to fit in with someone else. If Lucan was her husband, she would want him exactly the way he was, not trying to fit into something he thought he should be. Hell, it was his width and breadth that made it hard for her to take her eyes off him sometimes. Not that *that* meant anything.

'How did she die? If you don't mind talking about it that is.'

'I am not against discussing Isabelle's passing. It occurred many years ago now. Far longer ago than the length of time we were married.' He cleared his throat. 'It was not a dramatic death, although it was sad and painful to watch.' His shoulders lifted and then dropped. 'Isabelle caught a fever and although it went, she never recovered. Slowly she faded away until, one morning, she did not wake up. There was nothing I could do to stop it. I…'

She waited for him to carry on his sentence but he appeared to have stopped. 'You?' she prompted softly.

'I don't want you to think badly of me. I am not a monster, you understand. Despite looking like a mythical beast, I try to live my life well.'

She lightly touched his back, it was unlikely he would feel the gesture through his clothes but somehow it seemed important to reassure him. 'You should stop being so down on yourself. I do not think you look ill. In fact, I find you rather handsome.' Her stomach swooped as she realised what she had said, but then she dismissed it. He'd obviously been told he was not an attractive man in the past, and if the only thing she could do for him was to show him that was a lie, then what did it matter if she gave away a little of her pride.

'I swear that I will not think badly of you, whatever you say. Although what would it matter if I did? Once we are on English soil, we will never see each other again. Let us agree to be honest with one another about everything.'

For a long while, she did not think he was going to answer, and then, 'Handsome, hey?' Swivelling in the saddle, he looked down at her and for the first time she saw his smile in all its glory. His blue eyes twinkled, his lips parted, his teeth were visible, his whole face lit up with amusement and possibly joy. Her breath caught in her throat, she couldn't have said anything in response if she'd tried. All she was able to do was stare up at him and marvel at the change in him. She had thought him handsome before, but now he was beautiful. Really, truly magnificent. Slowly, his lips returned to normal, although the twinkle in his eyes stayed, along with something new, something soft.

Turning back towards the direction they were heading, she thought she heard him mutter the word *handsome* again but she wasn't sure. Now he wasn't looking at her, her own smile spread across her cheeks, her skin almost aching with the gesture. It was the first time she'd experienced happiness with someone else for a very long time.

Shifting on the saddle, he said, 'Very well, let us be completely honest with one another from here on in. Why not? As you say, soon enough we shall never see one another again.' *That* wiped the smile off her face. 'I was going to say that I liked my wife. Isabelle was a good woman who gave me my son, whom I adore. I am sure she would have made a fine mother and I am sad for my boy that he will grow up not knowing her. Her death changed something in me. It made me realise caring for someone only ever ends in pain. I love my son, but that is it for me. No one else will hold this power over me. As for the grand love, the one knights write about in their ridiculous courtly poetry—' he shook his head, some of his hair brushing against her forehead '—that does not exist.'

'You mean you don't believe that some men and women cannot live without one another?' He snorted, the sound somehow managing to convey complete disgust at the very thought of it, and she couldn't help her laugh escaping her. 'You surprise me, Lucan. I had you down as a romantic man.'

'Now I am starting to doubt your judgement.'

'And yet you didn't question it when I said you were handsome.'

'If we are being honest, that is when I began to doubt everything you have ever said.'

From his voice, she could tell he was smiling and she wished she could see it again.

'I think it exists,' she said. It was unlikely to be something she would experience for herself, but she liked the idea of it. The thought that some people would meet, fall in love and spend the rest of their days happy together, brought her a measure of happiness she could not explain. Even if she found the words, Lucan would likely scoff.

'Of course,' he said gruffly. 'I suppose it must, otherwise where did the bards get their inspiration from, but for me, no. My marriage was happy enough without it.'

It was the *enough* that was somehow mildly depressing, and yet Lucan believed he'd had a good marriage, and it was not as if she had anything to compare it to herself. Only two failed engagements. Or one failed engagement and another she was running from as hard as she could.

'She sounds lovely,' Jehanne's comment was lame in comparison to the laughter and honesty they had just shared, but it was all she could manage.

Tiredness seeped into every part of her; keeping her eyes open became a battle of wills. It was a fight she was losing miserably. Her head dropped, bumping against Lucan's broad back. She jerked upright, her skin burning, only to slump forward again moments later.

'Are you staging some sort of attack?' he asked after she'd repeated the process several more times. 'If so, it's surprisingly effective. Despite the gentleness with which your head is hitting my back, I am fairly sure the skin is going to be black and blue.'

There was laughter threaded through his voice, and she did not truly think he was cross with her, but she mumbled an apology anyway.

'Just sleep, Jehanne.' Her name in his deep, rumbling voice made her heart stutter. She did not think she had ever heard him say it before.

His command did not need to repeated. Resting her head between the solid space between his shoulder blades, she breathed in the rich leather of his tunic, the sharp tang of iron chain-mail and the delicious fragrance of his skin. The scents were comforting and warm and something else, something that pulled at her senses, urging her to press closer, to slide her arms around his waist, to hold on to him and not let go.

Everyone left eventually, everything ended: friendships, engagements, even parental love. Right now, in this blurry space between sleep and wakefulness, she could allow herself the dream that he was hers to keep forever, that there was no world outside of this moment. She allowed herself that innocent, fleeting fantasy as she drifted off to sleep.

Chapter Eleven

Lucan fought to keep his attention on the signs he was following, the bent branches and crushed undergrowth, and not on all the places Jehanne was resting on him. With every step the dun-coloured horse took, the effort became harder. With every sway of his body, she moved gently against his back, her thighs resting against his. All he could think about was tugging the horse to a stop, turning in the saddle and pulling her into his arms, so that her head rested against his chest. There he could keep her safe while she slept. It was a foolish notion. She would be no safer in front of him than behind, and it would only make it harder for him to control the irritated horse. The ridiculous urge was also a dangerous sign. It suggested that, despite his best efforts, he was developing protective feelings for his current companion. He could not allow those to develop. Even if he was brave enough to keep her in his life for longer than this short journey, if he ignored all his worries about losing another person, Lucan was not the man she was risking everything to be with. That privilege belonged to her previous betrothed.

The stallion tossed his head as if agreeing with Lucan that he lacked even a modicum of intelligence. Either this horse had been bad-tempered before they had taken it from its original rider or it was furious at being made to traipse through the endless woodland. Regardless of the reason, this was the most cantankerous beast he'd ever had the misfortune of riding, and the tiredness that weighed down Lucan's shoulders was making it even harder for him to control the horse as they navigated through densely packed woodland.

On top of that, signs of David and Rolf making their way through this part of the forest were getting harder to spot. Although Lucan was fighting it with everything that he had, his eyes kept sliding shut, staying closed for longer than a blink.

This tired and he might miss completely the damaged undergrowth that he hoped marked the Lord's passage through this endless forest. This tired and he might miss those who were following them from behind until it was too late. This tired and he might say something foolish to Jehanne, something that showed the direction in which his mind kept wandering.

When the horse whinnied in irritation, he jerked upright. Only realising he had fallen asleep when he saw things he had not noticed before.

'What is it?' slurred Jehanne, her voice heavy with sleep.

'I may have nodded off,' he said, or at least tried to say. His words were jumbled with exhaustion.

'Are you drunk?' Her voice was clearer now, but her head still rested against his back. The unhelpful thought occurred to him that this is what she would sound to wake up next to in the morning: soft and gentle but with a hint of a rasp at the back of her throat. It was an intimacy he could get used to.

'Of course I am,' he said, answering her flippant question with some irreverence of his own. 'While you dozed, I invited myself to a feast held by King Phillipe.'

'Ah. I suspect he was pleased to receive you.'

'He was shocked by my audacity at first, but he soon rallied and offered me some of his finest wines. I must say that he keeps a pleasingly wide variety.'

'Yet you returned here rather than continuing to enjoy yourself.'

'I was revelling in gorging myself on the table covered in succulent meat and stretching my body out in front of a roaring fire, but I realised that, if I stayed, I would miss sleeping on the painfully hard ground, clad in constantly damp clothes next to a woman whose snoring is surprisingly loud.'

Jehanne's body shaking as she laughed against his back was the most pleasant thing he'd experienced in months, possibly years.

'We should stop,' she said. 'You must rest. Or I could ride and you could sleep against me.'

Lucan could imagine it; his arms wrapped around her waist, his head resting against hers. The longing for it to happen was so intense it almost ruined him. He yearned to give in, to let it happen, and yet it was that desperation that held him off agreeing. He'd never wanted to depend on another person to keep him safe before now. Or rather, there had never been anyone who had offered prior to Jehanne. Everyone assumed he didn't need it and so he had learned never to ask, to depend only on himself. But the thought of letting someone else take charge while he rested, so tantalisingly close and yet so utterly impossible, nearly brought him to his knees.

'I would crush you,' was all he managed to say.

Her body shook with laughter again. Not only had no one ever offered relief of a duty before, no one had ever found him this amusing.

'I did not mean to be funny.' He didn't want her to get the wrong impression of him, for her to think that he was humorous. She might expect things from him then, things he would never be able to give her. Theirs was a relationship that should never have come about, one which would end as abruptly as it started. He was feared and respected in equal measure, people leaned on him or else avoided him. They did not come to him to laugh.

'I know. Only…'

'Only?' he prompted, interested to know what it was that he did that made her happy. Fool that he was, he wanted to keep doing it, even after telling himself that he shouldn't. He was not making sense to himself, which had to be down to exhaustion.

'Only,' she continued, 'you sound grumpy and you always look very fierce, but you're really quite sweet.'

'Sweet!' The word burst out of him, shock waking him up as surely as a bucket of cold water. 'Nobody has *ever* called me that before.'

'Perhaps nobody has noticed your true nature because you hide it behind a deep frown.'

'It's because there's nothing to notice. I am not sweet.' It was important that she know this. It would do neither of them any good if she started imagining things about him that were not true.

The saddle creaked as she moved backwards, lifting her head from its resting place, making him regret his harsh words until she said, 'For a man who's allowed me to sleep against his back, you seem very certain of that fact.'

'I could hardly throw you to the ground while you slept. I'm not sweet but I am not a monster.' If she carried on with this *handsome* and *sweet* nonsense, she might turn him soft, and then where would they be? Nowhere good, that was for sure. From the teasing note in her voice, he could tell she was laughing at him. He should stop this conversation before it went any further, but even though it was utterly preposterous, he found he did not want to end it after all.

'Even you arguing against me is adorable, thereby losing your own point while trying to make it.'

He could take it no longer, he had to see the smile he could hear in her voice. Turning in the saddle once more, he peered down at her. Whisps of hair clung to her face, her braid barely containing the strands anymore. Three streaks of mud crossed her cheek, her lip, which was no longer swollen, was curved into an inviting smile. Warmth shone in her eyes, laughter and affection lingering there. The urge to lower his mouth to hers washed over him, an almost painful longing that built in his ribcage, swelling and pushing against the bone as if trying to force its way free.

As he watched her, she reached up and smoothed his forehead with the tips of her fingers.

'There,' she said softly. 'You *can* get rid of the frown.'

Her fingers rested against his skin and that ache in his chest intensified. His heart thundered, the air around him stilled, bringing everything into sharper focus. Slowly, almost as if the action was happening to someone else, he dipped his head and pressed his lips to her palm. It was barely a kiss, barely even a brush of skin against skin and yet it was somehow more. A question, perhaps; one he did not know if he truly wanted to ask, but to which he also desperately wanted to know the answer. Everything was muddled, twisted in a way that turned what he believed and what he knew on its head. His mind no longer seemed to control his body.

He half-expected her to snatch her hand away and glower at him in disgust. But a delicate sigh escaped her and her fingers began to trace along his brow, a feather-light touch that torched his insides, rendering him almost mindless with want. He held himself still as her fingers brushed over his cheekbone, over the strands of his beard and down to his top lip.

He was barely breathing. It was agony not to move but to break the spell would be worse.

Her fingers ran over his lips, the light brush over his skin sending sparks rushing through him. He pressed another, barely there kiss against her skin and then another, harder this time, more obvious, impossible to deny.

Her hand dropped to his shoulder, applying gentle pressure, tugging him down towards her.

As if in a dream, he lowered his head, moving almost infinitesimally slowly in case he was misunderstanding her intentions. Instead of pulling away, she edged towards him, her thighs pressing against his. Her fingers slipped into the hair at the nape of his neck and sensation shot through his body, straight to his centre. Any restraint he'd been clinging to over the last few days was slipping away from him and he made no attempt to cling to it. She'd asked for the truth between them and this was his; he wanted her, desperately, to the edge of reason.

His lips skimmed over her forehead, the curve of her cheek, the edge of her jaw. Their breath mingled, mouths met, parted, met again. Her fingers flexed against him and the kiss deepened, the smooth slide of it intoxicating, like a glass of the richest red wine. He dropped his hold on the reins; the horse could do whatever it liked, take them wherever it wished. Having his hands free to touch her was far more important.

His fingers found her jaw and they trembled against her soft skin. If he had any thoughts left, he might have been embarrassed by that weakness. He traced down the length of her neck, to where her pulse was racing at its base. That reaction, the knowledge that she was as affected by him as he was by her, spurred him on, wiping away the last of his restraint. The kiss become a desperate, keening thing. Their tongues met and he caught her moan in his mouth. There was nothing he would not do for her, nothing he would not give her if only they could do this forever.

Her hands were in his hair, tugging at the strands, pulling him closer as she pushed her body into his.

Beneath them, the horse shifted, but he was hardly aware of it, he barely cared. If the world set alight, he would not notice as it burned around him. The longing he had tried to deny to himself that he was even feeling, poured out of him, consuming them both. There was nothing docile about her, nothing calm. The two of them together were a raging torrent that swept away every worry or concern.

Lucan would never know how it came about, but suddenly, the horse bucked up, rearing its front two legs and screaming with fury. Wrenching his mouth from Jehanne's, Lucan swore at the terror in her wide eyes. Time seemed to slow as the horse carried on with its rampage, desperate to unseat its riders.

The world snapped back into focus. Letting go of Jehanne, he twisted, grabbing the reins and fighting for control as the horse reared and bucked, intent on getting rid of them.

'Hold on,' he yelled over the angry snorting of the beast.

Jehanne screamed as they were thrown about in the saddle, the sound cutting through him sharper than any blade. She wrapped her arms tightly around his waist, clinging to him, although it would do little good if they both went down. He leaned back, not allowing the animal to lower its head.

'Stay calm,' he shouted, not sure to whom he was directing his command: the horse, Jehanne or himself.

Time seemed to stretch out as he battled the beast. Long frightening moments where the image of Jehanne falling to the ground and being trampled beneath stamping hooves kept flashing unhelpfully though his mind. Lucan never panicked, not even when they'd been captured by the French and he'd thought he might not see Richard, his son, again. But right now, fear had a hold of him. He did not want any harm to befall Jehanne; he would not be able to bear it if she got hurt because he had been careless with this animal.

Her arms were tight bands around his waist, anchoring them both to the world. Gradually the horse slowly began to calm, or perhaps the stallion realised he was not going to win this battle. He was still tossing his head and blowing great puffs of angry air through his wide nostrils but he was no longer trying to unseat them. Lucan's muscles were so taut, they ached.

'Are you hurt?' he asked Jehanne.

Against his back, he could feel the quick rise and fall of her chest, and all he heard was her harsh breathing. But there was no answer. Finally, after what seemed like a great age, she said, 'I'm…fine. I think. Scared. I'm not sure I will ever let go of your waist but… I'm not injured. Are you?'

He rubbed the length of her arm that crossed his stomach, not sure if he was reassuring her or himself. 'Fine. He's a foul-tempered animal, this one.'

Her quiet hum of agreement reverberated down his spine. Her face must be pressed up against his body but he couldn't turn to look at her without dislodging her from her position. 'Perhaps he is angry that we are making him carry us when all he wants is a rest,' she said.

'Maybe, but we don't have time to stop.' Goodness knows how long they had wasted with his mouth pressed against hers. It could have been a brief flash or days. Lucan could not say, but he could not do it again; Rolf was depending on him and his own future depended on him keeping his mind clear. 'He'll have to accept that we must go on, like we do.'

The horse was still tossing its head but it was making no further attempt to unseat them. In the battle for who was master, Lucan had won. At least for the time being. Jehanne made no further comment about stopping, neither did she try and entice him into kissing again. Lucan could not tell if he was relieved or disappointed.

They plodded on for a little while longer. Gradually, Jehanne released her death grip and slowly eased herself backwards away from him until there was no part of them touching. Lifting a branch over them both, he searched his mind for a suitable way to tell her what was in his mind, no idea if she would want to hear it or not. His life didn't involve talking much to women, and his lack of experience in this area was showing in this moment.

He did not know whether to confess to her that he had been craving that kiss for days, possibly even longer if he was truly honest with himself. From the moment he had caught sight of her on the castle battlements, she had intrigued him more than any woman he had ever laid eyes on. But even with all his wild imaginings, he had not dreamt up anything as spectacular as it had been. He doubted that, even if he lived for a hundred winters, he would ever experience anything so lovely again.

He could tell her all that, but then he would have to say that, despite all those things, he could not kiss her again. He wasn't as inexperienced not to know that kissing was often a prelude to more. More than he could think about now or he really would lose all concentration. If they lay together, they would be as good as married and that would disrupt both their plans. It was more sensible, if not as pleasurable, to stop now before they got carried away and entered a lifetime of regret.

Maybe the kiss wasn't something Jehanne would even want to discuss. He had very little experience of maidens, aside from his wife on the day that he married her. Occasionally forced to listen to courtly love poetry being performed on feast days at his modest castle, he had the vague idea that Jehanne might expect some romantic gesture from him now. Not only was he entirely incapable of giving one, he did not want her to form any expectation about his intentions. He would never marry again, never willingly take on caring for yet another person.

Moreover, he liked Jehanne, and the idea of hurting her was intolerable. He loathed being in this state of mind, when his thoughts went round and round in circles with no discernible outcome. Give him a problem, like a flooded wheat field and he could create a plan before anyone else was moving, but this…this was impossible.

When he thought his head might explode from overthinking, Jehanne finally broke the silence.

'I have never kissed anyone before,' she said casually, as if commenting on the colour of the sky.

Surprise caused him to only grunt in reply. He cursed himself for being an unfeeling brute with no manners, but he still couldn't find any words to express all he was thinking.

'Is it always like that?'

His throat was clogged. He cleared it, hoping, without really believing, that he would be able to sound as light-hearted as her when he spoke. 'Is what always like what?'

'I thought kissing someone would be disgusting. All that touching of tongues…' He felt her shudder.

Laughter rumbled out of him, of all the things he had thought about discussing with her, the actual process of what they had done had not occurred to him.

'That probably sounds very naive to you,' she said, mistaking the reason for his laughter. 'It's only that I haven't seen many people doing it, only on feast days when people lose their inhibitions to wine and ale. It's always looked a bit sloppy and never like something to be enjoyed.'

'You never kissed either of your fiancés?' The hot

surge of pride rising from his belly was not something he should be experiencing but he could not push it down, no matter how many times the gruff voice in his mind yelled at him to do so. The implication that she had enjoyed kissing him wasn't lost on him either.

'Goodness, no. William and I, well…' Now he knew the man's name; Lucan wished he hadn't asked. He didn't want to think about the man she was running to as a real person, preferring to think of him in the abstract instead. 'It never crossed my mind to kiss him.'

That shouldn't make Lucan feel better, but it did. Surely if she loved this man as much as Lucan suspected, she would want to kiss him, even if the idea in general didn't appeal to her. 'And the thought of kissing Urian.' Even though they weren't touching, he could still sense the revolt that coursed through her in the way that the muscles in her legs tightened. He couldn't agree more with that sentiment; he wouldn't want to get close to the vile pig let alone touch lips with him.

'So is it?' she finished.

By now, he had completely lost the thread of their conversation and, 'Huh,' was all he could manage.

Her sigh suggested he was witless. 'Does kissing someone normally feel all…bubbly and liquidy at the same time?'

Perhaps she was as bad at words as he was; he was fairly sure one of those wasn't a word at all. But he did know what she meant. The intense brush of lips had turned his bones to water, something he had never felt before. He should perhaps say that, but it might give away more than he wanted to at this stage. 'Do you think I go round kissing women all the time?'

No wonder she thought him brainless, he was. That was no answer at all.

'You have more experience than *me*.'

'Not much.' Did he really want to admit how little? They had said they would be truthful to one another, and it would not truly hurt to admit to what could be seen as a weakness. When this journey was over, they would never see one another again, the knowledge of that tipped him into confessing. 'I must have kissed Isabel, but I am ashamed to say I do not remember it. We were not wed long and she passed many years ago.'

'And since?'

He tugged on his tunic, somehow it was tighter and more uncomfortable than it had been earlier. 'Who would I kiss otherwise?'

'But surely…'

Damn it all to hell, she was not going to let this go, and there was nowhere he could storm off and hide. A trick he had employed in the past. 'I might not be a fancy lord, but I am a baron who runs his own castle. If I go around kissing the unmarried ladies, they would expect a wedding, and I'm not marrying again. I'm also not going to make a mockery of wedding vows and take another man's wife, so… I don't have whatever experience you imagine.'

He realised that his response was gruff, far harsher than he'd intended. Gentler, he said, 'But… In honesty, no, I don't think it does feel like that every time. I will remember what happened between us for a very long time.'

A long silence followed his confession. Perhaps he should not have made it. Jehanne might fix more meaning to what they had done than he'd meant to give. He was about to clarify that he had no intention of doing it again, when she said, 'Me too.'

After that, they fell into a deep silence. Her acknowledgement that the experience had been memorable for her warming his heart, even when he knew it shouldn't.

Chapter Twelve

Around mid-afternoon, it became obvious that Lucan could not keeping going. His whole body kept slumping forward before he would jerk upwards again. They hadn't spoken in some time, not since they had raided the packs attached to their grumpy horse's sides and found a dried loaf of bread. After they'd devoured it, alternately sucking on a water skin to wash it down, they kept going.

When she'd suggested he rest, Lucan had all but growled at her, unwilling as he was to let Lord David get too much of a lead on them.

'You need to sleep,' she murmured after Lucan fell forward for the sixth time.

Although his words were barely a mumble, she got the impression that he was trying to argue with her, which was absurd.

'Even if we catch up with Lord David, you will not be in a position to fight him for Rolf,' she said, when he didn't pull the horse to a stop. 'If indeed, that's what you intend to do.'

'Rain…tracks…foxes will make…' he trailed off with a snort that sounded suspiciously like a snore.

'That made no sense at all.'

He pulled himself upright, although his proud shoulders remained slumped. 'The rain might wash away their tracks,' he managed to get out. 'If we stop…sleep…the foxes…' he fell silent again, leaning forward and slightly to the side, she saw that his eyes had closed and he had fallen asleep mid-sentence.

If only the stubborn man would listen to her. Sliding her arms around his waist, she lightly gripped the reins and brought the horse to a standstill. When his eyes still did not open, she knew that she was right.

'Lucan.' She grabbed his shoulder and shook it. 'We need to stop here.' There was a small hollow only a few steps away. It didn't offer much in the way of protection from the elements and if someone was following them, there was nowhere for them to hide. But she had not seen anything better.

If Lucan wanted to keep going, she would not stop him. Physically, she was no match for him but it was not just that. She loathed decisions being made for her; it was yet another thing that stripped you of your personality. She was not about to do the same to anyone else, even if she believed they were making the wrong choice.

His only response was a deep rumble that might have been intended as words but certainly didn't come across that way. Given his size, he was probably unused to taking orders. She had seen the way he bristled whenever David had tried to tell him what to do, although the Lord's decrees were often ill thought out and easily ignored by all of them.

Swinging her legs over, she dropped down off the horse and led it to a partially collapsed tree. Its eyes rolled, as if it found her the most contemptuous being on Earth but it made no other protest.

'Come on,' she said briskly to Lucan. 'Get down.'

His eyes partially opened, before closing again. As he'd hated being called sweet earlier, he would probably loathe how adorable she found him right now. With his wide eyes closed, his long eyelashes almost seeming to rest against his cheeks and his large body slumped forward almost in half, she found him almost absurdly delightful.

Threading an arm around his waist, she tugged at him. Surprisingly he followed her silent directions without protest. Even barely standing upright, he still towered over her, his arm heavy around her shoulder. She wanted to lean her head against his chest and discover whether it was as comfortable and as safe as it looked, but he was too tired. Besides, it would be unfair to take refuge against him when he was the one who needed looking after.

'Over here,' she murmured, half-leading, half-dragging him over to the small hollow. He was barely able to stagger those few steps before he collapsed to the ground and went completely still.

The position he landed in did not look comfortable. In one of the packs, she had discovered a spare cloak while searching for food earlier. Fetching it, she rolled it into a ball. His long hair fell over her fingers as she carefully lifted his head from the ground. She couldn't hold it with one hand for long, so she stuffed the folded fabric underneath him as quickly as she could.

Moving backwards, she surveyed her handiwork. His neck was not bent in a strange angle anymore; hopefully he would not wake aching all over. Unclasping his cloak from around her, where he had insisted it remain even though it was his and the weather was turning colder, she lay it over him. It didn't cover him completely, but she made her way around him, tucking it in tightly, adjusting it so that it covered as much of his length as possible.

When that was done, she rocked back onto her heels and gazed down at him, hoping that whatever happened over the days and weeks, she would remember him like this. At rest, without his fierce frown, the skin of his forehead was much smoother. It made him look younger and, with his hands pinned to his side by his cloak, he looked vulnerable. The effect was endearing and she had to remind herself again not to get attached to a man who had shown no inclination to keep her with him.

Although they had been sleeping close by for several days, she had been so exhausted herself that she had tumbled into a deep sleep within moments of stopping for the day. Now she had the luxury of looking at him when he did not realise she was doing so. Perhaps it was a little untoward to stare at him, but there was no one around; the only person who would ever know was herself.

His red hair fell onto his cheek; she reached up and brushed it off, not letting her fingers linger on the softness of his beard. His lips were full, and now she knew how soft they were, how demanding they could be too.

She lightly touched her own mouth, fancying the skin still tingled from where he had pressed his lips against hers; the slide of his tongue against hers had burned itself onto her brain. If he'd let her, then she would like to do it again, to see if it truly had been as good as she'd thought or whether the unexpectedness of it had momentarily blinded her to the reality of it.

She hadn't lied to him when she had told him that she had believed kissing to be a repugnant pastime. The idea of someone's tongue against hers had always made her gag but when he had lightly brushed her fingers in the softest of kisses, she had wanted his mouth against hers more than she had ever wanted anything at all. And when he had kissed her, the whole world had fallen away. All that had mattered was him, the way he moved and the way he had made her feel.

If the horse hadn't bolted, she would have carried on forever. It was as well that it had. Worrying that being with Urian would strip her of her personal beliefs was pointless if she was just going to tumble into that with another man. Lucan could have far more power over her than her loathsome fiancé. Her dislike of Urian might have protected her soul from him, but allowing herself to get caught up in Lucan could be far more dangerous. He could make her care deeply for him, and when they parted her soul would be shattered.

Wind stirred, cold air brushing against her skin. She pulled her sleeves down over her fingers, wishing she could climb under the cloak and curl up next to Lucan, but she would not. Her mind was already too focussed on him. Over and again, she had relived that kiss, the taste, the feel of his lips moving over hers, the way he had woken something inside her, something she had not known was asleep.

She tried to imagine William plundering her mouth like that and found she couldn't. Her sweet, childhood friend was lovely, a kind and gentle boy she'd been grateful to be marrying. There had been no sign of him having a wild temper, no sense that Jehanne would live like her mother, constantly placating her husband over slights and injustices until she became a prop to her husband's temper and nothing more. As she and William had grown up and their union had neared, they had talked about the children they would have in the future. The concept had been abstract, she'd been able to see the children clearly but not the process of how they would come into existence. She still couldn't. Or at least not with William.

Gazing down at Lucan, she imagined his lips travelling down the length of her neck, as he nudged the edge of her dress to one side with his callused thumbs. She could almost feel his lips on her breasts, as he consumed them in the same way he had her mouth. She squirmed, the images floating through her mind, causing that delicious want to build again. Although, maybe he would not be soft and gentle, maybe he would devour her, his hands and mouth possessing her while his strong fingers pressed into the soft flesh of her thighs. She turned away from him, her breathing heavy.

As she stared into the heavy undergrowth, her heart pounding as if she had truly experienced the images which had played through her mind, she realised that his kiss had already changed her. Not once in all her years had she had thoughts even remotely close to this. Now it was all she could think about. While she should be planning for her future, working through the various scenarios that could befall her, these other, more physical thoughts were threatening to take over her mind completely. *This* was why it could not happen again. She had to maintain her grip on the reality of her life.

A sharp gust of wind shook the branches in front of her, the wood creaking under the strain before springing back into position. She wasn't worried for their safety, the trees had seen worse in their long history, but at least it snapped her out of her reverie. Lucan had stressed he was not going to marry again, and it was as well that he had done so. It reminded her not to put too much into their friendship, not to get too attached to him and the connection she was beginning to feel.

There was no expectation on her part that he would want to keep her with him after this was all over. That wasn't the way of things for her. It didn't matter how much people liked her, they didn't seem to mind walking away from her or letting her go when other priorities pressed.

When she and Lucan were separated, she wanted to remember him fondly and not with an edge of heartache. Although…if he wanted to kiss again, she could be persuaded. This might be the only time she ever got to experience physical pleasure with a man.

Pushing herself to her feet, she turned away from Lucan's sleeping form, making her way over to the horse.

'I think I shall name you Grincheux,' she said, running her hands along the stallion's long neck. 'It's a name that suits your temperament. I don't remember you from my father's castle, or at least no one has mentioned a stallion furious with the world. Is it our weight making you fractious or are you always bad-tempered?' The horse shook his head and she took that to mean he didn't care for the brush of her hand against his hair, but she did not know how else to soothe him.

She didn't dare take the packs from him to make his rest more pleasant. They might need to leave in a hurry and the things inside were too useful to leave behind. The only thing she could do was loosen the knot she'd made in the reins so that he could reach some of the grass nearby. Once he was busy munching, she settled back near Lucan, determined to stay awake to keep a look out for anyone who might want to do them harm.

Dusk was falling when Lucan finally stirred. Jehanne turned away from him, realising she'd gone back to watching him no matter how many times she had caught herself doing so and forcing herself to turn away.

His long arms stretched above his head, his fingers brushing against the ground. He groaned and rolled over onto his side, blinking at her. 'It wasn't a dream then?'

'I'm afraid not.'

'Damn,' he muttered, pushing himself upright. 'What's this?' He lifted the cloak she had placed under his head.

'You were sleeping at an odd angle. I thought your neck would be in agony if you had nothing to support it.' He stared down at it, as if uncomprehending her words or even that he held something in his hands. 'Did I do something wrong?'

His head snapped up, his gaze locking with hers. 'Of course not. I'm not used to people taking care of me, that's all.' His eyes flicked over where her arms were wrapped around herself. 'And you gave me my cloak too. Foolish girl, are you not freezing?'

She was, but she was not going to admit to it, even as her posture gave her away. 'I am exactly the temperature I want to be.'

Before she could move, he reached over and took her fingers in his large hand. 'Your skin is like ice.'

'As I said, that is exactly how I want it.'

Huffing a laugh, he stood and wrapped the spare cloak tightly around her, muttering to himself the whole time about wool-for-brains women. He clasped her hands in his and began to rub them, warming the skin. It was hard to stay annoyed at his insults when his actions were warming her for the first time since he'd last had his arms around her.

When he seemed satisfied by her temperature, he stepped away. 'Are you ready to ride again?'

'Of course.'

'Did you manage to get any sleep?'

'I thought it better that I keep a lookout.' He peered down at her, one eyebrow raised questioningly. 'This didn't seem like the best hiding place and I didn't want us to get caught unawares. Besides, your back made a good mattress earlier, I had plenty of rest.' His lips twitched. It wasn't his full, glorious smile, but it was enough to warm her from the inside. 'While you were sleeping, I named the stallion Grincheux. It seemed appropriate.'

This time, she caught the flash of teeth when he smiled. 'Aye, he is very grumpy. The name suits him perfectly.'

For most of last night and a large portion of the day, they had ridden together and she had not thought much of it. Perhaps because of her overwhelming exhaustion or because she had still been reeling from Lord David's contemptuous backhand or the fact that she and Lucan were pressed close together had not been an issue. This evening was completely different.

Once they started riding again, every movement brought the places where they touched into sharp focus. If she shifted in the saddle, her thighs brushed against his. If she tried to lean back, then the front of her body would somehow press into his back. It was almost impossible to sit still, or as still as she could manage while naturally swaying with the horse's movements. But she did try, because she did not want to feel the way she did whenever she brushed against him. Before yesterday, she barely noticed, but now sparks raced along her skin, pulling her back to the long moments of their kiss.

'Is something bothering you?' he asked when she adjusted her position for the one hundredth time.

'I am fine.'

'Are you sure ants have not crawled inside your clothing? It appears as if you have lost the ability to sit in one position.'

'I am only thinking…' Biting her lips, she paused. She did not want to confess as to what was truly on her mind. That marauding armies, furious fathers and her spiteful betrothed could all go hang themselves for all she cared, if only he would kiss her again. It was not a sentiment she was proud of, so she would keep it to herself. 'I was thinking,' she repeated, 'that it is strange that Lord David took Rolf and left us. Why not flee by himself, or try and persuade you to leave Rolf and me behind. We are the least useful and the most likely to slow you down in this escape attempt.'

Lucan stilled, his shoulders stiffening. Until this point, she had not truly been suspicious, but his reaction told her there was more to the tale. 'Do you know why he did?' she asked.

'I…' Lucan tried to shrug but the gesture did not look natural. 'Who knows what the man was thinking. He's not known for making clear decisions.'

While she could believe that last bit, she was not convinced by the first. Lucan knew exactly why Rolf had been taken, and that was why he had been pushing himself to get to the boy when all good sense should have made him stop. 'You can trust me,' she said. 'I will not betray you.'

He said nothing; his silence thunderous.

Although Lucan could not see her, she stared at his back, willing him to take her into his confidence, wanting, for once, to be worthy enough of someone else's secrets. But his silence crept on, his lack of trust settling like a heavy stone in the pit of her stomach. She and Lucan were enemies of a kind. Their countries were at war with one another and that meant they were on opposing sides, even if they had never argued personally. After all this time travelling together, she'd thought that the two of them had moved past their countries' antagonism. That because they held the common goal of getting out of France and to the places they thought of as home, they were more than two people who had been thrown together by circumstances.

She had begun to think of Lucan as her friend, a friend she admittedly wanted to do more with than was strictly platonic, but still… Discovering he did not feel the same way was crushing, the weight in her stomach seemed to be pulling her down towards the ground, even as she stayed where she was.

All her life, she had believed herself part of something, only to find that she was passed around when she was no longer necessary. At least, with Lucan, she had found out early on that he did not value her as highly as she did him. It gave her time to pause and to assess. Lucan was like all men in her life; not letting her in. There was no real harm because, although she found him very attractive, he did not have her heart. His rejection was annoying but was not personal, and the ache in her chest was as pointless as it was ridiculous.

An owl swooped overhead, its movement eerily silent. As she had sulked, dusk had fallen once again.

'There is smoke up ahead,' said Lucan. The first words he had uttered in a long while.

'Do you think it is them?' There was no need to elaborate, they had been chasing David and Rolf for nearly a day.

'With at least two groups of people chasing him, David is unlikely to risk drawing attention to himself. I think it is more likely to be a settlement, probably a small one.'

As they neared the edge of a line of trees, Jehanne saw what he meant. Nestled at the base of a large hill was a collection of several long houses, clumped closely together. Evidence of fires came from a few of the buildings, but not all. Before they emerged out into the open, Lucan brought Grincheux to a stop.

'Approaching could be risky,' he said, as they both stared at it.

'It could but we might be able to get some food and discover where we are.'

'If your father's men are there, we will not get away easily.'

'We can see no sign of anyone.'

'It does not mean that they are not within one of those buildings.'

'If they are, there could not be many, else we would see more evidence of it.'

He grunted. 'I'm not sure we should risk it, it could turn violent.'

'By that I take it you mean there could be a fight.'

'I do.'

'If there are not many, do you think you could win?' She believed he almost certainly would, but she would not want him to put himself in unnecessary danger, even if she was irritated by him.

'I might, but if there's a possibility that you will get hurt in the process then it is not something I would be willing to risk.'

With those words, her annoyance with him faded away. He was still staring towards the settlement, unaware of how those simple words had struck her deep inside. In a world where hardly anyone ever considered her well-being, his concern meant more to her than he would ever realise.

'Should we watch and wait for a while?' she suggested.

'Aye, good idea.'

They climbed down from the stallion, Jehanne stretching out her aching muscles. Lucan watched her for a few moments, before turning and rummaging around in one of the saddlebags.

'Do you think anyone will welcome us in at this time of night?' she asked as he handed her an oatcake, one of the last remaining items of food. Better by far than the foraged fruit they had been existing on.

'I doubt it. You'll have to do the talking.' His own oatcake was gone in two bites. 'But I found a few coins that your father's men were carrying. We can hand over one or two, even if that means we only get to sleep with the animals.'

'Smelly but warm, I'll take it.' Rather than brush the crumbs to the floor, she licked her fingers, intent on getting even the smallest amount of food into her.

Glancing up at him, she found his gaze locked on her hand. Noticing her looking, he turned away, colour staining his cheekbones. She had no idea what to make of that, so said nothing.

Darkness fell completely, and soon all they could make out of the settlement were the whisps of smoke coming from several of the houses.

'Would you consider staying here while I see what's down there?' he asked after a while.

'What? Why?'

The leather of his tunic creaked as he turned to face her. His fair skin was washed pale by the light of the moon but it was easy to make out the tightness of his jaw and the anxious narrowing of his eyes. 'I...' He stroked his chin. 'I might not be able to concentrate if I am worrying about your safety all the time. I could lose my edge and put us both in danger.'

Her heart thudded heavily, a painful reminder that this man was making it very hard to keep her distance. She had been fooling herself earlier when she had told herself that she did not have deeper feelings for him than a surface attraction. By words and deeds, he was showing her more care than anyone ever had. If he continued putting her safety and needs before any other consideration, walking away from him when it was time would be virtually impossible. She rubbed at her chest, trying to ease the ache inside. What he asked was impossible anyway. She would not let him go alone; waiting for his return would be torture.

'If my father's men are not there and you have to speak with anyone, it will be instantly obvious you are not from around here and that puts us in unnecessary danger.'

She took the deep rumbling sound he made as agreement, even if his deep frown made a reappearance.

'Just think, in a few moments,' she said, not giving him time to come up with a counterargument, 'we could be seated near a fire with some food in our bellies. It is worth the risk, is it not?' When that frown remained as deep as ever, she added. 'I have not been warm since we left the castle. I think my bones are becoming encased in ice.'

He rolled his eyes, crossing his thick arms over his chest. 'Well, we can't have that.' Another long pause where his gaze flicked between her and the settlement. 'We have Grincheux on our side. If it comes to it, he's angry enough to take on four men. I can deal with anyone else.'

'I am not completely useless,' she protested. 'David took me by surprise when he slapped me, but if I'm prepared, I'm sure I could…'

He stepped towards her, his body all rigid lines, harsh brackets around his mouth. 'Promise me that if there is danger, you will run away from it, not towards it.' He sounded almost breathless.

His urgency made her heart race. But even as her feelings for him tightened, curling and twisting around her body, much the same as ivy around a tree—and in a way that might be impossible to untangle later—she would do no such thing. His request was too big and went against her nature and the way she fiercely cared about this man. There was no way for her to express that, no way to say all that was in her mind without revealing too much. This blunt, practical man would not want to hear it. 'But what if you are hurt?'

'Leave me,' he snapped.

'I will not. You cannot ask or expect me to.'

He towered over her, his expression an unreadable mask. 'There will be nothing you can do for me, but you could save yourself. If I am wounded, take Grincheux and flee. You could return to your father's stronghold or carry on to England, but you cannot get harmed.'

Pushing herself up to her full height, she still didn't reach his wide shoulders, but she would be damned if she let him dictate her actions. She had risked too much to be told what to do by another man. 'We shall have to hope that no one tries or succeeds in hurting you, because I will not promise to abandon you. If fact, I shall do the opposite.'

He frowned, the lines on his forehead deep furrows. 'What do you mean by that?'

'I swear before God that should anything happen to you, I will stay by your side until my dying breath.'

His fingers curled around her elbow, tightening as she spoke. 'Jehanne, take that back. I will not have you throw away your life because of some foolish idea of chivalry. You are not a knight, but a young woman with all your future ahead of you.'

'It is too late. I may not have taken the sacred oaths of a squire on becoming a knight, but I know that once one is given it cannot be broken. To do so would mean terrible things for my soul.'

Long moments passed, his grip remained on her arm as he stared down at her. She had no idea what thoughts were passing behind his pale eyes. She wasn't sure who moved first, him or her, but there was nothing gentle about their kiss this time. It was bruising, almost a battle for dominance.

His tongue pressed against hers as if trying to prove a point. She pushed back, thrilled at the force rather than daunted. Whatever he could dish out, she could return a hundredfold. One large hand tugged on her braid, pleasure almost to the point of pain, skittered across her scalp. She scraped her nails over his scalp and into the soft flesh at the back of his neck. He grunted, pulling her closer, tighter against him. She went willingly, until she was flush against him. If this was a fight, both of them were winning.

He lifted his head, breathing heavily. 'You are infuriating.'

'Not as provoking as you.' Her breathing was ragged; she glowered up at him, not willing or able to concede. No matter what he did or said, she would not back down on this. 'I guess we will have to hope that no one causes us any harm, and then my word need not be put to the test.'

Although he was glaring at her, his arms remained banded around her, his grip on her hair as tight as ever, seemingly as unwilling as her to let go and step away. 'Aye,' he said, 'I guess we will.'

Chapter Thirteen

They approached the settlement slowly, Jehanne riding the horse with him leading. He'd told her that his size would be less obvious this way and, while she could see his point because he was lower down than her, Lucan was still a giant of a man. Even with his chain-mail off and stuffed into one of the packs, nothing could detract from the width of his shoulders. Anyone else might seem smaller next to the fractious stallion, whose nostrils were flared in irritation for a reason Jehanne could not fathom, but not Lucan. As Lucan was no longer telling her to take her oath back, she did not point out any of these things.

As they moved forward, they did not exchange any words. Perhaps Jehanne should have been dwelling on what was ahead of them. Her father or Urian could be lying in wait or the villagers might be hostile, but none of that held her concentration. Instead, her gaze kept snagging on the top of Lucan's head as he strode slightly in front of her. A bubble of amusement rose within her, and she pressed her hands to her cheeks to stop it erupting in a laugh. He might think that walking somehow diminished him, but he was doing nothing to hide the proud line of his body. Or the strength of his strides as he powered forward. He looked like he was a proud warrior.

They hadn't discussed their second kiss, there was no need to really. It had been born in the heat of the moment, a brief interlude when their tempers had flared and there was no other outlet. It would be forever seared into her memory, his demanding mouth, her passionate response, the tug of his hand on her braid contrasting with the soft silky strands of his hair falling over her fingers.

If only she'd brought a brush with her, she could have run it through his mane. Maybe he would have let her braid it so that it didn't fall across his face. The shock of red fascinated her, but tied back she would be able to see more of his face. She wondered if he would have the patience to sit still through such ministrations or whether he would shrug her off after a few strokes. The thought occupied her more than it should, considering the danger they were in.

When they were halfway from the trees towards the settlement, he said. 'Rolf's the English King's son.'

'What?' Air whooshed out of her, leaving her winded. 'He's what?'

'You heard me.' He did not turn back to look at her. 'I'll not repeat it.'

'How… What…' She could only gape at the back of his head; the announcement the most astonishing thing she had ever heard. 'Why… What…'

'You already said that last one.' Finally, he glanced back at her. In the darkness of the early evening, it was impossible to read his expression, though she fancied his lips were tilted in a half-smile.

'Oh, you are joking with me.' She pressed her hand to her chest where her heart was racing. 'I almost believed you then.'

His smile faded and he turned away, facing the settlement once more. 'I was amused at your inability to form a sentence. I do not have the ability to tell a joke, or at least I have never cared to tell one before. What I told you is the truth. Rolf is one of King Edward's sons. To clarify, he is not a prince. The King does not seem to believe in constancy towards his wife and as such has several, if not many, children born to other women. Rolf is one of them.'

If she'd been walking, she would have stopped dead in her tracks. As it was, she involuntarily jerked on the reins and Grincheux snorted angrily. Lucan tried to run a soothing hand down his neck, but the stallion bared his teeth. The world had stopped making sense. 'But… I don't understand. If what you say is true, why was Rolf sleeping on the floor of my father's courtyard? Why was he even in France in the first place? Surely the King would want to keep him safe and out of a country he is currently bent on laying to waste.'

'The only thing David and I agreed on was concealing Rolf's identity from anyone, even the others with whom we were travelling. As far as those other men we were with were concerned, Rolf was David's page. When your father's men captured us, we thought it wise not to tell them the details either. After what Edward has done to your country and, given how understandably furious your fellow countrymen are with him and with us, I think it was the correct move.'

'I…' Rolf was King Edward's son. Admittedly not one who would inherit his father's Kingdom but one who, when older, would play a significant role in the country, maybe even become one of the powers behind the throne. If her father had realised his importance…if Urian had…

She shuddered as she imagined what they would have done to the child. 'How… Why…?' she petered out…the revelation was so huge, she could not put into words everything that she wanted to know.

'I cannot answer questions you haven't asked.' It was hard to tell from his tone whether he was amused by her confusion or frustrated.

'I have three questions.'

'You'll need to make them quick, we are not far away now and I do not want to reveal Rolf's identity to anyone other than ourselves.'

He was right. They were drawing near the settlement, the smell of wood smoke becoming stronger. 'Why was Rolf in your care?'

'He wasn't.'

'But…' Rolf had not left Lucan's side the entire time Jehanne had known them. Lucan might not think he was looking after the boy, but it was evident Rolf did.

'He was in David's care, not mine. King Edward came up with the idea of Rolf acting as his page for the time we are in France, even though he has become a squire and lives with an entirely different family for most of the time. I told you that the King likes the Lord, although I have no idea why. I find him to be a cowardly insufferable bore, as does Rolf.'

'As do I.'

Lucan tilted his head in acknowledgement of her statement. 'But not even a son can argue with a King, and one who is not a prince has even less say over where and with whom he goes. David suggested he scout ahead for signs of King Phillipe's men. Of course, it was an offer designed to get him away from the fighting, because, as you know,

Phillipe has withdrawn further inland. but David presented his suggestion in such a way that made him sound brave and noble. Unfathomably, the King never doubted him at his word, or so it seemed to me.'

'Did the King pick you to travel with them too?'

Lucan shook his head. 'I volunteered. The King was reluctant at first. I assume he thought a man my size would stand out on the battlefield, but he saw that Rolf took a shine to me and agreed in the end.'

'Why did you want to be part of the scouting party when you despise David?'

'*Despise* is a strong word. I find him irritating rather than hateful. Spending time with him was preferable to bearing witness to the senseless waste the English were perpetrating on the innocent country folk. I refused to take part in the pointless destruction and will always feel shame that I did not find a way to put a stop to it. I could take it no longer, and I knew David would lead us away from conflict; he would not want to get hurt himself. Once we were underway and out of the King's gaze, David lost interest in Rolf. The boy stuck beside me over the other men, seeming to prefer my company over theirs.' He raised his shoulder in the way he did whenever he couldn't understand something. 'I don't know why.'

Jehanne could explain it. Rolf must see what she did, that this man, despite his gruffness, was solid and dependable. He might act like he wanted to rip the next foolish person's head off, but he was infinitely careful with the people he deemed worthy. An ache began to build beneath her ribs, a yearning to be the person who was loved by him, who would always be seen by him as deserving of his care and attention.

'What were your other questions?'

'You've already answered one of those. If Rolf was more taken with you than David, it stands to reason he was with you when you were captured, and I understand why you would not tell anyone who he was. I like to hope that Rolf would have been treated with dignity by my father's people, but you have seen Urian, and so I cannot say with all certainty that would be true. My third question is...why tell me now?'

'I trust you.'

At those simple words, light filled her, like the streaks of the sun blazing through dark clouds. To be worthy of this man's trust was heady indeed. There was no time to say more, to ask him why and to let him know that his sentiment was returned, because they were drawing very near the houses and someone was moving towards them. Someone carrying a very unwelcoming pitchfork. Lucan brought Grincheux to a stop.

A cool wind ruffled the long grass that separated them from this new person. Every line of Lucan's body was tensed, ready to strike, but Jehanne did not recognise the man. He was not from her father's stronghold, which meant he was only protecting the people within the settlement; a sentiment she could understand.

'*Bonne nuit*,' she called out before Lucan could say anything and make the situation worse. 'My husband and I mean no harm and wish we were not disturbing you late at night like this. We are not here to cause trouble. We are looking for sanctuary for the night and were hoping that we would be able to find some among you.'

The man shifted his pitchfork into his other hand, not lowering it but not using it to wave them off either.

'We have been sleeping outdoors for several nights and have heard terrible rumours of what the English are doing to anyone or anything they find. If you could take that worry from us, even for one night, we would be forever grateful.' She hoped she had not laid it on too thick and that the man had a kind side.

'We haven't seen any English here and we don't want to cause any sort of disturbance that might attract their attention,' said the man, his stare not leaving Lucan.

'We will not give you any.'

'Your man looks like trouble follows him.'

Jehanne reached out and lightly placed a hand on Lucan's head. The soft strands of his hair tickled her fingers. 'He is big but he's a gentle soul. Aren't you, love?'

Lucan nodded slowly, deliberately. The pitchfork changed hands again, the man's stance still showing no sign of relenting. Although this resistance was annoying, there was a tug of relief in her stomach. If her father's men were here, this man would not be reluctant to have them come closer. If the villagers were on the lookout for Jehanne and Lucan, Lucan was distinctive enough that even a brief description of him would make him easy to spot.

'We have coin,' Jehanne said, the last thing she could think of to persuade this stranger, 'and we're not asking to stay under anyone's roof with them. We'd take a night in with the animals. We...' She glanced around as if she had heard something, before turning back to the man. 'The English,' she continued. 'You understand.'

'How much coin?'

Lucan reached into one of the packs, pulling out some of the money they had found.

'Not him, you.' The pitchfork pointed in her direction.

Lucan handed over two of the coins they had found, muttering darkly under his breath. She brushed her fingers over his knuckles, trying to reassure him that all would be well. The money didn't add up to a great deal, but it was possibly more than the man had seen in a while. In a settlement like this, they probably saw money very rarely.

She closed the gap between them. Behind her, Lucan seemed to be emitting a deep rumbling noise, almost a feral growl. When she was close enough to see that the stranger had a weathered face, she held out her hand, palm up, to show him. Long bony fingers reached out to take them, but she closed her fist and took a step back. 'Do you have somewhere for us to stay?' she asked.

His hand still hovered in the air in front of her, his lined cheeks sucked inwards. 'It will be in with the animals and you'll be gone in the morning.'

'And food.' Her stomach was painfully empty.

'We'll make sure you are fed and have something to take with you, but you'll not come back.'

'You have our word on it.' Unfurling her fingers, she let him take the coins from her palm, his blunt fingernails scraping against the skin.

'I'm Denisot. You'll not be meeting anyone else.'

'If we are fed and have a roof over our heads, we will be more grateful than you will ever know.'

Nodding once briskly, he turned and led them through the densely packed settlement. Aside from the wind rushing over the thatched roofs, the space was eerily silent. The doors to each building were shut tight, no hint that there was anyone behind them. Denisot stopped outside one and told them to wait. The door opened and closed behind him before they had time to respond.

'Do you think he'll reemerge?' whispered Jehanne.

'He'd better,' Lucan, muttered, his voice barely audible even in the endless quiet.

Jehanne was about to say more when Denisot returned carrying with him two lit candles, each contained in a metal base for holding. He handed both to Jehanne, still apparently reluctant to get close to Lucan. Not wanting to let the flame go out, she moved slowly, holding her breath every time the wind blew.

It seemed to take forever to reach the far side of the settlement, but eventually they were there and Denisot threw open the door. 'We keep a few horses in here,' he told them. 'Yours is welcome to share in their feed. Make yourself comfortable and I'll be back shortly with some food.'

The man's demeanour was friendlier, perhaps he was happier now that he had received the coins or maybe having made the decision to trust them, he was going to go with it.

Jehanne feared the inside of the barn would be filled with the stench of unwashed animals but she was pleasantly surprised. Although not fresh, the air was lightly sweet, with the smell of horse dung mixed with the hay. Two mares barely even raised their heads at the newcomers. Grincheux raised his head haughtily as if unused to such inattention, but the ladies continued to ignore him. Jehanne rubbed her fingers together as the warmth of the space began to seep across her skin.

'Up there,' murmured Lucan, nodding to a short loft

accessed by a ladder leaning precariously against it. 'We could sleep up there.'

It would barely be enough space for both of them, but at least they would not have to risk being trampled by hooves while they slept. 'Good idea,' she agreed.

He took one of the candles from her. 'You see to Grincheux, I'll set it up.'

Not really understanding what he was saying, but trusting he knew what he was about, she placed her candle near her feet and began to loosen Grincheux's load. The stallion stood still, head held high as if he were a grand lord being tended to by one of his underlings. The mares continued to act as if he was not there, probably a great indignity to the proud beast. The packs and the saddle were easy to remove and when he was finally free of his burdens, she led him to where the females were making their way through some hay. Sliding himself into the group as if he belonged, Grincheux joined them, paying no further attention to Jehanne. Deciding he would not appreciate a friendly pat on the rump, she made her way back to where she had left the packs.

It had been harder than she'd like to admit to keep her eyes from turning to Lucan while she'd tended to Grincheux. While her fingers had moved over the various straps, she'd heard several quiet grunts, the slide of something heavy being moved across the ground and the creaking of wood. As intrigued as she was to discover what was going on, she'd known that if she'd stopped what she was doing to find out, it would have made carrying on with her own task much harder.

Now she was free to take him in. He'd already discarded his cloak, dumping it in a heap near the bottom of the ladder. Beneath the thin fabric of his undershirt, she could make out the shape of his muscles as he lifted a roll of hay and flung it over one shoulder. Using the ladder, he climbed effortlessly up to the loft and set his burden to the floor. She could just make out hay already up there and she realised that this was not the first load he had moved up there. As she watched, he worked methodically, spreading the hay around the area. Lifting his light every now and then, presumably to see what he was doing.

'Do you need any help?' she asked when she realised all she was doing was enjoying watching him labour. In all her years, she had never gazed at a man at work, nor had she taken pleasure in the simple act of looking at a man moving his arms.

The candlelight provided enough illumination to catch sight of his teeth when he grinned. 'You can carry on standing there, if you like.'

Fortunately, the barn door opened at that point, meaning she could turn her face away and hide her burning skin from him.

'Here,' said Denisot, passing her two steaming bowls of stew with a hunk of warm bread. 'You have blankets in those packs?'

'We haven't.' There was only the extra cloak to keep them warm and she was already wearing that.

Denisot tutted as if they were the two most foolish people he'd had the misfortune to meet before leaving without another word.

'Do you think that means he's coming back?' she asked Lucan, still not turning to look at him.

'I think he likes you. He'll be back.' Wood creaked again, the heavy sound of his boats on the rungs of the ladder and then the clomp of them on the barn floor as he moved towards her. 'Whatever is in that stew smells like it was sent from heaven.'

Her skin still hadn't cooled from the embarrassment at being caught shamelessly staring at him, but the light was such that he would not be able to see. Their fingers brushed when she handed him one of the bowls, yet he didn't seem to notice, even as tingles rushed along her skin from the brief contact. Not that she could blame him, it had been days since there had been hot food in front of her. For him, it was definitely longer. Tearing off a hunk of bread, he used it to shovel food into his mouth, his eyes fluttering closed, almost as if he were having a deeply religious experience. He groaned, the sound reminding her of the noise he made when his mouth was on hers, as if he was a desperate, drowning man. She pressed her legs together, an ache building between them, an ache she thought could only be satisfied by him somehow. How incredible to feel something like that when clutching a steaming bowl of stew.

As if reminding her that she had not eaten either, her stomach clenched painfully. Frustrated with herself for being distracted by the sight of Lucan again, she tore off her own chunk of the crusty loaf and began to eat too. Rich meat, mixed with root vegetables combined to create the best meal she had ever tasted. Perhaps it was hunger, days of living on foraged fruit, but as she tore through it, she could well believe she had never eaten anything this good before, despite her father being one of the wealthiest Comte's in all of France.

The creaking of the door alerted them to the wrinkled man returning. This time, he had a tiny, white-haired woman behind him who stared at them with unabashed curiosity. Jehanne was too hungry to pay her much attention. Denisot stacked some blankets by the door, before exchanging hushed words with his companion, who took a step towards Jehanne. That appeared to be too much for Denisot, who snatched what his companion was holding out of her hands, speaking quickly to her, making it hard to understand all the words. She got enough to realise Denisot was telling her to stay back from Lucan because he'd be able to crush them both with only one of his thumbs. She shot a quick look towards Lucan to see if he was following the conversation, but he was too busy mopping up whatever was left at the bottom of his bowl with more bread to pay attention to any at all.

It was only as Denisot drew closer that he lifted his head. Jehanne saw the moment Lucan realised the French man was carrying two more bowls of stew. His fingers tightened their grip, but to his credit he did not surge forward and grab them.

'One bowl is never enough for anyone,' Denisot said by way of explanation, as he placed the bowls on the ground near Jehanne's feet. 'My wife is the best cook for miles around.'

'In all of France,' said Jehanne. 'I have never tasted anything as delicious.'

Denisot beamed and the tiny woman began to bob her whole body up and down, a wide smile cutting through her crinkled cheeks. 'Big,' she said, pointing at Lucan.

'He is, but he is very gentle,' Jehanne reassured her. 'There is no need to be alarmed by his size. I promise he will not hurt anyone while we enjoy your hospitality.'

To Jehanne's surprise, the woman cackled, waving tiny

hands around her face as if dismissing Jehanne's reassurance. 'Big is good for you, no? That's what we women want, no? Big all over.' She chortled again, clearly very pleased with herself. 'Although the babies they will be big too, no?' She placed her hands on Jehanne's hips. 'Ach, you'll be fine.' Still laughing to herself, she followed her husband out of the barn and into the dark night.

Lucan's skin was aflame, so red it looked painful; she had to bite the inside of her cheek to stop herself from laughing. 'What did she mean by that?' she asked, willing herself to keep her lips straight.

Although not sure, she had a reasonably good idea what the old lady had been hinting at. Men liked to discuss the appendage between their legs more often than seemed relevant to Jehanne, but size or lack thereof seemed to be a prominent part of such conversations. Jehanne would not have commented at all had it not been for the colour of his skin; teasing him was an amusing way to pass the time.

'I think…' He swallowed, his gaze darting around the space, not landing on any one thing. 'It's possible that elderly lady was referring to my…um…' Jehanne could come to his rescue but his embarrassment was undeniably adorable.

'Your…'

He caught her look. 'Ah, you are teasing me.'

Widening her eyes to present the very image of innocence, she said, 'Was it the size of your hands? They make lifting things that much easier, do they? Or—' she scrunched her brow, hoping it made her look puzzled rather than lacking in wits '—perhaps she meant the size of your nose. Did you break it?' Reaching up, she ran her fingertip along the bridge of it, even there his skin was hot to the touch.

He stepped closer, the tips of his boots knocking against hers. His breath whispered over her skin and the smile she was holding in spread across her face, stretching her skin until it ached. The candlelight flickered over his red hair, so that it looked like the flames of a newly lit fire. Her fingers burned with the urge to reach up and run her fingers through it. He wouldn't resist, the light in his eyes similar to the moment before he'd last kissed her. Her hand flexed, fighting her mind for control. If she continued in this direction, she was definitely on the road to heartache. Adding that to running for her life wasn't sensible.

'I think,' said Lucan, his voice gravelly and slow, his blue eyes almost completely black, 'she was referring to my shoulders.' He raised one eyebrow, daring her to contradict him.

Humming appreciatively, Jehanne gave herself a long moment to appreciate their width. By the time her eyes returned to his face, his expression was nearly feral. Her heart quickened as the skin of her palms tingled with the need to touch and to feel. She licked her top lip, her mind blank, no teasing response ready. 'I…'

His quick grin turned her heart over. 'Not so funny now, is it?'

Laughter killed the tension that had been building between them. She wasn't sure if she was grateful to him or annoyed at him for turning the situation into something light-hearted. She was torn between being desperate to explore whatever it was that simmered between them and the need to squash it completely, so she no longer had to think about it.

The practical, rational side of her reminded her that, whatever happened, they would be separated shortly and that if she kissed him again, she might get more attached than she already was. Another side of her, the one she feared was winning, argued that the inevitable separation meant that she should enjoy herself, allow herself to sink into the desire and let it take her over. If she wasn't going to see him again, then there were no consequences. She need not be embarrassed or hurt when he lost interest. Instead this could be a brief, passionate moment out of time and they could both move on when they naturally parted.

As he watched her face, his smile slowly faded. 'What *are* you thinking?'

'Oh, I...' She glanced away from him; it was easier to think when she couldn't see his firm jaw. 'I was wondering what you were doing with the hay up there?' She nodded towards the small loft.

'Hopefully, I've made the place more comfortable for us to sleep. I think we deserve it after sleeping on the ground for so long. Even more for me than for you.' He rubbed his lower back, stretching into it. 'My bones creak when I move, they didn't do that before.'

Pain shot through her chest as she remembered all those nights he had spent chained to the wall of the castle. By sneaking food out to them whenever she could, she had tried to make it better. Crossing the courtyard, her stomach churning, sweat coating her forehead, knowing she would be made to pay dearly for her small compassion. But it had not been very much at all. Standing in front of the man who had proven himself to be brave and honourable, she was ashamed of how little she had done for him while he had suffered.

Far away from her father's temper, it was hard to remember what made him so frightening. The collective terror of everyone who lived in his shadow somehow made his presence that much larger than reality. Like everyone else, she avoided him when she could and obeyed him, without protest, when he gave an order. That behaviour had seen her betrothed to a man more loathsome than the plague. All that time worrying that marriage to Urian would destroy her soul and her father had already been eroding it without her realising it. If she truly wanted to fight for what she believed in, she should not have cowered away from asking her father to show mercy to his prisoners. She'd believed herself better than that, she would *be* better than that from now on.

Guessing that Lucan did not want her pity for his back, she said, 'I suspect your grinding joints has more to do with your age.'

She was rewarded by another flash of his teeth and her heart thrilled to see it. 'I doubt I am much older than you.'

That was most likely true, but she would not concede it. 'You just have an old face then.'

His eyes crinkled in the corners, but he shook his head, pretending to be disappointed in her reply. Reaching down, he picked up the second bowl of stew and proceeded to devour it in much the same way as the first. Swallowing a large chunk of bread, he said, 'This is the best food I have ever tasted. Is it reasonable for me to abduct that tiny lady and take her with me to England?'

It was a jest. Jehanne recognised that. The light-hearted words shouldn't hit her like a fist to the stomach. Lucan didn't even mean it. In her rational mind, she knew all this, but her body still ached as if she had received a blow. It was foolish to think about it, that he had never made a quip like that about keeping her. It must be tiredness making her maudlin because she wasn't normally this introspective.

Taking her time to pick up her bowl from the floor, she hid her face in case her reaction to his comment was evident from her expression. When she had herself under control, she straightened, the scent of the stew making her stomach rumble even though she had just finished a bowl of it.

'It's not unreasonable to take her with us at all. I'm sure we could fit her on the back of Grincheux alongside us. I'd even walk if she provided us with food as good as this every day.' She paused for a beat and then added. 'I don't think you need to seize her, she seemed quite taken with you.'

It was delicious to see his cheeks turn red once again; she giggled to herself, pleased to have the upper hand once more.

The loft was smaller than it had looked from below, or perhaps it was that Lucan took up much of the space, his long legs seeming to be everywhere at once. Neither of them could stand upright and when she tried to move, she accidentally kicked him in the shin. In trying to make amends, she twisted quickly away, only to knock her head into his chin.

'Are you still trying to kill me?' he asked, rubbing the spot where she had hit him.

'Slowly but surely,' she agreed. 'I debated whether to

use a direct hit but decided it would be obvious and you would be able to stop me, but occasionally hitting you with my head from various angles and you won't notice. Any day now, I will achieve my end and you will be no more.'

His laughter was a shocked bark, a noise she had not expected him to make. Her stomach fluttered, joy bubbling through her at achieving what had seemed impossible only days ago.

'For what purpose?' he asked.

If she mentioned they were natural enemies, the smile would be wiped from his face and their evening would be spoiled. 'I'm hungry and there's a lot of you.'

He raised an eyebrow. 'You plan to cook me?'

'I do.'

'Huh.' He settled along the far wall of the loft, putting his arm behind his head to keep it propped up. 'I don't think I'd taste very pleasant.'

'Taste doesn't matter to me as much as being full does.' Jehanne had spent an inordinate amount of time trying not to give in to the urge to lick his skin and wasn't sure she agreed with him.

Wrapping the cloak, that had become hers after they'd found it, around herself, she settled down next to him. There was nothing wrong with her cover. For all his draconian ways, her father did not spare his wealth and his soldiers' clothes were of the finest quality, but it didn't smell of Lucan and therefore was not as lovely as lying beneath his. It would not be fair to ask him to swap, hers would not fit over his body, but, more importantly, there was no way of explaining why she would want to without revealing too much.

Comfortable, warm and with a full belly for the first time in days, Jehanne waited for sleep to claim her. Maybe it was because she was too comfortable, or perhaps her body wanted to revel in having satisfying food within it, but her eyes refused to stay closed for more than a few short breaths. It was most likely due to the man lying next to her. His eyes were shut but she could tell he was not asleep.

'Should I blow out the candles?' she asked, because if she couldn't make out the shape of his lips, then she might stop thinking about pressing her mouth to them. 'We don't want to knock them over in our sleep and accidentally burn the barn down with us in it.'

His eyes flickered open, his gaze immediately meeting hers. 'Not to mention how furious that would make Grincheux. If we survived the blaze, he might try to throw us to our deaths again. Can you reach them?'

They'd left the candles towards the top of the ladder, not too far away from her. She rolled over onto her other side and wriggled forward. Blowing them out plunged the room into total darkness. Nothing was visible, not even her fingers so close to her face. Fear licked through her faster than any flame. Not frightened of the night or of heights, it had never occurred to her that the two combined would feel like a living hell. She hadn't realised she'd made a sound until Lucan said, 'Is there a problem?'

She cleared her throat, her lips parched. 'It's the dark… I… If I move, I'll plummet to my death.' She gripped her hands into fists, her palms slick beneath her fingers. On one level, she knew she should shimmy back in the direction her feet were facing. That was the way she had come. but fear held her insides, refusing to let her listen to the rational words. 'It is fine, I can lie like this all night.'

Except she couldn't. There was an edge near where she lay. Her mind had latched on to it and would not let it go. She would spend the entire night with her eyes wide open, her knees trembling and her heart racing.

A large hand closed around her ankle. 'I'm going to pull you towards me, let me know if it hurts.'

Her mouth was dry, as if she'd eaten a plate of dried lamb without taking a drink to ease the saltiness. 'I don't think you should.'

'Why?'

'What if you accidentally push instead of pull?'

There was a beat of silence. 'It's not something I've confused in the past.'

'There's always a first time.' Sweat pooled at the base of her spine, tears threatened. Very far below her, on the ground of the hard floor, hooves scuffed and horses huffed softly.

Fingers flexed against her leg and, without warning, disappeared. Terror at being left alone on the precipice made her squeak involuntarily, her heart racing so fast she feared it would burst out of her chest.

There was the rustle of hay moving and two hands clamped around her waist, one on either side. 'I am not going to let you fall, Jehanne. Come here.'

Without giving her more time to think, Lucan pulled her towards him, not stopping until her whole body was pressed up against him. One arm looped now under her head, the other still around her middle. 'There,' he said, his deep voice rumbling in her ear, 'you are safe now.'

Shamelessly burying her head in his neck, she allowed

herself the comfort of another person fully taking care of her. He asked no questions, did not tease or try to pull away; he only held her still, his strong arms a refuge.

Her fear gradually faded, slowly ebbing away until she could barely remember why she had been utterly terrified in the first instance. 'You saved me,' she breathed into the hollow between his shoulder and his chin.

'You were never in any danger.'

'I was about to hurtle to my death.'

'You were lying on a flat surface, not moving. If you had fallen, you would have been bruised at most. I don't want you to be grateful to me.'

It dawned on her that he was genuinely annoyed at the idea of her thinking he was her saviour. She briefly wondered if she should pull away from him but dismissed the thought. His arms were still tightly banded around her and showed no sign of loosening. If he no longer wanted her pressed up against him, she was sure he would let her know.

Slowly, she untucked her arm where it was pressed up against his stomach and slipped it around his waist, allowing her palm to slide up his spine until her hand was resting between his shoulder blades. If anything, he pulled her even tighter towards him. It was not her proximity that was annoying him, but something about her words.

'Why do you not want my gratitude?' she asked.

Beneath her ear she could hear the solid thud of his heart. 'Everyone depends on me, but not you. I like it.'

Right now, she relied on him for everything; if he left her to fend for herself, she didn't think she would last until the end of the week. Part of her didn't want to point this out; if he liked the way he thought she was, did she really want to show him that she wasn't that way at all. But then, they had promised to be truthful to one another, and there was her promise to herself that she would do better, be better. Lying about who she was in essence meant that he liked a version of her that didn't exist. It was no better than him not caring for her in the first place.

'I don't feel that is true. I think I am like everyone else, I do not know what I would do without you.'

Her soft confession seemed to fill the space around them, expanding, seeming to become an almost physical thing she could touch, when he didn't respond. The only thing stopping the fear creeping back in was his arms staying wrapped tightly around her.

Eventually, he said, 'You don't see yourself properly. You are strong and resourceful. If something happens to me, you will manage perfectly fine by yourself. You have been doing so for a lot longer than perhaps you even realise.'

'That makes no sense. We have been together for days. You may have relied on me for a few things, but I am depending on you for almost everything. You may not like that, but it is the truth, and we promised each other we would keep things true between us.'

'You are forgetting how long I was chained up within your father's castle walls. I saw a lot of you interacting with your family and other members of the stronghold. You held yourself apart from the rest of them. It was you who brought Rolf and I extra food; we would have starved if it had not been for that.'

'That's not true, you were...'

'Before you argue that we were fed by your father's people, you must have known that a man of my size could not last on the meagre rations I was being given, especially after the days of labour I worked through. I could have collapsed from lack of sustenance, and I don't think a single person would have cared.'

'Rolf would have minded; I would have cared.'

That deep rumble in his chest sounded, the one that showed he was experiencing a deep emotion that he couldn't quite articulate. That sound was quickly becoming something she adored.

'This is what I mean, you put other people before yourself more than you realise. I was your enemy, hell, I am still your enemy, and yet you would not have wanted to see me starve. You can claim it was because you do not like the smell of rotting bodies, but we both know that is not the reason you did the things you did. In those days I was dependent on you, not the other way around. And tonight, it was you who got us this shelter, this food. My size was a hindrance, not a help. You are strong, resourceful and full of courage. Without me, you would still be all of these things. You are an unstoppable force.'

Without thinking, she began to draw small circles on his back, around the ridges of his spine. 'When I asked you for help, you refused. Why was that?'

Lucan curled towards her slightly, allowing easier access to his back; she smiled against his chest. It seemed her big, fierce giant liked the gentle touch.

'Because the idea was a foolish one.'

'But…now you realise it wasn't.'

The straw rustled as he shook his head. 'Now, you have to agree that the whole escapade was, and has been, monumentally foolhardy.'

Her fingers stopped in their journey. 'I do not see that. We are free.'

'We are being chased across the country by your furious father and dangerously violent fiancé. We're sleeping in a barn meant for horses, and you're wrapped in the arms of a stranger. This is surely not what you had planned.'

'I did not think it would be easy. It was an impulsive request; I had not truly thought it through and I know you were right to refuse it. But, I would rather lie here in the arms of a man I know better than anyone else who has been in my life over the last year, than lie in the marital bed of a man I despise. But that is not the only reason you refused, is it?'

Another silence began, one she was not about to disrupt. She was coming to realise that he went quiet when pondering something. Her fingers began to trace his spine again, almost as if they had a will of their own.

'I… You are a very beautiful woman, Jehanne. Any man would be blessed to have you as his wife. Even before we had truly talked, I realised I could care for you deeply, and I do not want that.'

'I understand. People have a habit of letting you down if they let you in.'

'It is not that, although I am sorry that is your experienced. I have never been let down because I have not put my full trust in anyone. I have undergone loss in my life, my parents, a brother, my wife. Each time it has hurt, and I never want to endure such pain again. It makes you weak, and I am not a weak man.'

Her fingers reached the top of his spine and he shivered as she brushed over the base of his neck. There was no response to his words. He spoke the truth and yet it was a depressing view of the world. For her, the very reason for escaping her father's castle was to allow her to feel something more than dread. The uncertainty over her future might be daunting but at least she would experience lots of different emotions. Trying to be strong all her life would be painful.

'When were you set to marry Urian?' he asked eventually.

'There was no set date. I think my father was waiting for him to prove himself. The Comte is a forceful man, and Urian would emphasise his own violent side in order to win approval. My father was not so addle-brained as to not see through it and I lived in hope that Urian would bring about his own downfall.'

'Did not my fellow countrymen escaping do that? Your father's rant at his men was done in full view of me and Rolf, and he did not spare Urian. If you'd have stayed, it is unlikely you would have had to marry the man.'

'My father would have only betrothed me to someone else; who is to say that person was not worse. But, I agree, I may have stayed and risked the uncertain future. Urian found me and wanted to…' She swallowed. 'He was going to…'

Under her fingers, Lucan's muscles tensed. 'He was going to force himself on you?'

'He was.'

'How did you get away?' Lucan's fingers flexed against her shoulder. 'You *did* get away, didn't you?'

'I did. I persuaded him to speak to Lord David instead.'

'And he did that?'

'There is no need to sound so incredulous. I can be convincing when I need to be.'

'I do not doubt your abilities, only I find it hard to believe that a man intent on bedding you, could be compelled to do anything else.'

'I am not sure he would have wasted time finding a bed.'

Lucan's growl was deep, a sinister animalistic rumble. 'If he were here now, I would kill him. I *will* kill him.'

No one had ever shown a desire to protect her, not even William, the person she'd believed to be her greatest ally. It was making it very difficult for her not to put all her faith in Lucan. They were parting soon, and getting too attached would only bring her pain. Besides, she would not want any taint on his soul on her behalf. In truth there was nothing for him to defend.

'There is no need, it did not happen. If it had…well, I had resigned myself to having to lie with him anyway, or any man who became my husband even if I did not want to. You know how I felt about kissing; when I found out exactly what being in the marriage bed entailed, well… I nearly died.'

It was hard to tell if Luan's body was shaking with leftover anger or amusement. 'What is it that you find repellent about the idea?'

'It sounds very uncomfortable and undignified.'

'Hmm.' He was definitely laughing at her.

'Do you not think so?'

'If done properly, I do not think decorum and dignity will enter your mind.'

He sounded sincere but still Jehanne did not believe him. She had discussed it with Wiliam, in an abstract way, but she now realised they had not truly understood the finer details. After her return to France, she had heard other women discuss the marital act; some of it sounded horrific…

'I heard talk amongst wives of their husband wanting to put their appendage in their woman's mouth. Their mouths!' she repeated in case he didn't understand the full horror of the situation.

His shoulders were shaking violently now, his laughter muffled where he pressed his face against her hair.

'You don't seem to think that's disgusting,' she said. 'Have you done it?'

'Put my appendage in another man's mouth? I have not.' He paused. 'Nor have I had one in mine.'

'See.' Jehanne could not understand why Lucan was laughing. She had not spent a great deal of time studying that part of a man, but she had seen them. In the summer months, men would strip down and swim in the river, no care as to the watching women. The way it swung between their legs had been mildly alarming and not something she wanted her mouth anywhere near. A thought occurred to her, and once it was there, she could not let it go. 'What about putting yours in someone's mouth. Have you done that?' His whole body jolted at her question and she cringed. 'If that's too personal, pretend I never asked.'

His sigh was half-laughter, half-resignation. 'I am sure it is not the sort of thing a man should talk to a maiden about. I will probably go to hell for indulging in this conversation. But, I promised to speak the truth to you…' Another pause. 'It is not something I have ever done.'

'You agree then, it does not sound good.'

His body was still against hers. 'I didn't say that.'

'You *like* the idea?'

This time his pause seemed to go on forever. 'I…' His voice was strained. 'In the right circumstances, with the right person, I think it would be exceptionally pleasant.'

It was her turn to fall silent. Images flickered through her mind, skin taut, the press of fingers, the wet slide of tongues and that deep groan of desire Lucan made that almost seemed pulled from his very soul.

His muscles flexed beneath her cheek. 'I would give my castle and everything in it to know what you are thinking.'

'I…' It was like being at the edge of the ledge again, only this time she wanted to fall, even if the landing shook her very foundations.

'I never fully explained all my reasonings for refusing to help you when you first asked,' he said.

'Oh.' The abrupt turn of conversation bewildered her.

'I didn't think it was a good plan, that much is true. But my refusal was also my pride speaking. You see, I thought you had planned to ask me for help since the moment you saw me, and that was why you brought me bread and food. I thought you were like everyone else, that you regarded me as someone who did not need compassion because my size makes me impervious to any insult or attack.'

'Oh no, I…'

'I also…' he cleared his throat, the sound oddly nervous, given the circumstances. 'In the moments leading up to your request, when we were walking towards the castle, I thought, only briefly, you were flirting with me.' He gave an odd little chuckle that somehow hurt her heart. 'The disappointment I felt, when you wanted my help instead, clouded my judgement. I refused instantly when I should have talked to you about it.'

'I…'

But it appeared she was not going to get a full sentence out again. 'It's not your fault, you understand. I have been compared enough times to a mountain troll to know I am not a handsome man. A hint of kindness from a beautiful woman and my head was turned.'

Suddenly, not a single other thing mattered, not the ledge, not the running for her life, not the odious fiancé and the uncertain future. None of it. She didn't care if that made her fickle or flighty or foolish.

A giddy sensation flooded through her. Her entire life had been one long steady emotion, trying to keep herself calm in front of a domineering father and the knowledge that her future could change in an instant. She hadn't allowed herself to experience extreme emotion. But right now, in this smelly barn, her feelings had risen and spun, like a rushing river, tumbling and falling, heading towards something different and unknown. 'You think I am beautiful?'

'I don't think it, I know it,' he rumbled. 'I do not know why you are so surprised, you must be told that all the time.'

She laughed, happiness bubbling to the surface. 'I have never been told any such thing. It is the greatest gift I have received.'

'I am not in the habit of saying untruths. It is fact.'

'That is what makes your words better; you do not say things you do not mean. I am beautiful to you.'

'Not to me, to everyone.'

She was not going to argue with him, even though

she knew it was not true. She was invisible to most, and that had always been fine. If no one saw her, she could stay out of harm's way. To be beautiful to this man was something she would always treasure, especially when she found his wide shoulders and flaming red hair as captivating as she did. Tracing circles on his back was not enough, she wanted to touch every inch of him, to learn the planes of his back, the curve of his bicep. She settled for running her fingers down the full length of his spine.

He hissed out a breath and arched towards her, something firm pressing against her stomach. 'Is that…'

He shifted away, so that his hardness was no longer touching her. 'It is.'

'May I…'

'You may not,' he growled.

'You don't know what I was going to ask.'

'You were going to ask questions that I do not think I want to answer.' His voice was strained again, almost as if he were in pain.

If she didn't find out about it from him, who would tell her truthfully what she wanted to know. 'I have seen men bathing and it always looked soft and floppy, but yours…'

He groaned as if he were being tortured. Then on a big sigh, 'It is not always like that.'

'Then why…'

'When I first saw you, I thought you calm and controlled, a safe harbour in a storm but now…now it is as if you are the tempest. I am trying to hold on to safety and with every word you are dragging me away from it.'

'I… I did not mean to hurt you.' She began to shift away from him, hot humiliation staining her cheeks.

'You haven't. It's not that.' He groaned again. 'I am

making a mess of this. I see other men play with words and charm women with a smile, and I have always found it faintly amusing. In my head I have mocked them, but I would give anything for a splash of their charm in this moment. What I am trying to say is that, I have never met a woman like you. I want to touch you, for you to touch me. I want to show you what it is like between a man and a woman and to answer all your questions with my body, but it would be wrong. To have you in my arms, to have your hands on my back making me feel more than I ever have even with a simple touch, that is what the torture is.'

She squeezed her legs together, pressure was building there that she did not know how to ease, or even what it might mean. 'Why would it be wrong?'

'I am not going to marry you. I will not get you with child, no matter how much I might want to in this moment.'

His words were a blunt reminder that he did not want her forever, but he did want her for now, he had said as much. That would have to be enough. Tomorrow, the future, it was all a world away.

'I do not want to marry you either,' she told him, not sure if she was telling the truth. It hadn't occurred to her until he told her that he wouldn't. But this was not what this point in time was about. This was two strangers, thrown together by circumstance; two bodies that wanted to know each other. It did not have to mean anything, and nobody need ever know save themselves. She pressed forward, tilting her hips so they rested against his.

'Jehanne.' Her name was a warning, a plea.

Her fingers glided up his arm, stealing into his hair. 'It is only for now,' she whispered. 'For us, but not forever.'

For a heartbeat, she thought he might still refuse, but he gave in on a sigh. His lips were warm against hers, barely a whisper. A soft invitation and a gentle response. Twin hums of relief as they melted together, muscles softening as the world became only two people.

Her fingers deliberately traced every inch of his back, the dips and ridges of his spine and the broad width of his shoulders. The lazy slide of his tongue against hers had her craving more. Her dress melted away, the rough calluses on his fingers grazing against her sensitive skin, sending flashes of light through her. His thumb on the underside of her breast, his fingers tracing the valley between. His shirt disappeared, the shock of his skin against hers eliciting a gasp that was swallowed by his mouth.

His kiss became hotter, harder, more demanding and she was willing to give whatever he wanted. He rolled over her, pinning her to the floor. Even through the fabric separating them she could feel the hard press of his length. It seemed to fit exactly where she needed it.

His forearms held him off her, as he pressed open-mouthed kisses to her neck, her breasts, the curve of her stomach.

'Lucan,' she gasped. 'I need you to move.'

His mouth came back to hers, his hair falling across her brow. 'Like this,' he breathed.

He rocked his hips, applying more delicious pressure.

'More.' She clutched at his shoulders, pushing up against him, chasing the exquisite friction.

Muttering curse-words, he matched her movements, the tension building, ratcheting upwards, spiralling into more than she could name.

'Lucan,' she called, as the feeling became almost so she could burst.

His only answer was to press deeper, harder, pushing her over the edge so that all she could do was cling to him, riding out waves of pleasure that rushed through her.

When she came back to herself, she was staring unseeingly at the roof, his head slumped to the side of her, his weight pressing her down in a way that was surprisingly comfortable despite how heavy he was. She ran her fingernails down his back and he shuddered.

Questions bubbled up inside her. She'd heard women giggle about what had just happened to her, but Margot had told her it was a myth, that it was men who enjoyed what went on in a marital bed and not women. A pang of sympathy for her sister stirred her heart because Jehanne could never tell Margot she was wrong and that she should demand more from her husband. Hell, if the marriage bed was like that, Jehanne should have got married a long time ago. Her fingers stole into Lucan's hair; it was damp to the touch. Scraping her nails along his scalp elicited a groan.

'You do not know what you do to me, Jehanne.' He sounded drunk.

'It was good then? For you?'

'The best.' A kiss to her shoulder. 'Better than anything.' Lips on her throat, the underside of her jaw. 'You?'

'Well…'

He moved quickly, propping himself back up with his forearms. 'You did not like it? You should have said. I would not have kept going if…' He moved as if he were going to roll off her. She grabbed the tops of his arms before he could.

'I liked it.'

'Ah.' He settled back down. Not pressing all his weight on her, but enough for her to enjoy. His kiss this time was soft and gentle. 'Do you have any questions?' he asked.

'Are you going to answer them if I do?'

'It will be easier now I am not so distracted.'

'*That* I need you to explain.'

She felt his smile against her skin. 'Before, all I could think about was your body, touching it, tasting it and making it feel the way it did just now. Now we've done it, my mind can focus on other things.'

She let that thought sit with her for a moment. She wasn't convinced she could talk to him with any more clarity, her whole world was altered after those earth-shattering moments, but if he was willing to talk… 'What is this?' she asked, sliding a hand between them and touching a warm substance on her stomach. She had an idea, but no one had ever told her exactly what happened between a man and a woman and there would probably never be a better opportunity than now. 'And did it come from here?' she lightly touched his length, which was still lying between them.

He began to explain, but words soon turned into more touches and it turned out to be easy to distract him once more after all.

Chapter Fourteen

Lucan had barely said anything to Jehanne since they had left the small settlement slightly after dawn. There were many things he could talk about: the people they were running from, the places they were running to, the Lord they were chasing. These were all serious topics, ones he should address, but the words would not form. Instead, he both wanted to discuss last night and to never mention it again.

He'd told her he would not risk having another child and he had meant that with all his heart. Richard was his son and he loved him; there wasn't space inside him to feel that way about another person. When members of his stronghold had suggested he needed a spare heir, fury had turned his resolution into stone. Last night, if Jehanne had asked, he would have given in without a hesitation.

He was not a weak-willed man. That wasn't wishful thinking on his part, he knew it to be true; he was renowned for his strength of character. Stubbornness was what defined him. But one touch from Jehanne shattered all his restraint and that terrified him. It was like standing at the edge of a dark pond on a summer's day. The coolness invited you in, practically begged you to submit to its depths but there was no knowing what was beneath the surface, pleasure or the worst pain imaginable.

At least Grincheux was better tempered this morning. Perhaps a night with two mares had eased some of his tension. One night with one woman should have done the same for Lucan, but it had only made matters worse.

Moments after kissing her, he'd been moving against her, caught up in chasing his own pleasure, heightened by her gasps of delight. Nothing had prepared him for the onslaught of sensation—her skin against his, the scrape of her nails across his lower back, the softness of her body beneath. All of it had been more than he had imagined, and he had thought about it a lot in the days since he had first seen her looking down at him from her father's battlements.

The way she had thrust to meet him, as if she wanted him as much as he wanted her, had sent him out of his mind. Her enthusiasm for his body made him headier than a barrel full of ale. He'd spent himself embarrassingly quickly, his release like a raging fire through his whole body. Nothing had ever come close to feeling like that; not when he pleasured himself with his own hand and not, he was ashamed to admit, with his late wife.

Afterwards he'd lain there with a bone-deep contentment. King Edward's marauding soldiers could have skipped right past and he would not have cared. Her sweat-slicked skin against his was the most divine thing he had experienced on Earth. Reeling from the most earth-shattering experience of his life, he'd thought himself done, that he would be able to move on with a completely clear head now it was over.

Barely moments later, he was proving a mockery of

those thoughts. All it had taken was the lightest brush of her fingers against him and he had hardened faster than ever before. Desire he'd thought gone, proved only banked, roaring back to life, as urgently as if he had not spent himself in years.

Jehanne had been intent on exploring his body, her curious mind interested in the differences between them. He had been more than willing to let her. He'd rolled onto his back as she'd traced her fingers over his length and the soft skin beneath, bringing him to the edge over and over again without realising what she was doing. From the garbled words that had poured out of him, she'd learned exactly what to do to him to send him out of his mind. Before long his mouth was plundering her lips as his hips had bucked, seeking the pleasure she seemed so willing to give.

Even as his mind had given over to pleasure, he'd not wanted to be alone in the thrill of it. He had needed her to feel it too. At the first brush of his fingers, her legs had clamped tightly together. He said words, hopefully soothing, definitely begging, and gradually she had opened up to him. He'd been gentle at first, learning her in much the same way she had done him, listening to what made her gasp and what made her moan. It was not long before she was the one who was imploring him for more. He'd felt like a King, albeit one who was not above a little pleading of his own.

When she'd splintered around him, he'd spent himself again, the second time as powerful as the first. Lying in the dark, sucking in huge lungfuls of air, he couldn't believe his behaviour. Never before had he spent himself twice only moments apart. This is what she had done to him and she didn't even realise.

Jehanne had slumped against him, her head resting on his shoulder, slurring her words like a drunk woman on feast day. Words that stoked his ego, fabulous, soul changing. Words that terrified him, because they suggested she was grateful to discover what it could be like between a man and a woman. The thought of her with her hands on another man had turned his world red. He wanted to demand that she was his and no one else's. He'd choked the words down; they had no place in that warm, dark haven.

With the long, grey day stretching out in front of them, he was very glad he had not spoken. The post-coital bliss would have made him speak lies. Lies born in a moment of absolute satisfaction had no base on which to stand in the real world.

Love was what he felt for his son. The emotion was pure and simple and the best part of him. Nothing he felt for Jehanne was chaste. He paused for a moment, considering. That was not entirely true. He hoped whatever the next week, months and years brought made Jehanne as happy as it was possible for her to be, and for her to be as content and safe as she deserved. In that sense, his feelings were innocent and true. But they were not feelings which scrambled for dominance within him. With every league they covered, the need to pull Grincheux to a stop, find a comfortable place on the ground and spend what time they had left together worshipping her body became ever more pressing. He wanted to lie between her legs, to pleasure her until she was crying out his name once more, and it was becoming harder to remember why he was not doing so.

'Do you hear that?' asked Jehanne, breaking into his swirling thoughts. 'It sounds like running water.'

All he could hear was her breathing, but he would not say that.

'I think it is coming from somewhere to the left,' she continued.

'You want to stop?' he asked. They were no longer able to follow Lord David's tracks. A while ago, the footprints had led them to leaving the forest and out onto an open plain. Once there, the evidence had faded away and he had made the hard decision to stop trying to follow it. David had to be heading back towards the English invader's last known location, so he and Jehanne would go that way too. With no other option open to them, it was the only thing they could do. For a while now, they had been following a narrow path that led alongside a woodland and it was in that direction that Jehanne's head was turned.

'We can refill our waterskins,' said Jehanne. Lucan was about to argue that they were reasonably full after their stop, but stopped when she added. 'And we could wash.'

All other thoughts slithered out of his head, to be replaced with images of Jehanne bathing in a stream, her long dark hair clinging to her back as water ran from her skin. He was turning Grincheux off the path with no memory of making it happen.

They did not have to pick their way through much of the forest before they found the river. The water rushed over stones, swirling and bubbling as it raced on its journey. It did not look inviting but that was not going to deter Lucan. Now that he had the idea in his head, he was going to bathe. Even if Jehanne didn't join him, it had been weeks since his whole body had been submerged in water and he longed for its cool embrace.

Quickly removing his clothes, he made his way to the riverbank. Turning, he realised Jehanne was still standing next to Grincheux, her wide eyes fixed on his back. After last night, he hadn't thought to hide himself from her, but his skin prickled at his brazenness.

'Are you going to join me?' he asked, for want of anything better to say.

A slow smile crept across her face, and something inside him stuttered. 'I will, but for now I want to take in your magnificence.'

Heat rushed over him, burning him from the inside. Under her appreciative gaze, his cock hardened. Her gaze fell to it, and he held himself still rather than do something foolish, like beg her for a repeat of the night before or for something more.

Walking slowly towards him, she undid the clasp of her cloak and left it where it fell. By the time she was standing in front of him, only thin undergarments covered her body and he had no thoughts left in his mind. He was in thrall to her, completely and utterly.

'May I?' she asked, reaching out a hand to where he was straining towards her.

He huffed out a laugh. 'I will never refuse that from you.'

Her hand closed over him and his eyes fluttered shut at the pure perfection of the moment. Grunting, he forced them open, not wanting to miss a moment of this. Last night had been the most exquisite thing he had ever lived through, but being able to see her as she stroked him pushed his pleasure to the point of pain. Bolts of lightning travelled down the length of his spine, his legs trembled with the effort of holding him upright and he didn't think he would be able to hold on for much longer.

His hand closed over hers. 'Wait.'

'Do you not like it?' Her gaze flickered to his. Her pupils wide, her eyes hazy but a tiny frown worried her forehead.

'I love it.' He half-laughed, it was incredible to him that she could even doubt it. 'But if we carry on, it will all be over very quickly.'

'Is that a bad thing?' A slight breeze pushed the fabric of her undergarments close to her skin, outlining the shape of her breasts.

'I want to see you in the light, I want to take in every glorious detail of you.'

Tiny bumps rushed along the skin of her forearms at his words, and he traced them with his free hand until he reached the cuff of her sleeve at her elbow. Tugging at the material, he asked, 'Would you like to take this off.'

She nodded and dropped her hold on him. His body mourned the loss, even as he reassured himself that it would be worth it. She bent over, reaching for the hem near her ankles. It seemed to take her forever to pull the material up over her calves, her knees, her thighs. His palms itched the need to take over, but his stare remained fixed to the point where the material inched ever upwards, revealing miles of pale skin. By the time, she pulled the garment from her body, he was almost whimpering with need and he wasn't even embarrassed about it. Never had he been as undone as this.

Her nipples were puckered; he leaned over and took one in his mouth, the skin cold against the warmth of his tongue. Her moan nearly sent him to his knees. Her fingers slipped into his hair, holding him in place as he poured his attention onto one and then the other. When he lifted his head to claim her mouth with his own, she stumbled into him. His hands roamed down, over her hips, her buttocks, his kiss a frantic desperate thing.

Wrenching his head upright, he managed to say, 'Let's bathe.' His chest was heaving, as if he had run for miles and his cockstand was almost painful, but any day could be his last with her, and he didn't want to spend himself only moments after taking her into his arms. When he was older, he wanted to remember this as the perfect moment out of time.

Her lips were swollen, the skin around them slightly red from where his beard has rubbed against her. A primitive need to mark her swept over him and before he could give into the strange impulse, he stepped back. Cold air rushed between them and she shivered.

'The water will be cold,' she murmured.

'We'd better get it over quickly then.' Perhaps it would give them cooler heads before they completely lost control.

Her grin was mischievous and made his heart flip oddly. 'You can go first.'

'Why don't we go in together?'

'If you squeal, I will know it is too cold for me.'

'This was your idea.'

'I only wanted to see you naked. I've achieved that so…' She shrugged.

He laughed, shocked at her honest words. No one had ever given him reason to believe his body was anything to admire. Too big, too unwieldy, too like a bear, were comments he'd heard often enough to make him believe they were true. But Jehanne seemed to genuinely enjoy the way he looked. He was not a vain man, he had no cause to be, but he wanted to bask in her admiration, like a cat lying in a pool of sunlight.

Touching a foot to the water, he ducked his head to hide the shock of the icy temperature. 'It feels warm to me.'

'Is that so?' She crossed her arms underneath her chest, drawing attention to her breasts. He tried not to let that distract him.

'Definitely.' Pricks of pain covered his skin where the water rushed over it.

'Why are you not following that foot into the water then?'

'I am waiting for you.'

Her lips were curling softly and his heart swelled. Spending a lifetime making her look like that didn't seem like a bad option after all. Before he could follow that train of thought and completely lose sight of everything, he stepped into the water. The shock of the cold seemed to push all of the air out of his lungs, and only his steely willpower gave him the ability to stride over the slippery rocks towards the middle of the river, where it raced around his middle. Ducking down, he covered his shoulders with the water; goose bumps erupted over every inch of his skin, knocking romantic thoughts out of him.

'The current is strong,' he shouted across to her on the riverbank. 'If you are not a good swimmer, I would stay near the edge.'

He should have known those words would only goad her into action. No sooner had he finished speaking, she was stepping into the water, squealing as the icy water hit her calves. 'You lied,' she yelled at him. 'It is freezing.'

He laughed, realising that he'd done that more in the last few days than he had for years, possibly his whole life. She was dangerous for his equilibrium, but he would worry about that later. Shouting curse words with every step she took, she reached him in the centre of the river.

'I didn't know a maiden knew such words,' he teased.

'I didn't know I knew them either.'

'Are you going to get in completely?'

She glowered at him and he wanted to laugh again. She was adorable in her anger. 'I will never forgive you for this.'

'You don't have to go under, if you are not able to.' He was coming to learn that the best way to get her to do something was to tease her into it.

Without warning, she dropped, completely disappearing beneath the rushing water. She emerged, gasping, water running down her body in a torrent. Even if someone tried to drag him away, he would not be able to take his eyes off her. 'You are the one who is magnificent,' he said.

Her smile lit up the world. Without thinking, he stood and wrapped his arms around her. Her skin slipped against his, cold and wet. Her hair was a curtain of black that fell against his forearms. Then they were kissing and he was lifting her, his hands on her thighs. Her legs came around his waist, her hands gripped his hair.

He had no recollection of making it back to the water's edge, no memory of placing her on the ground, but he would always remember the journey his lips took as they moved down her body, the sweep of his tongue on her pebbled nipples, the soft giggle as his beard tickled her stomach and the noise she made when his mouth found her core.

He'd never touched a woman this way, but he already knew her. From their night together, he knew where she liked to be touched, knew how much pressure to apply to make her cry out and when to lighten the brush of his tongue to make her garble demands for more. When she reached her peak, her hips bucked from the ground and her fingers tightened in his hair, to an almost painful degree. As she came down the other side, he stayed where he was, his touch gentling as she slowly relaxed back down to the ground. Lifting his head, he was greeted by the most beautiful view. His woman, her legs open to him, her breasts bare to the sky and her eyes wide with shock.

He kissed the inside of her thigh, the curve of her waist, her shoulder. Lying to her side, he gathered her in his arms, triumph roaring through him at finding her trembling. 'You are beautiful,' he murmured.

She turned to him, her mouth meeting his in a gentle kiss. 'Right now, I feel it.' She reached up and smoothed some hair off his forehead and softly kissed him again.

Shards of light seemed to be streaming though him, lighting him up from the inside. There were only a few times in his life when he'd experienced true happiness: holding his son in his arms for the first time, watching him take his first steps and hearing him laugh. Now he could add this moment to that short list.

He was marvelling in that revelation when he realised she was moving down his body, her lips tracing over his ribs, pausing at a long, thin scar that bisected his abdomen. He held his breath as he realised her intention. 'You don't have to do that,' he wheezed, as her tongue touched the very tip of him and his world nearly imploded.

'I want to.' Her breath whispered over his sensitive flesh and he had to force himself to remain still and not thrust mindlessly towards her.

'You said…disgusting…you…' He had lost the ability to form a full sentence, as her lips moved over him.

'You said it would feel good with the right person.'

'Meant me…me feel…' But there were no more words, only the slide of her tongue and the warmth of her body against his. While he had been learning what she liked, she had been doing the same for him. Every move she made heightened his pleasure until there was nothing in the world but the pure luxury of her attention.

This time his climax went on forever, an endless release in which he swore he could see stars behind his eyelids. Words spilled from him, compliments to her beauty, praise for the way she had made him feel and adulation for her. None of it made sense, it was a garbled nonsense but he hoped she understood that no one had given him a greater gift than she had. No one had ever made him feel as if his body were meant to be built exactly this way, because any differently and this moment would not have been as sublime.

When she curled into his side and he pulled their cloaks over them both, he had never known such bone deep contentment.

Chapter Fifteen

The autumnal sun finally broke through the clouds, drying Jehanne's hair as she lay curled in Lucan's arms. He was sleeping deeply, giving her a moment to study him. His large body was completely relaxed, no sign of the normal, deep frown marring his forehead. Some smaller strands of hair clung to his cheek as they dried, merging with his beard, but she didn't reach over and brush them off. To do so might wake him and she didn't want anything to end this fleeting interlude. Soon enough, he would awaken and reality would insert itself. They would carry on with their journey. Today or tomorrow or in a few days, they would meet up with the English, and before long she would be on her way to England and William's family.

Less than two weeks ago, that knowledge would have filled her with relief, but now… She had become attached to the man who slept next to her; she cared for him more than she ever had another person. Even knowing that he had no intention of marrying her hadn't stopped her from developing feelings that should never had come into existence, let alone grow into something she could not stop or control.

She'd believed the marriage bed was something to

dread and fear. Lucan had shown her that it could be a joyful place full of pleasure and laughter. She was glad to know it, glad she'd experienced such passion with a man she liked and respected, even if that meant she was destined to have her heart broken. Even knowing this had an end didn't make her regret anything they had done.

But he was a stubborn mule of a man. She'd seen that when he had refused to dim his anger in front of his captors, even if that might have meant better treatment from them. He'd made up his mind that he was not going to allow himself to feel for her and he felt, to her, that he was like a large boulder, impossible for one woman to shift. Even though she could see a future with Lucan in it, she was not sure she was strong enough to risk yet another rejection by someone she cared about.

She was still watching his sleeping face, pondering her next move when, from further downstream, birds burst from the trees, squawking madly as they flew high into the air. Lucan was standing before she'd even had time to realise the sound had woken him. They both stared at the sky as more birds emerged, adding to the shrieking. The muscles in his thighs were taut, the skin stretched tight. 'Something is happening.'

'It could be a wolf hunting a deer.'

'Perhaps.' He began pulling clothes on.

'But you don't think so.'

'I hope it is, but chaos follows David, and he has Rolf. If that cacophony is anything to do with them, I owe it to the boy to find out.' Before he had finished speaking, she was rushing down towards the stream, grabbing her clothes from where she had dropped them earlier. 'You can stay here,' he said, as she pulled her undergarments on over her head, briefly getting stuck in a sleeve before fighting her way out.

'If you try and leave without me, I shall only follow.' Rolf was someone else she shouldn't care about, but did. He might be the son of the most hated man in France, but that was no fault of his. She was an excellent example of children not being the same as their father.

Instead of an argument, she got a terse nod of his head. A tacit acknowledgement that he was not thrilled by this development but would not stop her, and she was glad for it. In a world where men always controlled her, he let her follow her own decisions, even if he didn't agree with them.

Grincheux seemed to grasp the urgency as Lucan urged him into motion. They were flying towards the commotion before she'd had time to mourn that their quiet interlude was over forever.

As they neared, the deep roar of angry men sounded through the densely packed trees. Jehanne strained to hear what was being said, but it was all jumbled together without one coherent thread to latch on to.

Lucan slowly brought Grincheux to a stop. 'We need to proceed on foot. Whoever is out there will not be listening for our arrival, but they do not sound in the mood for strangers arriving in their midst. We do not want to alert them to our approach by thundering up to them on the large stallion.'

They secured Grincheux by tying his reins to a tree stump, and together they pushed their way through the woodland, the unmistakable sound of metal against metal reaching them. As swords clanged together, Lucan hesitated; Jehanne braced herself for a plea for her to return to Grincheux, but after a moment, he only shook his head.

For a large man, Lucan moved almost silently. She tried to step where he did but somehow twigs snapped underfoot, the sound seeming to fill the forest as clearly as if she had shouted an alert that they were approaching. Lucan made no comment.

A distinct shout, the clear sound of the word, 'Bastard,' had her coming to a complete stop.

Lucan half-turned, raising one eyebrow in query.

'Urian.' She was sure of it, had heard him yell that word often, would recognise it anywhere. Cold seeped through her veins, turning her insides to ice. She'd truly begun to believe she would never see him again, but he was only a few steps away.

'Are you sure?'

There was no way to explain how the imprint of his voice was etched onto her soul. She would never mistake Urian for a different man. 'It is him.'

She would have stayed rooted to the spot forever but a scream rent the air, the sound obviously made by a child, and she was moving without thinking, Lucan powered ahead of her, his long legs eating up the ground far quicker than hers.

Lucan's curse was vehement and several heartbeats later, she discovered why. Lying on the ground, blood spreading across the forest floor was David. A few paces away, Urian held a struggling Rolf around the waist.

'I knew you were lying,' Urian screamed. 'I knew they were with you.'

'Urian, put the boy down.' Terror was pounding through Jehanne, turning her legs to water but she would not let her betrothed hurt Rolf, not if there was anything she could do to stop him. 'He is only a child.'

'He's a liar, trying to keep you hidden.' Urian's skin was mottled purple and white, his eyes blazing inhumanly. 'Well, the English will discover what we do to traitorous pigs.'

'He is not lying to you, Urian. He did not know where I was.'

Urian's lips curled, more wolf-like than man.

'We were separated a few days ago. I heard your voice and I came straight to you. Whatever has happened, none of it is the boy's fault. You can let him go.'

She couldn't look at Rolf, one glance at his pale skin and she would lose her nerve.

'Do you know what hell I have been through?' screamed Urian, not loosening his grip on the boy. 'And all because the English scum thought they could defy me. I don't care if he is a child, he will pay for all the times your father has treated me like a fool.' Spit was flying from his lips, the cords of his neck protruding in angry lines.

'It's all over now,' she said as soothingly as she could manage, stepping towards him with her hands raised. 'You have rescued me and we can return home. All will be well, you will see.'

Urian barked out a laugh devoid of any amusement. 'My reputation has been destroyed. Nothing will make it right again unless I return with you alive and these three dead.'

Jehanne had been so close to freedom, so close to getting away from his man. She'd allowed herself to hope and to believe that she would never have to see him again.

Now she knew the only way to save Rolf was to offer herself up in exchange. Once she got him to let go of the boy, he could escape with Lucan and she would never see them again. There wouldn't be time for a proper goodbye. There was no other way.

She pressed her lips together as tears pricked the backs of her eyes. She would not cry; if she was going to do it, she would do it with her head held high, knowing that her sacrifice was worth it.

She tried to take a step forward, but a large hand clamped around her upper arm.

'You hurt the boy and you will never see your fiancée again,' Lucan growled.

Pain erupted in her chest. She believed with her whole heart that Lucan would not hurt her and that he would lyingly threaten her for Rolf's sake. But his words were still brutal.

'I'll kill the boy and then run you through with my sword like the wild boar you are,' snarled Urian.

Rolf's eyes were wide, a silent plea for all this to be over. His gaze locked with hers and she attempted a small, reassuring smile. But she did not really see a way out of this situation that didn't either end with her leaving with Urian or at least one more person fatally wounded.

Urian's knuckles were white on the hilt of his sword. He'd yet to use it on the child, but the sharp metal was barely a hair's breadth from Rolf's innocent skin. There was a chance Lucan could get it from him, without a weapon of his own, he still had strength on his side. But it wasn't Urian's only deadly blade. Somewhere about his person there would be a dagger, probably two or more. One lucky swipe and Lucan could get hit. Urian would show him no mercy. Jehanne knew her own limitations; she would be no help in a physical fight.

The only thing she could do is offer herself up in exchange. Her soul screamed, but looking at Rolf's pale skin and terrified eyes, she knew she had to do it. She had talked Urian down before, but she had never seen him this wild and unhinged. Her stomach turned watery, fear washing through her. Taking a deep breath, she prepared to speak but she never had a chance.

With no warning, Lucan dropped her arm and leapt across the gap that separated him and Urian. His roar of rage sent wildlife skittering away from where they stood, the sudden exodus adding to the noise and confusion. Jehanne barely had time to blink before Rolf was running towards her, his arms outstretched. She had time to brace herself before he flung his arms around her waist and buried his head in her shoulder. She held him back, squeezing him fiercely, not sure who was lending their strength to whom.

Urian swung wildly, his sword narrowly missing Lucan's face. Terror lanced through her; she had to find a way to help. She could not bear it if he were to be injured, could not even contemplate the idea that he might die.

'Rolf,' she said, holding him at arm's length. 'Did David have any weapons on him?' She realised she was already talking about the man in the past tense when she hadn't even checked to see if he was still breathing.

'He found a dagger in one of the packs.' Rolf stepped back, dropping his hold as he blinked slowly up at her. 'He tried to use it on Urian, which is when he got stabbed in the stomach.'

'Did you see where it went?'

Rolf shook his head, turning so white he was almost ghostly. 'You cannot get involved in the fight. You must stay safe.' Lucan kicked out at Urian, making contact with his shin and causing him to stumble back a few paces. 'If we can get the weapon to Lucan, he might stand a chance.'

'I… I think it is near him, but I didn't check.'

Rolf made to go in the direction of the lost weapon but she grabbed him by the arm, stopping him in his tracks. 'Rolf, it's time for you to go. Head in that direction.' She pointed towards the way she and Lucan had come. 'You'll find an irritable stallion by the name Grincheux. Wait for us there. But, and you must promise me this: if, for any reason, you suspect that Urian has won this bout, do not hesitate to ride him away from here. We have been heading north to find the coast. Do you know how to work out which way that is?'

He nodded briskly, tears swimming in his eyes.

'Do not stop to talk to anyone. Do not get off Grincheux. Ride until you reach the sea. Once there follow the coast to the east. You will eventually get to Port Einon, a place sympathetic to the English. There you can seek refuge until you are reunited with your…the King's men. Do you understand?'

Rolf nodded again.

'Then go.'

There was an almighty crack and Jehanne turned to see Lucan scrambling to right himself. A tree was crashing to the ground, knocked over by his weight. Only several steps away, Urian was pulling his sword free from a trunk. There was no time to waste.

'Go, Rolf. Go now and don't look back.'

With one last anguished look at Lucan, the boy turned

and disappeared through the trees, becoming one less thing to worry about. Back on his feet, Lucan grabbed a log and charged towards Urian. Managing to get his sword free in time, Urian blocked the blow, but stumbled back a few steps.

Tearing her gaze away, Jehanne searched the ground, looking for the fallen dagger. Careful to avoid getting close to the fighting men, she reached David's body. The man's chest rose and fell but there was a wet sound to it and Jehanne did not think he had long left. A pang of sadness hit her at the futility of it all. They might never discover why David set off without her and Lucan, but he had paid a very harsh price for his rash actions. There was no time to sit by him and hold his hand to show him he was not alone at the end of his life.

Scouring the ground, she saw a glint of metal a little way from the fallen man's feet. Her fingers curled around the handle just as her hair was yanked upwards from behind.

Pain lanced across her scalp, and she screamed as she was pulled to her feet. 'Why were you talking to the boy?' snarled Urian, his fetid breath making her gag.

'He's just a child, Urian. I…'

He yanked on her hair again. 'That's not an answer.'

Lucan prowled nearby, but didn't come closer. If he ran now, Jehanne wouldn't blame him. He could get away with Rolf and forget that they ever met. As pain ricocheted down her neck, she had one, last desperate thought. Urian couldn't speak English, she had never known him to at any rate. Taking a huge risk, she spoke to Lucan in the language of his country. 'Lucan, you can go now. Rolf is with the horse. Urian will not hurt me, he values the status marrying me will bring me too much for that.'

'What are you saying?' screamed Urian. 'Do not talk to him. He is our enemy!'

'Go, Lucan. Go home to your son. You do not need to save me. All that will happen to me is that I will return to my home. I may not like it, but I can endure it. You must not risk never getting to see your son. Go.'

Urian shook her by her hair and spots swum in her vision. Biting her lip to stop herself from crying out, she tasted blood.

'What did you say to him?' screamed Urian again.

'I was telling him, he cannot win against you. You are too good a swordsman and he is unarmed. I told him to surrender.' Her voice was calm. He would not know how violently her knees shook.

Her simple flattery did not dim the rage in his eyes or get him to loosen his tight grip in her hair. Her scalp was burning but she would not give up. 'You have done well to find me. In all the days in which I was lost no one else has even come close.' She was not getting through to him, the anger burned brighter than ever, but at least he was looking at her and not Lucan. Lucan could use this time to get away. Her heart cracked a little at the thought of never seeing him and Rolf again, but at least they would both be free. Lucan would see his son and be happy.

'You have done well, Urian. I was frightened and alone without you, but you found me, and now I will see my family again. I will tell my father how bravely you fought the English.' She was laying it on thick now, hoping she could still reach his vanity through his rage. He was strong and one twist of his hand would bring her to otherworldly pain, but she wouldn't think on that.

She tried again, 'Think how it will be when you return with me. Think of how proud my father will be of you.'

'Your father is a bastard.' His lips were a slash of red against purple skin.

'I know he is difficult, but you will see how...'

She never got to finish her sentence. Lucan barrelled into the man's side, taking them all to the ground. Her wrist landed awkwardly as she fell, the dagger tumbling from her fingers. She rolled away, scrambling to her feet as soon as she could.

The two men were a blur of fists with the occasional flash of steel. It was almost impossible to follow the frenzied movement but she did not miss the way Urian's fingers scrambled at his thigh—or the sharp blade he pulled from its sheath there.

'Lucan,' she screamed, 'he has a dagger.'

Urian moved like lightning, his arm coming up, the deadly knife going straight for Lucan's exposed neck.

The world seemed to slow, the sound of the woodland fading away as the blade made an arc through the air. Before it could plunge into his soft flesh, Lucan was twisting his body, moving with almost inhuman speed, using his size and strength to turn the blade on his opponent instead.

The fight ended on a soft grunt. No less haunting for its lack of drama. When it was over, Urian was lying motionless on the ground with Lucan breathing heavily, hovering slightly above him.

A heartbeat passed, then another.

'Is he dead?' she asked. Once again she was surprised

by how steady her voice sounded. Surely she should be feeling some sort of emotion, but now the terror was gone, her body was still.

Lucan pressed a hand against the other man's neck, feeling for a pulse. After a while, he said. 'He is.'

Jehanne's knees gave way then and she sank to the floor. For so long, she had hated Urian and now he was no more, it was difficult for it to sink in.

'Lord David?' Lucan was nodding towards the other man. Jehanne did not need to stand to see that his chest was no longer moving.

'He is dead also,' she said. Two men gone and for what? There was no sense to it, not really. They were fighting over nothing, enemies because their respective Kings had decided it was to be so. In another life, Urian and David would probably have found common ground, both believing themselves to be the most important person around. But one had killed the other and Urian had been unable to see reason.

Lucan pushed himself to his feet, his gaze never leaving Urian's body. 'Did you mean it?' he asked.

'Mean what?'

'When you told me to go.'

'I did.'

He grunted; she couldn't tell whether he was happy with her offer or not.

'Telling you to leave was the only way I could think of to save you. You didn't have a weapon to defend yourself. I was sure you were a good fighter but I knew he would have three blades. I was worried you could not beat that or that you would get hurt in the process. I did not want you to die for my freedom, it was not worth it.'

He squeezed his eyes tightly shut as if he was warding off physical pain. 'You're a good person, Jehanne. I swear to you that I will get you to England, to safety and to the people who care for you. You deserve, more than anyone I have ever met, to be happy.'

She wasn't sure what to make of that statement. It looked as if his words had cost him something, though she could not fathom what. Besides, he was wrong. 'I don't think it's true that I am good. I feel no pity now Urian is dead. Surely I should experience some emotion, even if it is relief. I was supposed to be marrying the man.'

He scrubbed a hand down his face, finally turning his body away from Urian and looking towards her. His blue eyes were shockingly bright against the pale skin of his face. 'It will come. You will feel it soon. Right now, it probably doesn't seem real to you. Death never does at first.'

There was a pause while his words sank in. It was true that nothing about this felt real. Whatever happened now, even if she did return to her father, she would never have to marry Urian. He was gone, never to hurt an innocent person again. Still no emotion came to her, only this strange stillness.

Lucan was looking around the clearing. 'Where's Rolf?'

'I directed him back to Grincheux and told him to head with all possible speed to the English if something happened to us. We should head back to him if we do not want him to flee. I am tired of chasing people through forests.' She smiled to show she wasn't serious and wondered at herself for making light of the situation while two men lay at their feet. 'Do you want to...' She gestured to where David lay, not sure what she was suggesting. It was not as if they could provide the men with a burial befitting their status.

He nodded briskly, somehow understanding her intent. 'I'll cover them both up. You return to Rolf. I'll follow you shortly.'

'Very well.' She wanted to go to him, to offer him comfort with the slide of her hand against his skin, but he was turning away from her, no indication that he wanted or needed her touch.

Rolf's eyes were red-rimmed. As she approached him, he ducked his head, trying to hide the fact he had been crying. She pulled him into a hug and let him sob into her shoulder, still surprised that she felt no emotion at all.

'Is Lucan alive?' he asked thickly, his words muted by the press of his face against her.

'Lucan is fine. He will be with us shortly.'

'What about David? That Frenchman plunged a sword into his stomach.' He shuddered and she held him tighter.

'David and Urian have both passed away.' The words softer than the brutality of their ends.

Rolf absorbed this news quietly. 'They were both bad men,' he said eventually.

Jehanne didn't know enough about David to comment. He had seemed selfish and reckless, but that did not mean he deserved his fate. Urian was different. No man should die alone, far from home with no one to mourn him, but the man had been intent on killing Lucan, had wanted to force himself on her and thought nothing of beating a man in chains. He had proven himself, over and over, to be a bad person. Perhaps that was why she was experiencing no emotion at his death.

Presently, Lucan joined them, leading two horses. Rolf ran to greet him, throwing his arms around the large man. Lucan gruffly patted him on the back, his gaze meeting hers over the boy's head. He didn't need to say anything to her, she already knew. The idyll of the last two days were over; everything was different now.

Chapter Sixteen

They became aware of King Edward's camp before they saw it. The deep rumble of thousands of men talking over each other, the clanging of blacksmiths working non-stop to produce weapons and the heavy air of many burning fires.

Snakes writhed in Jehanne's stomach at the reality of being surrounded by the enemy of her people. It was a necessary evil to reach somewhere safe from her father, but even knowing that did nothing to settle her.

'I am sure Father will grant you permission to return home,' said Rolf to Lucan as they rode towards the noise. They were astride Grincheux, slightly ahead of where she was riding the horse David had stolen. 'You saved my life more than once and that will count for something. You will be seeing Richard soon.'

Jehanne didn't hear Lucan's reply, but she could picture his face. Whenever he thought of his son, his lips curved slightly and his ferocious glare softened into something near a smile.

Rolf twisted in his seat to glance back at her. 'And he will take care of you too, Jehanne. You will see, he is not as bad as the French say.'

Since being rescued, Rolf had made no secret of his

parentage in front of her, repeatedly reassuring them both that his father would treat them well because of what they had done for him. Ridiculous though it seemed now, with the rumble of the English camp ahead of her, Jehanne had not thought about how the English would receive her. Getting away from Urian had been her primary concern, but now that fear was gone, she was free to worry about many other things instead. Perhaps the reaction of King Edward to the daughter of a French nobleman in his camp should have been the highest on her list, but it wasn't.

The heavy dread that weighed her down was her inevitable separation from Lucan. She was not ready for it, could not begin to contemplate a time when he was not in her life. They had not known each other long, but even though they had been running for their lives, life had never felt so vibrant and free as it did when she was with him.

Twice now she had asked him if she could come with him, and twice he had turned her down. Both times his rejection had stung, even though she had come to understand his reasoning. But it had to be worth asking him one more time. Her fingers curled around the soft leather of the reins as she debated whether to wait and ask once they were inside the camp, or now, while they were not among the English.

Glancing at the horizon, she realised she had left it too late. Riders were already coming towards them, the blues and reds of King Edward's royal banner fluttering in the wind as the incomers held it aloft.

'Lucan,' she called, nudging her horse forward so that she was riding alongside him. Perhaps there would be time to ask now before they had company. 'I need to...'

'All will be fine, Jehanne. I will not let them hurt you.'

The riders thundered closer, every beat of the horses feet marking the time slipping away from her. 'It's not that, I...'

But Lucan's gaze was shuttered, his eyes locked on the approaching men. Every trace of the man she had come to know had faded away and the defensive warrior was back, each line of him solid and menacing.

'Are we expecting trouble?' she asked quietly.

Lucan's fists were curled tightly as he controlled Grincheux with his legs. 'It is safe to assume that we always are. Stay behind me.'

It was only then that it dawned on her that his threatening stance was all for her. Neither he nor Rolf had anything to fear from these men. A fine tremor ran over her and she fell back, letting Lucan take the lead.

The riders slowed as they neared. Even at a distance, Jehanne could see the way they shifted on their saddles as they took in the grim look on Lucan's face and the way his muscles bunched beneath his long sleeves.

'My Lord,' said the man carrying the standard. 'We had feared you and your party dead.'

It was a jolt to hear Lucan addressed formally but she supposed it was correct. He was a baron. Not as high up as David, but more senior than the men before you.

'There is much to discuss,' said Lucan. 'I must meet with the King with the utmost urgency.'

'And the lady, My Lord?'

'She stays with me, as does the boy.'

The two men exchanged glances.

'Is there a problem?' Lucan's voice was a low rumble full of menace and unspoken threats.

'Of course not, My Lord.'

The two men turned and the five of them continued on their way towards the camp. Jehanne rode behind. No one looked at her, and the horribly familiar sense that she was no one important, no one who needed to be cared about, slowly descended on her once more. She'd hoped never to experience it again, had believed that possible but now it was worse because she knew what it was like to live without the sensation. It tried to wrap itself around her heart but she fought it off. She hadn't gone through so much, risked so much, to become the person she had always been.

Chapter Seventeen

Much to Lucan's disgust, the two riders flanked them as they walked to King Edward's tent at the centre of the encampment. Jehanne hadn't spoken a word since they had encountered the other Englishmen. Although his gaze kept darting towards her, she did not appear to look in his direction once. Her shoulders were stiff, her face turned resolutely in the direction they were walking.

He wondered if she'd considered this part of her plan when she'd decided to escape her father's castle. In the depths of her enemy's camp, perhaps a marriage to Urian didn't seem so bad to her now. She needn't worry. King Edward might have destroyed the French countryside in his bid to engage King Phillipe in battle but he was not a hot-headed man who acted on a whim, unlike her father and late fiancé. With Rolf on her side, the English King should treat her with respect, unless, of course, he had another plan for her. Lucan was not a man of court, could not be obsequious or pretend to be someone other than he was, but for Jehanne he would try.

Hopefully she would soon be on her way to England and could marry the man she had loved since she was little more than a child. It would not be long before they were reunited now, and then she would be happy. Rage ripped through Lucan, hot and potent, at the thought of her smiling up at some faceless man. The sensation was so vividly real he stumbled.

Rolf glanced up at him, a thin eyebrow raised but he shook his head. There was no way he could explain to the boy the pure, unadulterated fury that was pounding though his bloodstream. He could not explain it to himself. He did not want another wife for himself, had known that truth for years now, and yet his body revolted against the idea of Jehanne wed to a man who wasn't him.

King Edward's tent was larger than the others. Two men stood on either side of the entrance, each holding their own standards. They paused outside. Jehanne was close to him now, close enough that he could feel the fine trembling her body. He brushed the back of her hand with his fingers. Her skin was icy, but before he could say anything reassuring, they were ushered into the tent and came to stand before the most powerful man in England.

Rolf didn't rush forward to greet his father, who was seated on the only chair in the tent. Instead, he bowed as low as Jehanne and Lucan did.

'Rolf,' said the King when they all straightened. 'I feared something terrible had happened to you. I am glad to see my worries were unfounded.'

Although the words were kind, Edward did not rush over and hold his son to his chest, not like Lucan planned to do when he next saw Richard. Lucan planned to let his son know exactly how he felt about the length of their separation, it would be clear that Lucan loved him with every word and every deed. This was not the relationship Edward had with his own son, although perhaps that was because he was one of many.

The urge to fidget pressed down on Lucan; he managed to stay still through sheer force of will. Rolf had convinced him that his relationship with Edward was good, that he would be able to persuade his father to let Jehanne travel to Borne, but this stilted formality did not bode well for her.

'Where are the rest of the scouts who travelled with you?' asked King Edward.

'We became separated,' said Rolf. 'They were not good men, they abandoned me. It was only Lucan and Mademoiselle Jehanne who have protected me since I last saw you, My Lord.'

Edward's unease began to build, pushing against his skin, making his fingers twitch against his thighs. Those in the Royal household addressed King Edward by his given name; that Rolf not doing so suggested they were not as close as the young lad believed.

'*Mademoiselle* Jehanne,' said Edward, his attention focusing on the woman. Slowly standing, the King kept her in his gaze as he slowly walked towards her. Lucan started forward, putting himself in front of her. In that moment, he knew he would commit treason to keep her safe, and that frightened him more than anything ever had in his whole existence. Lucan was supposed to keep himself alive to see his son again. If he denied his King anything, that would not happen. 'She is French,' King Edward said to Lucan, part question, part statement.

'She is, My Lord. But she is not our enemy.'

'I see.' Lucan watched as the King's jewel-heavy hand waved around in the air, as if he could pluck words from the air. 'Perhaps Mademoiselle Jehanne can be taken to one of the family tents to freshen up while we discuss all that has passed since I last saw you.' Without waiting for any of them to agree, he turned to one of the guards. 'See that this lady is treated with the greatest courtesy. She is our honoured guest.'

Lucan had to force himself to stand very still. There was no hidden message in the King's words. Edward was the epitome of a chivalrous knight; Jehanne would be treated with utmost civility. Unless the King decreed otherwise. The wrong reaction now and Lucan could make the situation worse. But it hurt like the very devil to watch her leave and do nothing about it, especially as she did not glance in his direction.

'Now,' said the King, his smile showing far too many teeth for Lucan's liking, 'Tell me everything that happened since I sent you on a scouting mission.'

Chapter Eighteen

Pacing around the inside of the richly furnished tent did nothing to speed up time. Even in clean clothes and with a body freshly scrubbed clean, Jehanne itched from restlessness. It wouldn't be safe to burst out of her surroundings and head back to the King's tent. Although she had been treated with polite deference, she was their enemy and a potential threat to the safety of the English King.

She had put all of her trust in Lucan. Deep down, she knew that was the right decision. He would not let her down, not let anything bad happen to her. He was a man who stood by his word, even if that word was not one that she liked.

Now that their situations were reversed, she understood what a vulnerable position he had been in her father's castle and the remarkable bravery he had shown by never appearing cowed.

She wanted to show that level of bravery, to expose her feelings once again and hope that she wasn't cut down by the man she had come to care for more than anyone else. She would ask him one more time if she could stay with him. If he told her no again, she would have to learn to live with that answer.

A rustle at the tents opening had her spinning round. 'Lucan.'

She rushed to him, flinging her arms around his neck, pushing herself against him even when he didn't hold her back. She thought his fingers might have lightly traced her spine, but she must have been mistaken because he was pulling away from her, stepping into the tent and putting distance between them. She wrapped her arms around herself instead.

'Did it go badly?' she asked. For that could be the reason for Lucan's cold reaction.

'It went very well.'

'Then why aren't you smiling?'

One corner of his mouth lifted slightly. 'Do I ever?'

'Your eyes…' Her words petered out not knowing how to explain the flatness in his eyes. She had seen them blaze with fury, amusement and passion but never dead like this.

When she didn't carry on, he shrugged his shoulders. 'I am not a man at ease at court. Dealing with the King is not something I enjoy.' She felt there was more to it than this, but she held her tongue. 'The King has agreed for an escort to take you directly to Borne. Rolf will return to England with you, so you can be assured that your security will be of the highest order.'

'But…'

'Someone will remain with you at Borne while it is established whether your future is secure there. If, for whatever reason, it is not, then further arrangements will be made. You need never return to Comte de Balladur's residence.'

This information was more than she could have ever

hoped for. Knowing that she would be out of her father's control forever was miraculous. But a chill was creeping across her heart that had nothing to do with her future and everything to do with the man standing in front of her, aloof and stern and nothing like the person she had come to know over the last couple of months.

'What about you?' she asked.

'Once my duty to the King is complete, I will return to my stronghold and Richard.' His lips curved in an approximation of a smile but it still did not meet his eyes.

She folded her fingers into the skirts of her new dress, hiding their trembling. She would have to ask him her question now, even if his stance showed him to be as impenetrable as a fortress.

'Lucan.' His blue eyes met hers for the first time since he had entered the tent, and she pressed her lips together to stop a gasp. The look in his eyes was colder than ice. It could not matter. She had to go on, she might not get another chance. 'May I stay with you?'

For the longest time, he said nothing. The cold, fathomless blue of his gaze did not warm or waver. 'Why?' he asked eventually.

'Because…' She searched for a way to say what was in her heart in a way that would not burden him. 'I want to be with you. I think I make you happy and…'

But he would not let her go on. 'We have been on a romantic adventure together. Like the one in those courtly love poems I do not agree with. Let us not make more of it than that. You will be disappointed with a life that ties you to me.'

Even braced for rejection, his words still lanced through her but instead of causing pain they stirred her fury. 'You of all people should know how much I detest decisions being made for me. You do not know my feelings, so do not belittle them.'

An answering spark flared in his gaze, and for a moment, she felt hope that he would fight back, but the flame died and his eyes became flat once more. 'I am not going against your will, or forcing you do something detestable to you. You wanted to go to Borne, you were willing to risk your life for it. I have aided you in every possible way.'

'And I will be forever grateful. But that's not what I mean and you know it.'

'My response remains the same.'

'Then you are nothing but a coward.'

He reared back then as if she had struck him. 'I may be many things, but a coward is not one of them.'

She pointed a finger at his chest, no longer caring what he thought of her. 'Physically, of course you are not. But you hide behind that ferocious body of yours, not letting anyone get close to you. Too afraid to risk getting hurt from feeling things. You may think that you are brave, but I know differently.'

'You think you know me, but you don't. We hardly know each other.'

Her eyes burned, but she would not cry. She had cried when she had been sent away from France to make an alliance in England. She had wept when those she cared for in that home would not fight for her. But she would be damned if she cried now. 'I know you better than you will ever know yourself. I see you for the frightened man you think you aren't. Once you leave this tent, I will not see you again, and you will regret that for the rest of your life.'

Every line of his body was taut. She hoped, beyond reason, that he would stay and fight with her, even if he could not fight for her. Yet in the end he only strode out of the tent, without saying another word.

Chapter Nineteen

After the quietness of the French countryside, the bustling port at Einon was a shock to the senses. French and English voices called to one another over the slap of water hitting the wooden docks. Large gulls swooped and dived overhead, their screeching adding to a sense of urgency that filled the whole area. A large ship, its sails down, was moored slightly out to sea, waiting for a favourable tide to bring it in and allow its passengers to board.

Jehanne and Rolf sat outside a tavern, gazing out at it, neither of them on a hurry to climb aboard a vessel that rocked violently even without moving in any direction. Since her confrontation with Lucan in the English tent two days ago, everything had moved very quickly. She had not seen Lucan again, he had not come forward to say farewell to her as she had left with Rolf and their guards. Tears had threatened once again, but she'd managed to hold them back. If he was not able to risk anything for her, then he was not worthy of her broken heart.

'I am not looking forward to the crossing,' said Rolf.

'Me neither.'

'But it will be worth it for you. You will be reunited with…William, is it?'

'That's right, William. I do hope to see my friend again.'

'Friend?' Rolf's nose wrinkled. 'I understood you were going to marry him as soon as you were reunited. Lucan said he was the love of your life.'

'When did he say that?'

'When he was bargaining with the King.'

A sick, swooping sensation swept through her, like being dropped from a height. 'What do you mean by *bargaining*?'

'My father wanted to ransom you to your father. He was trying to think of a way to do it that might finally persuade King Phillipe to engage in battle, but Lucan pointed out all that was wrong with that idea. My father still wasn't convinced, so they struck a deal.'

Jehanne's heart thundered in her chest. 'What sort of a deal?'

'Rather than return to his fortress, Lucan is to head a force to the North. It is rumoured that the French King has an encampment there. Edward wants him to stage some raids on them. He hopes it will finally get Phillipe to react and engage in battle.'

'King Edward has asked Lucan to fight and Lucan has agreed to it?'

'That's right. My father believes drawing the French King out to the battlefield due to raids on his supplies might be the way to go. He thinks Lucan's size might work in their favour. It might not, but my father's siege at Cambrais failed, so he is willing to attempt other means to engage with him.'

'But Lucan doesn't like to fight.'

Rolf raised a bony shoulder. 'He might not, but he

doesn't really have a choice. At least not now that he has struck this deal.'

As Rolf's words sank in, Jehanne's world slowed to a stop. Lucan had given up his chance to return to his son, so that she could go to William at Borne. Despite the time they had spent together, Lucan hadn't realised what he had come to mean to her. He thought that William was the love of her life, because all he saw was her running to him and not that the point of her escape was to forge her own destiny. Lucan had given up his dream for her, and instead of showing gratitude, she had railed at him and called him a coward.

'Why didn't he tell me?' she asked softly.

She'd been half-speaking to herself but Rolf responded to her question anyway. 'I found he is better at gestures than words.'

'But I told him I wanted to stay with him—he refused. Why would he do that?'

Rolf didn't respond, for which she couldn't blame him. Rolf was only a child, and if she didn't have the answer, then she could hardly expect him to know either.

In all the time she had known Lucan, all he had been fixated on was seeing his son again. The love and devotion he clearly felt for his son was one of the things that had struck her so forcibly. After a lifetime of being a pawn for her own father, it had been refreshing to find that not all men were like that. And yet, he had given up reuniting with him anytime soon, so that she could achieve what she wanted.

Part of her was almost giddy at the knowledge that someone would make such a selfless gesture on her behalf. It had to mean that his feelings for her were far deeper than he had acknowledged. The other part of her was filled with red-hot fury. If he'd listened to her, if he'd understood what she had been asking, he need not have made the gesture at all. But he had rather risked his life than his heart. He'd rather ride to battle than end up with his feelings hurt should things go sour between them. What a wonderful yet foolish man.

'Oh dear,' said Rolf. 'The ship is coming and the sea looks no calmer. We shall be tossed about all afternoon. I should not have eaten that bread earlier.'

Sure enough, the vessel that was to see them to England was turning about, ready to come into port. Pushing herself to her feet, she brushed debris that clung to her dress to the floor. 'Run along and fetch your belongings,' she told him. 'We don't want to keep anyone waiting and the sooner we leave, the sooner we can recover from the seasickness on the other side.'

Whatever Lucan's actions might tell her, his words had told her a different story. Three times she had asked to stay with him, and three times he had told her that she could not. To ask a fourth time would show a level of foolishness she did not possess.

Chapter Twenty

Lucan stood at the end of the dock staring out to sea. It would not be long now and the ship's sails would disappear over the horizon, taking Jehanne ever closer to Borne. All his life he'd made careful decisions, always choosing a path that would be easiest, that would cause the least strife. Not once had he regretted any that he had made until now.

Walking away from Jehanne, refusing to let her stay with him had been the most mindless thing he had ever done. He'd done it to protect his heart, not realising it was already too late. When she had ridden away from King Edward's camp and not looked back, it had dawned on him she was taking a piece of him with her and that he would never be the same again.

In that last horrible meeting, she'd risked being vulnerable in front of him, asking him for a third time to stay with him, and he had crushed her by refusing. He was a coward, just like she had said. Too afraid of opening his heart to another person. She probably, quite rightly, hated him now. Hell, he couldn't stand himself after the things he had said.

He blinked and the ship was finally lost to sight. He bent double as the reality of the situation hit him. Jehanne was gone, returning to England and possibly her first love. He could chase after her; the journey wasn't long, but if the increasingly fractious weather turned worse, he could get stuck in England for days or weeks, and he would not be able to complete the mission Edward had tasked him with.

Defying his King was not a good idea, not if he ever wanted to see his son again. Land could be taken from you, whether you were a baron or not. Not that he cared about that for himself, but he did not want his son thrown from the only home he had ever known. It meant Lucan could not follow her until this latest mission was completed. That could take weeks or months. By then, she might have already married William and Lucan's one shot of finding true happiness with Jehanne would be over.

Seawater had to be getting into his eyes, because they were stinging. He dropped his head and considered the planks of wood beneath his feet. To hell with it, he was going to follow her, stop her before she reached William, offer her marriage and a life with him. If he was able to return quickly, then he would. If not, he would make sure that his son was safe from the King's wrath over Lucan's defiance.

He turned on his heel. Decision made, he wanted to get on with it.

Only, he came to an abrupt stop. There, up ahead of him, standing facing him, was Jehanne.

A slight breeze stirred her skirts. She was not an image he had conjured up from the desperate depths of his imagination but a real woman, sea-spray curling whisps of her hair.

In three long strides he was in front of her. 'You're here.'

Amusement danced in her dark eyes. 'I am, and so are you.'

'Shouldn't you be on that boat?'

'I know that is what you arranged and what you sacrificed to get me on it, but I'm afraid I could not go after all.'

It occurred to him then that there might be a whole host of reasons for her remaining in France. Perhaps she did not want to travel to England after all, maybe she wanted to remain with her family. It might not have anything to do with him. Why would she risk putting herself in a vulnerable position once more when he had turned her down three times already?

It was his turn now to show bravery. As she had said, he might be strong when it came to his body but now it was time to show he was worthy of her.

'Jehanne.' He reached out and threaded his fingers through hers because not touching her was torture. 'You were right to call me a coward.'

A small frown creased her forehead. 'That was unkind of me and it is untrue.'

He squeezed her hand. 'It was the truth and I needed to hear it. I have been afraid, not of physical pain but of risking my heart. I thought it could only contain enough love for one person and my son had that. If you would be willing to give me a second chance, I would like to show you how wrong I was. I love you, and I want to spend the rest of my life showing you exactly how much.'

The wait for her to respond stretched on forever. Now he knew what she must have experienced every time she asked him if she could stay with him. He'd rather be manacled to her father's walls for eternity than wait a moment longer for her words.

Stepping closer to him, she reached up on tiptoes and pressed a fleeting kiss against his mouth. 'Your gestures always speak louder than your words, Lucan. I will have to learn to listen. You should have told me that you had postponed your return to England in exchange for me returning to Borne. I would have known then that you loved me. I would never have left King Edward's camp. No matter what you said to me from that moment on, would have convinced me that you did not care for me.'

'Why did you not board the boat?' He wanted to be sure about her motives, even though there were only two choices from here. Marry her if she loved him too or spend the rest of his time persuading her he was worthy of her love—and then marry her.

'Because you are in France. Wherever you are, that is where I am going to be, so long as you will let me. And I so very much want you to let me, because I love you too.'

Happiness rushed through him, turning his knees to water. 'Then you will marry me.'

'I will.'

'Today.'

'Today.' Her eyes shone with happiness as she gazed up at him. 'I do love that smile of yours. You should show it to the world more often.'

'With you by my side, that will be the easiest thing I have ever done.'

Epilogue

England 1346

'Richard,' Jehanne called.

'Would you take this to your father?' she asked, handing him a water flask. 'It's hot out there today.'

'I will, Ma.'

At twelve summers, Richard did not like to be called 'darling boy' before his peers but that was what he always would be to Jehanne. She'd fallen in love with him the moment she had laid eyes on him six years ago and the feeling had been entirely mutual. In looks, he was almost identical to his father, although Lucan would comment gruffly that he was grateful the lad had more of his mother's temperament. Lucan's daughter was another matter altogether. Getting the four-year-old to behave was very difficult, some might say, an impossible task.

'Ma,' said Richard before he left the room, 'Margot is climbing the bed curtains again.'

She managed to grab her daughter, named after the sister Jehanne would never see again, before she reached the top. The girl's shrieks of laughter over getting caught could probably be heard in France. And, fanciful though it was, Jehanne hoped her sister would sense she was happy and free.

'What is going on here?' asked her husband, his broad frame filling the doorway.

'Papa.' Margot ran to Lucan, flinging her arms around his legs. 'Ma stopped me climbing.'

'A good thing too. You are not a squirrel.' Margot's laughter rang out once more; her father's wide grin a sight to behold. 'Remember what I told you before, you must look after your mother.'

Margot nodded sagely. 'Because of the babe.'

'That's right.'

'When is he coming?'

Lucan ran an appreciative eye over her. Her husband seemed to find her even more irresistible when she was with child, which was incredible given how insatiable he had been when she wasn't. 'Soon. Why don't you run along, Margot, and see what your brother is up to. I think he is going to practice sword fighting.'

'You shouldn't encourage her to learn how to duel. Before you know it, the kingdom will have fallen to her.'

Lucan laughed. He did a lot of that these days, and Jehanne never got tired of hearing it.

'I thought you might appreciate a lie-down,' said her husband, prowling towards her.

'How thoughtful of you. I would like a rest.'

'I'll join you,' said Lucan, lifting her as if she weighed nothing and setting her down on their bed. 'You know how I don't like to be lonely.' His lips ghosted along her neck and she arched towards him to allow him better access.

'You are very generous,' she murmured, as his mouth

continued its journey along her collarbone to the base of her throat.

'I live to keep you happy.'

The words, said in jest, were true.

* * * * *

If you enjoyed this story, make sure to check out The Knight's Mission miniseries

The Knight's Rebellious Maiden
The Knight's Bride Prize
The Disgraced Knight's Redemption

And why not pick up the A Season to Wed miniseries, featuring Ella Matthews's captivating romance

Only an Heiress Will Do *by Virginia Heath*
The Viscount's Forbidden Flirtation *by Sarah Rodi*
Their Second Chance Season *by Ella Matthews*
The Lord's Maddening Miss *by Lucy Morris*